MARRIAGE AND MALICE

KIRA COLE

Copyright © 2024 by Kira Cole

All rights reserved.

No part of this book may be reproduced in any form or by any electronic or mechanical means, including information storage and retrieval systems, without written permission from the author, except for the use of brief quotations in a book review.

1

CHRISTIAN

I groan as I glance out the window.

The crew dashes across the tarmac, getting the private jet ready for takeoff.

In a few minutes, I'll be leaving Georgia.

My phone starts ringing as I kick my feet up and lean back against the seat.

Ruben's name flashes, and I accept the call. "I'm on the plane now."

"Great." Ruben sighs as something shatters in the background. "I swear, these people act more like destructive children each day. I know you don't want to come home and get married, boss, but I'll be glad to have you back."

"Just remind them who's in charge in my absence." I close my eyes for a moment. "You know, Georgia was supposed to be a vacation for me. Some time away before I have to marry a woman I never laid my eyes on."

Ruben's been my closest friend for years. He's one of the few people I can be open and honest with.

And though he might be new to the concept of being

my right hand, and he might complain, as soon as he gets off the phone, he is going to handle it.

He's tough but fair, and he's knocked out more than one man for disrespecting him.

"I'm sorry the wedding needed to be moved up. But with more names leaked, we can't chance it."

"I know, I just wish I could have stayed in Georgia a little longer. Leaving Billie's resort opening is shitty, even if she understands."

On the other hand, going away means I don't have to endure their constant displays of happiness and love, envious of a life I will never have.

It's the kind of happiness I don't deserve or want.

This arrangement is going to work much better for my life, even if it means the end of an era.

"You could always go back after the wedding," Ruben says, the noise in the background growing softer as a door closes somewhere close to him.

I'm starting to think moving us back to Tennessee was a mistake.

"If we were still in Colombia, I wouldn't even entertain the idea of marriage." I lean back in my seat and close my eyes, running a hand down my face. "At least there, I didn't have to worry about the authorities breathing down my neck."

And I wouldn't be forced to form a family, to put someone else's life at risk by being associated with me.

"That's why you're coming home, boss. So you can get married, and we can stop worrying about our enemies leaking information about us and getting our people arrested."

"And the cost is marrying a woman I don't even know. Then I get the joy of spending my life with her."

Ruben chuckles. "It's going to be fine. You're doing this for the right reasons, even if you might wish it didn't have to happen."

"I *do* wish that. This is a shot in the dark. I'm hoping that a marriage will be enough to protect my people, but I don't really know."

And that is why I keep hesitating.

If I was one hundred percent sure this marriage would protect my people, I wouldn't bat an eye at it. Hell, I'd be hitched already.

But there is something else to consider. "Besides, what about the woman on the other end of this? I have to set expectations with her from the beginning. She is going to expect a husband who might grow to love her. I'm not capable of that. All feelings do is ruin you."

"Come on, man. I know you. We both know that this is not the life you would have chosen for yourself. So, maybe this is the change you need."

A door slams and Ruben groans. "Camila just took off. Said she was going to meet you at the airport when you landed."

Fuck.

"Of course, she is." As much as I've missed her, I don't want to rehash this entire conversation with her. "Think you could stop her?"

Ruben laughs. "No way. If I go after her, she'll put me in the ground where I stand. Your sister is as terrifying as she is beautiful."

"Stay the fuck away from my baby sister." I sit forward, ready to punch his face even though he is thousands of miles away. "You're my friend, Ruben, but if I find you so much as lay a finger on her, I'll cut it off."

"I'm not doing anything with Camila. Hell, half of the

trouble over the last few days is convincing the men she sent to the hospital not to go after her."

"She did *what?*" I pinch the bridge of my nose and close my eyes. "Ruben, please tell me that when I land, the only thing I'm going to have to worry about is a wedding that shouldn't be happening."

"I promise, you have nothing to worry about. Well, except, of course, your wedding."

"Ugh. I'll see you in a few hours."

"Safe flight, boss."

I end the call and glance out the window.

The car that dropped me off starts driving away.

In my mind, I get off the plane, call the car back, and go spend the rest of my planned week with my friends.

God, what am even I going back for? An arrangement that benefits both parties, but none of us actually wants? If only I knew who is targeting my men. Who is targeting me.

The pilot opens the door to the cockpit and peeks out. "Sorry to interrupt. We'll be taking off in a few moments if that is alright with you."

I nod and sit up straighter, fastening my seatbelt. "Yes, thank you. Let's head home."

As the pilot returns to the cockpit, and the plane starts to move, all I can think about is the fact that in no time, I'll be standing in front of an officiant reciting my vows.

My stomach lurches just thinking about it.

Though I asked Ruben to do a full background check on her, I never really cared to look. I just wanted to know if she was safe.

I don't know this woman, and it doesn't matter in the grand scheme of things. After all, this isn't a love connection. I had those before and look what that got me.

No, this is a business transaction. A trade.

So, we'll get married and then we'll come to an understanding of what our lives are to look like together, one way or another.

My head falls against the head rest, and my eyes close.

This is going to be a giant mess.

I don't have time for another person in my life. Let alone a woman who might come with unreal expectations.

I already put the marriage off for as long as possible.

Now there is no escaping reality.

The last men I lost made everything that much more urgent. So, I have to get married as soon as possible. Sooner than scheduled.

Too soon. Which means my ass is back on a plane and flying home to claim my bride.

Only, I'm not ready. Not happy.

But fuck if I'm failing my men.

The plane lifts off, ever higher, the people on the ground growing tiny.

As my eyes stay glued to the window, the rest of the world fades away.

I really should have stayed in Colombia.

"CHEER UP, BIG BROTHER." Camila gets out of the waiting car with her arms open to the sides. "You should be excited to be back home and see your sister."

I hug her and shake my head. "You didn't have to come pick me up from the airport."

"Of course, I did. I've been waiting to talk to you about this marriage plan you have."

I sigh. "Not up for discussion. It needs to happen."

Guilt courses through me at the way her gaze drifts around the tarmac.

When Ruben, Camila, and I had the meeting to discuss the marriage, she opposed it. But by then, it was no longer a matter of *if* it would happen. It was a matter of when.

This is my life. My choice.

I'll never marry for love. Never thought I'd be married at all. And if this marriage wasn't happening now, I'd be single forever.

Better than falling in love and having the person ripped away from you.

The pain of losing a loved one is the worst kind of pain. And I never want to be the reason someone else loses their life. Because associating with me is dangerous.

Loving me is deadly.

Love is supposed to be a good thing. But I know better.

This life doesn't lend itself to love. Not where I'm concerned.

One day, Camila is going to take over the cartel. It's not what I'd want for her, but it's what she wants for her life, and if I'm being honest, I'm looking forward to a break.

However, that's not going to happen until she's ready.

Right now, she is working her way through medical school. How she is going to run the cartel and act as their doctor, I have no idea, but if anyone can make it work, it's her.

But right now, she doesn't need to try and figure out how to help the cartel when this marriage can do just that.

Her focus should be on school so her life can be more than just killing people.

I wish my life was more than just killing people.

Camila shrugs and pulls her dark hair over one shoulder, combing her fingers through it. "I know. I don't like it, though. You should be marrying a woman you love. Not one who gives you an advantage. I hate you being lonely, but I'm not so sure this is the right move for you."

"I'm not lonely."

"Right." She rolls her eyes. She has the uncanny ability of seeing right through me.

I grin. "I promise you I'm not. You know as well as I do that running the cartel takes up a lot of time. If we add the legitimate businesses I have, it leaves me no time to even think about relationships, let alone a serious one."

"That's bullshit, and we both know it. You had to go to *another state* to spend time with your friends. Sure, you may be working with Jovan and Alessio in an alliance, but they're your friends. Hadley and Billie are great too, so don't feed me that bullshit about being too busy to maintain relationships."

"Look at you, thinking that you know everything."

She laughs, turning to head to the car that is waiting on the tarmac to take us home. "You're right. I do know everything. Billie told me that she's your best friend, and you talk about girls together."

I groan and run a hand down my face. "I talked to her once! About one situation!"

Camila laughs, the sound easing some of the tension in my chest.

Neither of us has had an easy life, but seeing her happy and thriving makes my day. For years, when we were younger, I thought I would never see her smile again.

"I like them," Camila says. "You're going to have to invite them all to come visit us again soon. Their trip here a few weeks ago was the best. I loved getting to meet them."

"One of these days. You have to focus on school, though."

"You want me to focus on school so I stop focusing on the fact that you're marrying yourself off."

Sighing, I search for the words to best explain this to her.

For so long, it's just been the two of us.

I hate the thought of letting her down again. I've already done it too many times in the past.

"Camila, this is the best way forward. I promise, I'm not lonely. This marriage is going to work, and everything will be fine. I can deal with this."

I hate the way she purses her lips and nods, as if she doesn't quite believe me.

"Camila, I'm doing what I have to do. Now come on, let's go home."

I open the passenger side back door, and she gets inside, not bothering to say another word.

She's going to give me the cold shoulder the entire drive home, I can see it now.

I can handle the silent treatment if it means I get to keep her in my life. I can't lose any more family.

Closing the door with her inside, I turn around and grab my bag, slinging it over my shoulder.

I have less than twenty-four hours to kill before the wedding, and I don't know what to do with my time.

If I asked Ruben, he would want to go get drunk at one of the clubs downtown.

I'm getting too old for that shit, though. Even if I wasn't, something doesn't sit right with me about getting drunk the night before my wedding.

Arranged marriage or not, it's the only one I get, so I still want to remember it.

As I open the trunk and toss my bag inside, a gunshot rings out.

The bullet grazes the arm holding the trunk door open and lodges into the side of the jet.

I reach into my bag and pull out my gun before crouching behind the car.

The locks on the car thud into place at the sound of the gunshot.

Even though Camila is going to be pissed, she's locked inside. It's where she is safest.

Protect the heir at all costs. It's what my men are trained to do.

I peek over the side of the car to scan my surroundings. My gaze flies to all the possible hideouts.

Nothing on the left side. I go to the other side and do the same. Nothing.

I'm about to move to get closer to the front when my eyes land on a man in a fluorescent vest with a gun in his hands.

Bastard is hiding behind one of those boarding stairs.

Great. Murder before marriage. Can my day get any better?

The man shoots again, missing me as I hide behind the armored car.

I lean around the side again, aiming at the man and pulling the trigger.

The bullet buries itself in his thigh, blood pouring down his leg as he drops to the ground.

I hurry out from my hiding place, shooting his hand as he tries to aim his gun at me.

The man groans, the gun falling from his grip, and he uses his other hand to cradle the injured one.

Gun trained on him, I bend down to take his piece.

When he reaches for me, I press my foot against the bullet wound in his leg.

"You really should have thought this through."

Standing up, I aim at the space between his eyes and squeeze the trigger, watching the life drain from his eyes as blood trickles onto the ground.

My phone starts ringing as I tuck my gun in my waistband.

With a sigh, I pull it out and swipe my thumb across the screen.

"If this is about the wedding, we can talk about it later."

"The deal is off."

2

ZOE

Don't cry. Just keep folding your jeans and do not cry. You have to be strong. You need to be strong.

"You look like you're going to throw up," my sister Ava says as she walks into my room and takes a seat at my desk. "What's going on in your head?"

I shrug. If I look at her or start talking about the marriage now, I might start crying. If I start crying, I don't think I'm ever going to stop.

This isn't the way I thought my life was going to go. I had no intention of getting married. Not any time soon.

I had dreams. A whole life ahead of me.

Now, I have a wedding to go to. *My* wedding. And I have no idea who I'm even marrying.

But I'm going to do whatever it takes to keep my father safe.

"Zoe, talk to me." Ava gets up and heads to my closet, pulling out some of my dresses. "Look, this might be a good thing. You might not have to go to any more state dinners. Dad won't make you play the part of the perfect daughter."

Laughing, I shake my head. "There is no end to being

the daughter of the Head of State. We both know that. Even when he retires, he's going to want to drag us out to dinners with cameras so he can make sure everybody knows he's living the perfect life."

I'm trying to make light of this whole thing, but my breath catches in my throat as I try to hold it together.

Ava shrugs and piles the dresses on a free corner of the bed. "I know. You can dream, though. You might have more time to work on your music too."

I scoff and drop the pile of folded jeans into my suitcase. "Doubt it. We live in Nashville, but nobody around me seems to think I can make it in music. Sometimes, I think I should give up on my dreams. Save myself the heartache."

Music is my life, the one true solace I have in life, and thinking about giving it up hurts more than can be put to words.

And Ava is the only safe space I have right now. She is the one person I can talk to.

"I'm scared, Ava. I'm terrified of everything happening right now. Music was the one good thing I have. What if I have to let it go? To give it up?"

"That won't happen. You are really talented, and I believe in you."

"But what if—"

"You are smart, and you are strong, Zoe, so whatever happens, you will survive. If you are afraid that might happen, then you need to have a back-up plan in place."

She comes over and holds my hands in hers. It gives me comfort if nothing else.

"If music is what you want to do, then I know you're going to do it, but I want you to be prepared in case anything goes wrong."

My chest constricts. "I don't know. There's a little voice

in my head, telling me I'm not good enough. And it won't even matter if whoever I marry will just push me to be the perfect housewife."

"Whoever you marry might be fine with you performing." Ava reaches out to run her hand over my back as the first tears start to roll down my cheeks.

I wipe them away, determined not to cry. "I doubt that, Aves. This guy is looking to arrange a marriage, so he is going to be a control freak who wants his wife to do whatever he wants. I'm not sure I can live my life like that anymore. I've been doing that my whole life already."

Oh god, I haven't even met my future husband, and I'm already a disappointment.

I turn my back and head to my suitcase, squishing things and pretending to be busy.

I hate having to do this. I hate having to give up my life.

But I'll do it. Today and any other day of the week. Family first. Always.

I just wish it wasn't at the expense of my dreams. My freedom.

I sit on the bed, elbows on my knees and face in my hands. "There is no way that I'm going to be able to keep working on my songs and writing an album. I may as well give up on my dreams now because they're not going to come true."

Ava pulls me up and into a tight hug. "It's going to be okay. You don't have to do this if you don't want to. We can find a way to get you out of this."

Mom walks into the room. "That's *not* going to happen."

She glances around, her upper lip curling. "Why aren't you packed yet? You know how important this marriage is to your father."

Ava spins around to face our mother. "You could have an ounce of compassion. You're not the one being forced to marry a stranger."

Mom arches an eyebrow and puts her hands on her hips. "Zoe knew what she was doing when she agreed to help your father. Stay out of it, Ava."

Then she turns and points her finger at me. "And *you*. You are a grown woman, and I expect you to start acting like it."

I've played the part of the perfect daughter my entire life, or tried to, at least.

And yet, nothing I do will ever be good enough for my mother.

As fire and ice battle inside me, shame and anger fighting to manifest, Ava's face turns a bright red.

I grab her hand and pull her back.

She and Mom have never been on the same page about anything.

But unlike me, she is not shy about letting people know she is not happy.

I wish I could speak up for myself too.

Maybe this marriage can be the start of my new life. My clean slate. My chance to reinvent myself.

Mom waves her hand in the direction of my suitcase. "So, stop lazing around and finish packing your things. You're getting married tomorrow."

Her outstretched finger turns to my sister. "And Ava, you better fall in line at the wedding. I will not have you disappointing the family yet again. It's bad enough that you spend your days around criminals."

Ava throws her hands up in the air. "I'm a registered nurse working at a prison! It's not like I'm there to hang out with them or that I'm up to no good. Besides, why does it matter where I work? I help people."

I smother my smile.

My sister is like a dog with a bone when it comes to her job. She is amazing at what she does, and she isn't afraid to walk into a room full of dangerous men.

Hell, I'm pretty sure most of them are scared of her. Ava can be terrifying when she gets going.

Ava glares at Mom while I continue packing. "You know what? I'm not going to stand here and argue about this with you."

Facing our mom, hands on her hips, Ava tips her chin up. "How can you stand there and let Dad treat Zoe as some sort of offering? Don't you care about all the sacrifices she's already made for the family?"

Mom steps closer to Ava, looming over her. "We've all made sacrifices."

To her credit, Ava only takes a step closer.

"And Zoe has sacrificed the most, yet you still demand more. So, don't come in here and boss her around when she is already making the ultimate sacrifice for Dad."

Mom shakes her head. "The way you are talking, it's like she is about to walk down death row or something."

Then her eyes find mine. "Believe me, Zoe, this is not the marriage I had planned for you, but your father needs this."

A lump rises in my throat. "I'm aware I have to do this for Dad. Everything will be okay. We'll all be okay."

Mom nods and walks into my closet. She rummages through the drawers, pulling out more clothing to pack in a second empty suitcase.

"Mom, if there was another way to fix Dad's problems,

would I still be getting married tomorrow?" My voice waivers, but I fight to hold myself together.

"Your father needs this wedding to happen, so get your head out of the what-ifs and finish packing, Zoe." She gets up and carries a pile of clothing over to the other empty suitcase. "You need to stop whining and do what you're told."

After dumping the clothing in the suitcase, she shakes her head and stares at me for a moment.

Though I hope for a hug, some words of comfort, or even love, I know better.

She grips my chin and pulls my face closer to her.

"Pull it together, Zoe. I don't have time to deal with your silliness right now. Act like the grown woman you are and do what you have to do to protect this family."

As she lets go of my chin, I wonder if my mother is ever going to be the person I need her to be. The mother who fights for her daughter. Like Ava fights for me.

Like I need to learn to fight for myself.

Mom takes a step back from me, her expression blank. The same poker face I've seen a thousand different times growing up.

"It's pointless to sit here and talk about the things that could be. We are looking at what is right now. You are getting married, and your father won't have to worry anymore. This is a great opportunity for you."

She lifts her chin up. "You should be happy your father thinks you can do this. God knows if it were up to Ava, we'd find him dead in a gutter soon enough."

Ava's jaw drops as my chest constricts.

"Thanks, Mom," I say, my voice cracking. "It's nice to know I can count on you to be there for me through this."

"I *am* here for you." Her eyes narrow as her lip curls for a split second before the curtains are drawn again.

"Someone has to make sure things are going to schedule. We're doing what has to be done as we always have."

Mom spins on her heel and walks out of the room.

I wait until she's gone before turning to my suitcase and start packing again. I can't look at my sister right now without breaking down.

Ava scowls and crosses her arms. I know that she's about to give me another one of her lectures.

"Zoe, I love you, and I know you love our parents, but that doesn't mean you have to sit there and take everything they throw at you. You need to stand up for yourself, even when it comes to our parents. They're not going to die if you tell them to give you some space."

"Damn, Ava, why don't you tell me how you *really* feel?"

"See?" She points at me. "That's the kind of attitude I'm talking about. Don't pretend that you don't have a little bit of a backbone in there. You have no problem standing up to me when I push it too far."

"That's different. I know that at the end of the day you will always be there for me. Mom and Dad are different. I know they love me, but it feels wrong to go against them. It feels like I have to be the perfect daughter for them. Like I always have to prove my worth."

"You don't." Ava launches herself at me in a tight hug again. "You're perfect the way you are, Zoe. I know that this is the last thing you want to be doing, but it's going to be okay. If you feel you have to do this, then don't let the man you're marrying push you around. Go into this marriage prepared to stand up for yourself. Let yourself be angry for once, okay? Promise me."

I laugh, a couple tears rolling down my cheeks. "I promise I will let myself be angry and stand up for myself."

But I don't know if that is a promise I can keep. I want to be the person who goes after what she wants, the kind of person that speaks up for herself. But more often than not, I'm the kind of person who appeases others, who sacrifices for others, and it's killing me bit by bit.

The truth is, I don't know how to be that person. But I wish I did.

"Good." Ava holds me at arm's length, her own eyes watery. "I'm sorry that you have to get married. If I could change this for you, I would."

Dad says as he appears in the doorway. "Well, good news."

His smile stretches across his face as Ava turns to face him. The suspicion is clear in her eyes.

They've been fighting since she found out I'm getting married to help him.

"What? You've sold off her firstborn too?" Ava crosses her arms, but she looks like she's coiled tight and ready to strike if he says the wrong thing.

"No." Dad tucks his hands into his pockets and leans against the doorframe, his smile melting off his face. "I know you don't agree with some of the things I have to ask the family to do, Ava, but I would appreciate it if you stopped looking at me like I need to watch my back."

Ava shrugs and sits down on the edge of the bed. "Then don't make Zoe get married."

"That's the good news." His eyes turn to me, and he smiles again. "Zoe, the wedding is off, sweetie. I've found another way to deal with everything going on."

"You're serious?" I ask, hope making me a thousand times lighter. "I really don't have to go through with the marriage?"

"Nope. I'm sorry that I asked you to do that in the first place, honey. Everything is going to be fine, though."

"Does that mean I can perform tonight?" I abandon my suitcases, eager to get changed and head to the bar where I'm supposed to have a gig.

Dad told me a few days ago to call the bar to let them know I wouldn't be there, but I didn't.

I've worked all my life to get my foot in the door of the music industry. This recurring gig is my chance.

I wasn't going to cancel the one bar who offered me a semi-permanent half hour time slot to perform.

"Yes." He sighs and shakes his head. "You need to think about what you're going to do for a living. Get a real job. You're twenty-four, Zoe. It's time that you start going after a career and leave this silly hobby behind."

"We can deal with that tomorrow," Ava says, walking over to the door and giving Dad a gentle push out of the room. "Right now, we have to get ready for Zoe's show."

She closes the door before turning to me. Her smile is blinding as she jumps up and down squealing.

I laugh, bouncing with her before the high starts to wear off. As my eyes roam though my bedroom, falling on my packed clothing, my only thought is there is no way I'm going to bother with unpacking right now.

"What am I going to wear tonight?" I ask Ava as I start digging through one of the piles for my favorite pair of black ripped jeans. "You're going to help me with my makeup and hair, right?"

Ava laughs and tugs on a lock of my hair. "I'm sure I can do something with this for you. I also brought a new crop top with me you're going to love. It's a little black bustier. It was going to be an *I'm sorry you have to get married against your will* gift, but since that's not happening, now it's an *I'm so glad you don't have to get married against your will* gift."

I laugh.

As I hurry to get ready, I'm on cloud nine.

Maybe I don't have to give up the future I've always dreamed of after all.

3

CHRISTIAN

"Hold on, Jeremiah, what do you mean the deal's off?"

I scowl at the dead body at my feet, wishing he were alive so I would have an outlet for my anger. "I came back to Tennessee to get married tomorrow, and now you're calling this off?"

Jeremiah Redford has been nothing but a pain in my ass since he first brought up working together.

He reached out to me when some of my men had been taken by the cops after their names were leaked. He told me he could protect my people, keep the authorities away from my cartel, if I protected his family against some bad people.

Marrying his daughter was supposed to be the signature to the deal, ensuring that our families would be tied together.

"You heard me. You're on your own. The wedding is off." Jeremiah chuckles, and for a moment, I wish I could reach through the phone and strangle him. "You're a smart man, Christian. You'll figure it out, I'm sure. However, my daughter will not be marrying you tomorrow."

"You have no clue what you've just done," I say as I step away from the body.

I pace back and forth, running a hand through my hair. "This is the one and only chance I'm going to give you, Jeremiah. I'll pretend you didn't just say that, and we continue with the wedding tomorrow."

"Not happening. I love my daughter, and I'm not going to force her into a life with you."

I bark out a short laugh. "You're fucking kidding me, right? You love your daughter, but you're willing to marry her off to a complete stranger? A criminal you approached to make a deal. How do you think she's going to react when she finds out what kind of man you are? Although, I'm sure she already has a guess. What kind of man marries off his daughter?"

"I do what I have to do to protect my family. From what I know, that is a concept you are quite familiar with."

The line goes dead.

I throw my phone, watching it shatter against the tarmac.

The pilot looks over at me from where he stands beside the plane before looking down at the body.

"Do you want me to deal with this mess, boss?"

I link my hands together behind my head, looking up at the fat white clouds drifting across the sky. "Yes. Handle this, and do it discreetly. Forget you heard that conversation, and there will be a bonus in it for you."

The pilot nods and walks over to the body. He doesn't say a word as he picks up the man's body and carries him over to the little truck that transports bags from the airport to the plane. He stuffs the body in the bed before looking down at the blood on the ground.

I don't have time to stand around for this. I need to

figure out how I'm going to be able to protect my cartel without Jeremiah keeping the authorities away from me.

My people are like fish in a barrel.

I've had to sit back and watch as people I've known and trusted for years get locked away because someone has been leaking their names and linking them to crimes through irrefutable evidence.

My men are familiar with the dangers associated with life in a cartel. Having people locked away due to a snitch was not supposed to be one of them.

Jeremiah has the power to talk with the district attorney and the police chief and get them to back off. Without this deal, I'm left with my pants down around my ankles, wondering how the hell I'm going to fix this.

Jeremiah is going to pay for fucking me over.

As I walk to my car, I sort through my options.

I could kill him right now, but that's only going to draw attention to me.

He's not a stupid man. You don't get to be the Head of State without making sure that you have contingency plans in place.

If I kill him, there is no doubt in my mind that somebody will be coming after me.

I need a way to make him uphold his end of our deal. He may not want my protection anymore, but I still need his.

And he's going to learn what happens when he crosses the cartel.

I get inside the car and, as expected, Camila is fuming. She turns her head away from me.

Good. I need the quiet to come up with a plan anyway.

As our driver puts the car in motion, I drum my fingers on my leg before glancing at the time.

It's getting later in the day, and soon, musicians are going to be flocking to the bars.

I might not have wanted this marriage, but as soon as I agreed, I had Ruben do some digging. I wanted to know the sort of person I was bringing into my home.

Jeremiah's younger daughter is a musician, and she spends every moment she can in the bars, trying to sing and play guitar for the crowds.

Ruben got the name of the bar where she's performing at for the next several weeks and her slotted times, which is why I know where she'll be tonight and when I can catch her there.

A plan starts to come together in my mind.

I know how to get what I want and how to piss Jeremiah off at the same time.

Guess I'm going to go pay his precious little daughter a visit.

ZOE GRINS as she waves to the crowd before getting off the stage.

My gaze drags up her long legs before settling on her face.

I don't miss the sparkle in those green eyes as she walks the dim room over to where I'm sitting at the bar.

Though she doesn't know who I am, I got her name and picture a couple of hours ago.

Ruben tried to give me her information when he was doing her background check.

At the time, I didn't think the information would be all that useful, but it's important to know your enemy and what that enemy is offering.

I just wasn't ready to put a face or name on her yet. The marriage could remain an abstract problem for a little while longer. I just wanted to be told she was safe to bring home.

Thanks to her dad's antics, I was forced to get acquainted with her a bit sooner than I had prepared for.

So, here we are.

"You were amazing up there," I say as she stands beside me.

Her long hair is tousled like she's just had the best sex of her life. The makeup around her eyes is dark and smokey. Any other place and time, I'd drag her off into a corner.

"Thanks," Zoe says, her smile too sweet.

She's not the kind of woman who would be able to withstand life in the cartel, that much is clear.

"Can I buy you a drink?"

I'm already motioning to the bartender and taking out my wallet. "You're the kind of woman who looks like she enjoys sex on the beach."

Bright red cheeks frame that perfect smile.

My cock stiffens as I consider what that blush would look like if she was on her knees for me.

Despite the ripped jeans and messy hair, Zoe is the kind of woman who screams innocence.

I could ruin that innocence without a second thought.

And she would love every second of it and beg for more.

"I'm more of a whiskey on ice kind of girl." Her gaze drags up and down my body, her tongue darting out to lick her full bottom lip.

The neon lights shining above reflect off the little gold nose ring she wears.

Not quite as innocent as some would like her to be, then. I doubt her dad likes all those piercings.

It makes me think there may be a slight rebellious streak

in Zoe. Just enough to keep things interesting when I screw up her father's plans.

I look back at the bartender, pulling out a couple of bills and putting them on the counter. "Two whiskeys on ice. Keep the change."

As the bartender takes the money and makes the drinks, I watch Zoe.

She sways her hips to the music, drumming her fingers on the counter. She watches me from the corner of her eye, not quite looking my way.

"Want to dance?" I ask as the bartender hands us our drinks.

She eyes the traditional Colombian tattoos spiraling up my arms before her gaze settles on the band shirt I'm wearing.

With a wicked little grin, she downs her whiskey and puts the ice-filled glass on the counter.

"Only because you seem to have good taste in music."

I chuckle and chug my own drink. "Well, if you give me one of your shirts, I will gladly prove that my taste in music is even better than you think."

Zoe rolls her eyes and takes my hand, her fingers weaving through mine. She leads me to a dark corner of the dance floor, away from prying eyes. "What's your name, pretty boy?"

I spin her around, drawing her back to me.

Her back presses against my chest, her head just below my chin.

Her ass grinds against me as I run my hands up and down her curves.

My cock only grows harder as she arches her back and tilts her head to look up at me.

"Christian." My fingers dig into her hips a little harder. "And what's yours?"

"Zoe."

She spins in my arms, running her hands down my chest.

The corner of her mouth tilts up as her hands slide back up my chest and over my shoulders. The softness of her body pressed against mine is driving me wild.

Though she might seem innocent, there's a part of her that knows how to wrap a man around her finger without a second thought.

It's not surprising, given she is the daughter of a politician.

Hell, I would be disappointed if she didn't know the power she has over people.

It's that same power that has me leaning in to get a taste of her.

Zoe links her hands together behind my neck, her lips moving against mine. She moans as I bite her bottom lip and slide my hands down to her round ass.

Her little whimper as my tongue tangles with hers drives me wild.

I pick her up, groaning when her legs wrap around my waist.

My cock strains as I carry her into a small hallway and press her back against the wall. Her fingers run through my hair as I slide my hands beneath her shirt.

I groan as she grinds against me.

Zoe gasps as I brush my thumb over her nipple through the thin lace over her breast.

Her back arches off the wall as I toy with her nipple, teasing it into a stiff peak.

I kiss my way down her neck as her hands roam down to grip my shoulders.

As I pull the neckline of her shirt down, her eyes go wide.

She shakes her head and puts her hands on my chest, pushing me back a step.

"I'm sorry," she says, fixing her shirt. "I shouldn't have done that. One drink is enough to cloud my judgment, apparently."

"It's alright," I say, tucking my hands in my pockets and taking a step back to give her some space. "Although my judgment definitely wasn't clouded."

My gaze darts down to the dark little mark I've put on her neck.

She's mine now.

Her cheeks flush. "I have to get going. I didn't realize how late it was."

"Let me walk you to your car." I'm not going to let her out of my sight for a moment.

I don't trust her father not to swoop in and take off with her to another country in a sad attempt to hide her from the consequences of his actions.

Too bad the consequence of his actions got to her first.

"Sure." She tucks her hands in her pockets.

I put a hand on the small of her back, grinning when she shivers.

"Thank you."

The walk to her car is short and neither of us says anything on the way there. It's a comfortable kind of silence, but one that I doubt is going to last much longer.

She stands on her toes to peck my cheek before getting into her car.

"You only had the one drink, right?" I ask, catching the

door before she shuts it. "I'm not going to let you drive if you've had anything more than that."

She shakes her head. "Just the one drink, and we danced the alcohol off afterward. I'm good to drive."

I nod and close the door for her. "Drive safe."

Zoe smiles and starts the car.

I wait until she's leaving the parking lot before getting in my car and following her. I keep a safe distance back, though I doubt she is going to think much of another small silver car on the road.

It's only when she turns up her driveway that I turn on the next street and park my car. I watch as the lights go on in her bedroom, her silhouette against the window.

Now, I wait.

4

ZOE

I want to scream, but a hand clamps over my mouth before I get the chance.

Moonlight streams through the window, illuminating the man from behind as his weight settles over me in the bed.

His thighs bracket my arms, pinning them to my body.

I don't have a fighting chance.

I'm going to die. There's nothing I can do to help myself right now. I'm going to die.

"I'm going to take my hand off your mouth, but you're not going to scream. If you scream, I'm going to have to knock you out, and I really don't want to hurt you."

The voice is familiar, but it's not quite coming to me.

I squint my eyes, trying to see through the darkness, but the man keeps his face in the shadows.

My entire body feels like it's frozen in place, but my heart is racing.

I have to fight. If I fight, someone might hear me. They might come in and save me.

I start thrashing, though I'm not sure if it will do any good.

With the way the man is sitting on me, I can't get my arms free.

I try to drive my knee into his back, but I can't quite bend to do it.

"Damn it, Zoe." The man reaches over and turns on the bedside light. "I said that I don't want to hurt you, but I will if I have to."

His cold and detached tone makes me believe him.

I stop fighting, my vision blurring as I lean back in the pillows. I blink away the tears, looking up at him.

Christian looks down at me, grinning as his thumb drifts over my cheek.

How did he get in here? Why is he doing this to me?

I shouldn't have kissed him. I know that it's bad to hook up with strangers. I should have seen this coming.

Nothing good ever comes from kissing strange men in the dark.

Is he going to kill me? Is he going to do something worse?

"Now, I know that this wakeup call is a little rude, but it's good to see that your bags are packed. I've already taken the liberty of taking them to my car. Took a couple of your guitars too. You're the last thing to go. You can either decide to climb out of the window on your own, or I will knock you out and carry you down."

I shake my head, hating myself for the rush of heat that floods my core as he shifts lower on my body.

Going to bed with the memory of his hardened cock pressing against me only hours ago proved to be almost impossible. Now, feeling him pressed against me again, I'm wide awake.

My body is buzzing with energy as I stare up at him.

"I'm going to take my hand off your mouth now, and you're going to make your decision." Christian starts to pull his hand back, watching for any signs of me screaming.

I know better than to try to scream, though.

He will knock me out and drag me out that window before anyone could get to me. I can see it in the way his dark eyes watch me.

He's waiting for me to make a mistake—to do something stupid so he can throw his power around.

It's not going to happen. I'm not going to give him the satisfaction. "I'll go out the window," I say, wriggling around beneath him. "Let me up."

I don't want to go with him, but there isn't another option right now.

He's already proven that he can get to me if he wants to. There's no doubt in my mind that he can overpower me if he wants to.

The best option I have is going along with what he wants and hoping that my family notices I'm missing a soon as possible.

"If you keep moving like that when you're under me, there isn't going to be any getting up." Christian makes a point of shifting, moving some of his weight off me. "You'll be begging for it."

"Screw you." I glare at him, wondering how much he would have to move for me to be able to drive my knee into his balls. "I said I would go with you. Now get off me."

I have no idea what is happening, but talking back to him is just as easy as it is with Ava.

I'm so glad that I'm finding my inner strength. At least I hope that's what this is.

Well, regardless, I'm fighting back somehow.

He gets off me and holds out a hand.

Scowling, I smack his hand away from me and drag myself out of the warm blankets.

Christian's low groan when he sees the tiny black silk nightie I'm wearing sends panic coursing through me.

There is no way this is happening. This is just a dream. It's not happening.

Am I ever going to see my family again?

I want to ask him, but I don't think I'll get the answer I want.

My hands are shaking as I try to focus on staying alive for now.

"Where are we going?" I ask, proud when my voice doesn't waver. "Why me?"

"That's my business. Now, hurry up. I don't have time to waste with your questions."

Another question is on the tip of my tongue, but I shove it down.

Just stay alive. All I have to do is stay alive, do what he says, and then I might get to see my family again someday.

The thought plays on repeat through my head as I walk to the glass doors that lead to my balcony.

He follows me out, standing just behind me as I look down at the post he must have climbed to get up here.

The stone balcony is cold against my bare feet.

"One second," Christian says, shrugging off the leather jacket he wears and holding it out to me. "You're going to catch a cold, walking around like that in the middle of the night."

"You could give me time to go back in and change."

He scoffs and waves the jacket in my face. "And give you the chance to hit a hidden panic button? Fuck no. Put the coat on and get your tight little ass shimmying down the post."

I snatch the coat from him as the breeze grows colder.

He reaches back inside my room and produces the pair of heels I was wearing at the bar.

They're not going to be the easiest shoe to wear while climbing, but it's the only option I'm being given.

"You're not going to pull anything funny on the way down," Christian says, crossing his arms.

I watch the way his tattoos move with his flexing muscles, my core clenching.

"I'm not stupid."

"I don't think you are, but I think that being in a situation like yours makes people do stupid things. Sure, you're going to get to the bottom before me, but you're not going to run. I would catch you. You're not going to alert your family. You don't want me to hurt them."

My heart skips a beat at the mention of hurting my family. I feel sick to my stomach as I climb over the edge of the balcony without saying a word.

He's right and we both know it.

I'm out of options.

Hopefully, my family finds me soon enough.

"Where are we?" I ask as Christian parks the car in front of a house.

It's too dark to be able to get any details.

"My house. We're almost late to our wedding, Zoe, but don't worry. It will all be over soon. You just have to repeat the vows, we kiss at the end, and then we figure out what married life is going to look like."

My stomach plummets to my feet, and I feel like I'm

going to be sick. "Who the hell are you? Why are we getting married?"

"I would have thought that your father told you about the deal."

The pieces of the puzzle start to click into place as I stare at him in horror.

I knew that I was supposed to marry someone to keep my father alive, I didn't know my future husband was the man at the bar.

"Did you know who I was when we danced together?"

Christian chuckles. "Yes. I did my research, though it appears that you didn't. Now, we're going to go inside, and you're not going to cause a scene. I will not be embarrassed by my wife on our wedding day."

I'm definitely going to throw up. I can't marry a man who kidnaps women from their beds.

He gets out of the car as I consider my chances of running.

The door flies open before I can do anything.

Christian smirks as he unbuckles my seatbelt before picking me up and tossing me over his shoulder.

I hit his back with my fists, kicking and thrashing, but his grip is too tight.

"I'm not going to marry you! You're insane! This isn't happening!" I kick him again, pain radiating through my foot as he grunts. "I'm not going to do it."

"Wrong." He carries me up the front steps and into the house.

As soon as he sets me down and flicks on the light, I can see that several men surround us.

One of them steps around us to lock the door and stand in front of it while Christian sets me on the ground.

"I'm going to be honest with you, Zoe." Christian nods

to a man with a small book in his hands. "You can either marry me now, or I'll find some other less pleasant way to collect the debt your father owes me. It's your choice."

The world comes to a screeching halt as my mouth drops open. Is he threatening to kill my father? Could he do it?

I don't have to ask because I know the answer to that.

Tears gather in my eyes, but I'm not going to cry. Not for him.

I grit my teeth together and nod, tucking my hands into my pockets.

If marrying this monster is what it takes to keep my father safe, alive, then that's what I'm going to do.

I was already supposed to get married to help my father, wasn't I?

"Good. Now that we have that settled, let's get this wedding underway."

The men around us watch as the officiant opens his book.

I try to go numb, repeating the words I'm supposed to say while drowning out the rest of the world. If I let myself think about what is happening right now, I know I'm going to break.

I can't break. My family needs me to be strong. I have to protect them.

Even if it destroys mee.

Christian doesn't look happy about the marriage, which is perhaps the most shocking part.

For a person who went to the effort of kidnapping me to marry me, he doesn't look like this is what he wants either.

Anger courses through me as I stare at him.

This isn't the way my night was supposed to go. I met a

cute stranger at the bar. I made out with that cute stranger at the bar, thinking that I was due to have a good night.

And then this is how my night ends.

Dad said the deal was off, that the marriage was off.

So, why is he marrying me anyway? Or is this another man who is using me because of my dad?

God, what is going on?

"You may now kiss the bride," the officiant says.

Christian leans toward me, the kiss short and chaste.

It's nothing like the way he kissed me in the bar.

I hate the way disappointment curls through me when he pulls away.

A few minutes later, the marriage license is signed, and I'm alone in a home I don't know with a man who screwed me over.

"Well, this is home now," Christian says, nodding to a long hallway to his right. "There's a staircase at the end of that hallway that leads to your room. I've already had your belongings brought up there while we were getting married."

I shake my head, taking a step back from him. "Why? Why are you doing this?"

"Do you think that this is the way I wanted things to go? Do you think I really want to force you to marry me?" He gives a bitter laugh and crosses his arms.

"Let's get one thing clear, Zoe. If it were up to me, I wouldn't be married to you at all. Unfortunately, there are decisions to be made that are bigger than the both of us. I've done what I had to."

"You're a bastard."

I turn and head down the hall, needing to get away from him before I explode.

My body feels like it's vibrating with anger as I climb the stairs to the second floor of the house.

I look in the open doors, finding a massive room with my bags sitting near the doors to a large balcony.

Slamming the door shut, I take a minute to try and gather myself.

I want to scream and shout, but it's not going to do any good. This is what my life looks like now.

Let yourself be angry for once. Ava's words echo through my head as I look around my new room.

There is too much going through my mind to take any of it in. The anger bubbles to the surface as I allow myself to truly feel it for once.

I need to break something. I need to scream and make something look the way I feel on the inside. All I need is a distraction from how helpless and angry I feel.

Looking around the room, I spot a white vase sitting on the bedside table.

I pick it up, feeling the weight of it for a moment before screaming and hurling it at the wall on the opposite side of the room. Some of the anger leaves my body as the thing shatters with a crash, jagged little pieces flying everywhere.

I pick up a glass figurine from the bookshelf and throw that too. Glass rains down onto the dark hardwood floors.

As I stare at the destruction I caused, the anger starts to fade, giving way to exhaustion and sadness. But a stronger feeling arises.

Oh god. What have I done?

Tears roll down my cheeks as I hurry over to the pile of glass and ceramic.

I need to clean it before Christian walks in here and sees the mess. I don't know what he'll do to me if he finds out that I'm breaking his things.

I kneel down, and a sharp sting travels up my leg making me scream.

Tears start flowing as I sit back and look at the large piece of glass wedged in my leg.

The door to my room bursts open, and Christian comes running in, a gun in his hand.

"What the hell is going on in here?" He looks around the room before his gaze lands on me.

He tucks the gun into his waistband and shakes his head. "You know, if you want things to break, I have an entire set of dishes put away just for that purpose. My little sister likes to break shit when she's pissed off too."

"How would I know that?" I sit back and stretch my leg out in front of me.

My head starts to spin as I look at the blood trickling down my leg. "Do you have a bandage?"

"Come here," Christian says, crouching and scooping me up into his arms. "You look like you're going to be sick."

"I don't do well with blood."

He doesn't say another word as he carries me into the ensuite washroom and sets me on the edge of a massive tub.

I look out the window at the woods that surround the backyard.

It's a stunning view and one that I know I won't get tired of looking at for however long I'm here.

Christian is silent as he works, pulling the glass out of my leg with a pair of tweezers he found in a drawer.

White towels get stained red as he cleans up the blood and looks at the wound.

"You shouldn't need stitches, but I'm going to send a picture to the doctor to make sure." He pulls out his phone and takes a quick picture before returning his attention to my leg. "I'm sorry you're involved in this mess. I don't want your life here to be difficult."

"Somehow, I think it's going to be difficult whether you want it to be or not."

He just smiles and continues dabbing at the wound, sitting there with my leg in his lap and humming along to a song that only he can hear.

As he sits there with me for who knows how long, I wonder if there is more to him than meets the eye.

5

___

CHRISTIAN

My phone starts ringing before the sun comes up.

I groan as I get up from my position on the floor just outside Zoe's door.

After I finished cleaning her leg up last night, I carried her to bed and cleaned up the broken glass.

She didn't say a word to me, but I could see the quivering in her bottom lip the entire time.

It was only when I left the room and closed the door that her sobs started. Which is why my back is now stiff after sleeping in the hall in case she needed help.

I'm in so far over my fucking head with this.

I walk down the hall so Zoe doesn't wake up. "Hello, Jeremiah,"

I know I'm going to have to explain everything to her one day, but that day is not today.

It's clear that Jeremiah didn't bother to tell her my name which makes me think he's been trying to find a way out of the wedding since he arranged it.

"What the fuck do you think you're doing, Herrera?"

His voice is barely more than a hiss. "Do you think that this is some sort of fucking game?"

"No," I say as I head down the stairs.

If I'm going to be dealing with him this early in the morning, I'm going to need a lot of coffee. "But you seem to think it is. Tell me, Jeremiah, what did you think would happen when you went back on our deal? I know you're not a stupid man, but that seems like something a stupid man would do."

"You don't know what you've done."

"I did what I had to do to protect my family." Venom drips from my tone, and I end the call.

I don't need to deal with him at all. I have what he wants, which means he is going to do what I want whether he likes it or not.

The sun is starting to rise as I walk into the kitchen and dump grinds into the coffee machine.

I yawn and stretch, my back popping as I lean down to open the fridge and search for the cream.

I don't know how she takes her coffee.

Running my hand through my hair, I shut the fridge.

I should let her sleep. She's had a long night and she's going to be in pain when she wakes up.

I put a bottle of painkillers beside her bed while she was sleeping last night, but I don't know if those are going to be enough.

Even though the cut didn't need stitches, it looked like she was going to be in pain once the shock of everything that happened yesterday wore off.

My phone starts ringing again the moment I step onto my back porch with a steaming mug of coffee in my hand.

I shut the door behind me before taking a seat on one of the loungers by the pool and pulling out my phone.

"How is the problem back home?" Billie asks the second I answer her call.

"Good morning to you too. You do know that the sun is just now coming up, don't you? I haven't even had a sip of my coffee yet."

Billie laughs, completely unbothered. "I needed to make sure that you got home okay. You didn't seem happy when you left here. What's been going on since you got back home?"

"I'm not talking to you about it." I take a long sip of coffee before setting the mug on the table beside me. "Not a chance in hell. Now, tell me about how the party for the resort's opening went. And how is being engaged?"

"You're trying to change the subject. That means that there is girl trouble brewing. You have to tell me what's going on. Now. Or I swear I will be getting on a plane today."

Fuck. I know she's serious. "Fine."

I run my hand down my face. "It's girl problems. Well, girl adjacent. I have some people that have been after me for a very long time. Names from my men are leaked. Cops show up and arrest my people. I kill the rat. Wash, rinse, repeat."

"And what does the girl have to do with it?"

"Well, I made a deal. Mutually beneficial. The girl was supposed to be the signature on the deal. The marriage I was telling you about."

Billie gasps. "Christian! What did you do?"

I scowl at the pool. "Why do you think that I did something?"

"Because you don't talk to me about your girl problems unless you *did* do something. What did you do?"

"Well, the wedding was supposed to be today, but they

called me when I landed to back out of the deal. So, I kidnapped her and forced her to fulfill her end of the bargain. Not that she knew it was me she was supposed to be marrying."

"You're an asshole," Billie says, amusement in her voice. "A massive asshole. Fucking criminals and their damn honor codes."

I laugh and reach for my coffee. "You talk as if you aren't a criminal as bad as the rest of us."

"That's not the point." She sighs.

I can imagine the disapproving look she would be giving me if she was here right now.

"Look, I understand that you took her to make a point and ensure the safety of your people, but this is going to be hard for her. You need to go easy on her."

"Maybe I should start calling Hadley for girl advice."

"Screw you." Billie laughs as something crashes in the background. "I have to get going. Some of the new capos have decided to fight over a girl and nobody else is here to kick their asses for it."

"Look at you. I remember when you wanted to get out of the life."

"Things change. People change. Soften yourself for this girl, Christian. She might be worth it if you're going to have to spend a lot of time with her."

The call ends, leaving me staring down at my mug of coffee, wondering if Billie is right.

I know I can't be as hard with Zoe as I am with others.

She doesn't know what she's walked into yet, but I'm going to have to show her. And fast.

Zoe is going to need to know the dangers of this world and what happens if she disobeys me.

Which I'm sure will be a challenge all on its own if her

smashing things last night is any indication of how our relationship is going to go.

It's almost dinner time when Zoe finally makes her way out of her room.

She wraps her arms around herself as she stands beside the kitchen island and watches me dish out the crawfish boil I made for dinner. Her stomach growls as she sits on one of the stools.

"How are you feeling?" I push the bowl toward her, sticking a fork in it.

She grabs the fork and spears one of the chunks of potato.

"Is the cut bothering you at all? Did you remember to clean it?"

"I cleaned it," she says, her voice monotone as she looks up at me. She bites her bottom lip for a moment, pushing food around her bowl.

"What's bothering you, Zoe? You look like there's something you want to say. When it is just the two of us here, you are free to say what you want."

Her eyebrows furrow as I dig into my food. "Am I trapped here?"

"I would say so. That's usually what happens when you get kidnapped."

"So, that means that you won't let me go to my gig tonight? I'm supposed to be performing at the same bar I was last night."

Her eyes are watery, but she doesn't let a tear fall. Within a couple seconds, the wounded look in her eyes is gone.

I sigh and run my hand through my hair.

I don't like the idea of taking her out where her father could get to her. I don't want to lose her this soon. Not when so much is on the line.

If I have Zoe, her father isn't going to let the authorities come after my cartel. He'll be too worried about what I will do if he does.

On the other hand, I don't want her to be miserable here. She is just the pawn in the middle of a dangerous game, and she doesn't deserve to be kept from her passions.

I watched her entire set last night. Zoe comes alive when she is on stage, and it's clear that being in the music world turns her into the person she is deep inside.

The shell of a woman sitting in front of me right now, docile and looking down at her plate like she's already given up, is just the façade she presents for her parents and the media.

I want to bring out that fire that's burning in her. The anger that I can see simmering just below the surface.

If she gets nothing else out of this, I want her to be able to stand up to shitbags like her father.

"Zoe, I know that the chances of you liking it here are low, and that's fine with me. You can hate me and the rest of the people here. It won't matter to me one bit."

Confusion shines in her eyes. "It won't?"

"No."

She is in the middle of my problems with her father, but that doesn't mean she needs to like me. It might be easier if she does, but I'm not holding my breath.

If I'm being honest, I don't want us to like each other. It complicates things.

Everything about my life would be easier if we act like we are just two people who live in the same house. Roommates. Although, trying to think of her as only a roommate is hard when I know what her soft curves feel like beneath my hands.

Zoe nods. "Well, that's good, then. I happen to think you're a heartless bastard."

I laugh and shrug. "Think what you want. I'll take care of you while you're here, and that means allowing you to continue to pursue your career."

Her mouth drops open, and her fork clatters to the plate. "Really?"

"I have a stipulation, though. For my peace of mind. It's one that I will not budge on, so do not try to negotiate with me."

Her eyes narrow like she is waiting for me to deliver the worst news of her life. "What is it?"

"You need to take a protection detail with you. If I'm there, then you won't need to, but on nights I can't go with you, I expect other people to be with you."

Zoe purses her lips and nods. "Okay."

"Good. Now that we have that settled, eat your dinner. We have a show to go to tonight."

I finish off my food and leave the room before I can do something stupid. Though I don't know what that stupid thing may be.

When it comes to Zoe and those big green eyes, I don't know if there's anything I wouldn't do.

Having her here is a risk I probably shouldn't have taken.

6

ZOE

I smooth down the ripped denim skirt, looking at myself in the mirror.

Tonight, the eyeliner is darker than ever, and my lips are painted a deep shade of burgundy. The makeup is an armor against the rest of the world.

I can't cry if I have to worry about my makeup rolling down my cheeks.

As I step out of the washroom at the bar, I see the several men who have to follow me around. Christian promised that they wouldn't be there if he was around, but something came up before the show, and he had to take off.

I toss my hair over my shoulder, trying to maintain a false sense of bravado as I walk down the hall and back onto the dance floor.

The men disperse, hiding among the crowd as I start to dance. I have time to kill before my set, and I want to spend that time dancing away the nerves.

The last thing I thought I was going to be able to do was chase my dreams. When I got married last night, I thought my life was going to come to an end.

Even though I don't like having a bunch of men follow me around, it's better than the alternative. I could have to kiss my dreams goodbye, but Christian doesn't seem to want that.

The busier I am, the less time he has to spend with me.

The thought is fleeting.

Spending as little time with Christian as possible should be a good thing. I don't want any part of whatever he is involved in. Because whatever it might be, I suspect it isn't good.

Why else would he have to force me to marry him.

"You look stunning tonight." Christian appears at my side with a grin that promises nothing but trouble. "It's like another version of you comes to life when it's time to perform."

"Yeah, I guess you could say that." I stop dancing, my attention lasered in on him.

My stomach does a little flip flop when the smile falls, and his gaze drifts up and down my body.

"What is it? Should I have worn something else?"

He raises an eyebrow and shakes his head.

"Why would I want you to wear anything else? You look amazing. Although, I should probably get you a ring or something. I'm not the kind of man who is going to enjoy people hitting on my wife."

My cheeks warm as I roll my eyes. "I might be your wife, but that doesn't mean that we have to act like it. You can carry on with your life, and I can carry on with mine."

Christian leans closer to me, stealing the air from my lungs with a single heated look.

I hate how flustered I feel when I'm around him. He just looks in my direction, and I feel like I'm melting into a puddle at his feet.

It has to be the tattoos. No man has any business looking that good and *having tattoos. It's not fair.*

"What makes you think that carrying on with our lives would be in any way acceptable to me?" he asks, his tone low as he takes my hand and pulls me to him. "We're married. Which means that you're not going to be seeing anyone else."

I snatch my hand back from him, crossing my arms. "And what about you? Do you get to sleep around with whoever you want?"

The corner of his mouth twitches, and he shrugs. "Would it matter to you?"

"If I don't get to sleep around, then neither do you!"

Not that I sleep around at all. Hell, I have never even slept with a man, not that I'm going to tell him that.

The closest I've gotten to sleeping with someone was when he had me pressed up against the wall last night.

He chuckles and straightens up. "I guess that's only fair. Until you come begging for me to make you feel good."

I roll my eyes. "I doubt whatever you're working with could ever make me feel good."

As I stand there, considering whether or not to wipe the smug smirk off his face, I wonder why I can't be this version of myself all the time.

This is the version I like the best. The Zoe who doesn't let other people take advantage of her. The Zoe who is kind but is still able to speak up for herself.

That's the person I want to be all the time, but I've always struggled to come to terms with her.

Christian grabs my hand and spins me around, pulling me back against his chest.

His heartbeat races against me as his arms wrap around

my waist. His head rests on my shoulder, his teeth grazing my earlobe.

"I could make you feel all kinds of things, Zoe. You just have to beg for it."

My cheeks flame, and when I turn to look at him, he's laughing.

I flip him off as the band on stage finishes their last song.

"Funny. You think this entire thing is funny. I could blow your entire plan for whatever it is you're doing right now."

He lifts a shoulder and drops it. "You could, but then I would leave you in the capable hands of your protection detail while I go speak with your father. Now, if you want to play stupid games, I have a whole line up of stupid prizes for you. However, I really don't want to give them to you."

"You're infuriating." I poke a finger into his chest. "You think you can do what you did, then come here and rile me up? You have another thing coming."

Christian grabs my finger, holding it tight. "You're lucky that I'm the only one who can hear you right now."

I swallow hard, my heart racing.

He's a dangerous man. I should know better than to toe the line with him. After all, he was willing to kidnap me in the middle of the night and force me into a marriage to get what he wants.

Don't make stupid mistakes, Zoe. You still don't know what this man is capable of.

If there wasn't a security detail posted around the bar, I might have a chance at running. However, they would catch me before I got through the doors.

It's too risky to even try.

And he did say that I could still perform. He's not

making my dreams seem like they're a waste of time like Mom and Dad do.

This entire situation is ridiculous.

"Zoe!" The owner of the bar, Joe, comes over with a smile on his face.

He loops his arm over my shoulder, completely ignoring the murderous look Christian gives him. "You were great up there tonight. I knew that making you a regular here was going to draw in the crowds."

"Thanks, Joe." I shrug my way out from beneath his arm.

I'm already in enough trouble with Christian. I don't want anything else to happen.

"I mean it. There were some agents in the crowd tonight. I have no doubt that you'll have people approaching you with some deals before you know it."

He looks over at Christian and holds out his hand. "Joe Tellegato. I'm the owner of this place and the person who keeps telling Zoe that she has to start performing more."

Christian takes his hand and shakes it. "She is something of a songbird. I agree with you, though. It would be a shame not to go after her dreams when she is so good at it."

I stare at him with wide eyes, not quite believing what I'm hearing.

My heart thuds against my chest, conflicting feelings racing through my mind.

I should be upset with him for this entire ordeal, but it's hard to get over the high of performing.

Especially when he thinks that I should follow my dream.

"Well, I'm going to leave you two to the rest of your night. Have a good time. I'll see you next week, Zoe. Put on another performance like that, and I'm sure you'll have those agents knocking down your door soon."

Joe disappears back into the crowd, heading to the bar while my cheeks warm.

Christian watches me for a moment, his gaze unnerving.

I shift my weight from one side to the other, not quite sure what he's expecting from me right now.

All the confidence I felt earlier has flown out the window, giving way to the need to be whatever I'm supposed to be in this moment.

"You look nervous," he says, the corner of his mouth twitching. "Do I make you nervous?"

"Wouldn't you be nervous?"

Christian shrugs and tucks his hands in his pockets. "I think you'd be stupid to let your guard down around me. I'm not a good man, and I've hurt a lot of people."

"You said you wouldn't hurt me." My gaze connects with his and I hold it, some of the nerves fading away. "I have a hard time believing you are the kind of man who would go back on his word, even if you are a criminal."

Christian chuckles and steps closer to me, his chest brushing against mine. "You don't know the first thing about me."

My heart threatens to pound out of my chest. "You're right, I don't. But we're married now. Aren't I supposed to be getting to know you?"

I want to run, but I know that I can't. I have to stay with him to keep Dad alive, which means that I need to play the game.

If that means that I have to play along with this marriage, then that's what I'm going to do.

Even if it's terrifying to think of getting close to this man.

Christian smirks and shakes his head like I've made the biggest mistake of my life. "Well then, let's get out of here, and we can get to know each other."

THE CAR FEELS TOO small as we drive along a winding road through the woods.

I can't shake the feeling that something bad is going to happen, even though all we've done is listen to music.

When the car finally comes to a stop beside a lake, my heart stops in my chest.

"Did you bring me out here to kill me?" My voice wavers as I look over at him.

Christian laughs and turns the music down. "Why the hell would I kill you when you're still useful to me?"

I feel like I'm going to be sick. "I don't know what you actually want with me, but I think killing me in general would be a bad idea."

"I'm not going to kill you."

He sighs and hits a button, his chair moving all the way back and tilting a bit. "I like to come out to the lake when I need time to think. It's quiet. There's not a lot of quiet when you run a cartel. There's always some sort of problem and someone wanting something."

"Cartel." I exhale, trying to process that piece of information.

I knew he was involved with something dangerous, but I didn't think it was the cartel. "As in guns and drugs and sex trafficking?"

"Not the sex trafficking," he says, his tone sharp. "Only

sick bastards sell people like they're fucking commodities. My cartel may be involved in all kinds of crimes, but human trafficking of any kind isn't one of those crimes."

I bite my bottom lip, watching as the wind outside creates waves on the lake. "Why are you telling me this?"

"You might not have chosen this life, but it is yours now. You should be prepared for the dangers that you're going to have to face eventually."

Great. More danger.

My pulse races as I kick off my heels and lean back against my seat.

"I don't know what to think about this."

Christian looks over at me, the dim lights from the dashboard illuminating his face. "Ask me whatever questions you want right now. I'll answer what I can."

There are several different places I could start.

I want to know what he gains by being married to me. I could ask him how long I have to be trapped in a loveless marriage to him. However, none of those are what is bothering me the most.

When it comes to what he gains and how long I have to be with him, I already expect the worst.

It's the freedom he is giving me that seems to get under my skin.

"Why did you let me go to the performance tonight?" I twist in my seat to face him, leaning against the door.

Christian takes my leg, running his hands up and down my calf. Everywhere he touches makes my nerves feel like they're on fire.

He inspects the bandage on my leg before pealing a corner off and looking at the cut beneath.

"You're a pawn in a chess game you don't need to understand," he says, leaning closer to get a good look.

"There's no sign of infection but you have to make sure you clean it again when we get home tonight."

He puts the bandage back in place but leaves my foot in his lap.

His hand strokes up and down my leg but he doesn't seem to even notice he is doing it. And I'm not going to ask him to stop either.

Even if he scares me, there is no denying the chemistry between us. The way I feel when he touches me is the same way I feel when I perform.

"I'll make sure I clean it again." I pull away from him, needing a clear head. "What do you mean, I'm a pawn?"

"I'm not going to go there with you right now," he says, his tone stern. "You don't need to know about all the monsters that lurk in the dark. Just know that you are safe with me."

"Are you going to let me keep performing?" I change the subject, knowing that it's not good to press right now.

If there is one thing a lifetime of people-pleasing has taught me, it's when to back off.

Christian has a look in his eyes that says he isn't going to tell me what's going on behind the scenes. The last thing I want to do is make him angry when I have no idea what he's capable of.

"Yes," he says without giving it a second thought. "You're amazing up there. I've never seen a performance quite like it. You have a way of connecting with the audience that makes me feel like I was part of the show. It was something else entirely."

My cheeks warm and butterflies erupt in my stomach. "Do you really think that?"

"I have no reason to lie to you, Zoe. You were so good up there. I'm sure that one of the agents is going to contact you soon. Someone is going to want to sign you before another label has the chance to snatch you up."

I shift in my seat, shaking my head. "That's not going to happen. I'm good, but I'm not that good. I don't have enough time to really work on music. My family wants me to focus on building another career for myself."

"Good news," Christian says with a boyish smile. He leans closer to me, his face inches from mine. "You're no longer with them. You can do whatever the hell you want."

"As long as it's alright with you."

His gaze darkens and drops to my mouth. "You would like that, wouldn't you? Someone to take charge and tell you what to do. You want someone who is going to tell you that it's okay to go after what you want."

I don't know what to say.

The car seems to grow a thousand degrees hotter as he closes the distance between us.

His mouth moves against mine as his hands slide up my legs.

Then, he grabs me before he lifts me and moves me to his lap.

Straddling him is a whole new sensation.

He grins as he pulls away to look up at me.

"If I'm going to be the one to tell you what to do, then I want you to ride my face. Right now."

"What?" My mouth drops open, and my cheeks feel like they're on fire.

"Every major accomplishment should be celebrated with an orgasm," he says, like it's obvious. "Don't worry, Zoe. I don't want anything else in return. I just want to make you feel good. I can see you getting lost in the things going on in your head. Just let go and have what you want for one night."

"And what makes you think an orgasm is what I want?" I'm stalling, and I know it. Though I've gotten myself off multiple times, I've never had a man tease me with his tongue until I come.

"Because you were dry humping me in a bar last night. Let me make you feel good, and then we can go home and pretend it never happened."

I should tell him no. I should demand to get more answers about what is happening to me, but for tonight, I just want to let go. I want to give in to the fire burning bright in his eyes as he leans his seat all the way back.

He shifts down the seat, making enough room for my knees on either side of his head. "Come on, Zoe, let me taste you. Just once."

"You know, it's pretty hard to turn you down when you say it like that."

Maybe an orgasm is all I need to break this strange tension between us. The heat between us will leave and then I can move on with my life.

And I want him.

Even though I know it's a bad idea, I really do want him.

I move to hover over him, gripping the back of the seats behind us to keep myself upright while his tongue traces along my wet slit.

My hips rock as he dips one finger into me.

"Fuck," I say, breathless as he sucks my clit. I roll my hips, trying to get more of him as he slides a second finger into me.

My pussy clenches around him as he takes his time to thrust his fingers inside me.

He groans, his tongue circling my clit.

Christian massages my inner walls while his free hand grips my hip, guiding the rocking of my hips.

As he continues to tease me, my core starts to clench.

He sucks on my clit again, sharp waves of pleasure rolling through me.

His fingers move faster as wetness coats my inner thighs.

His hand digging into the flesh of my hip only turns me on more. I know that there are going to be bruises in the morning, but I don't care.

Right now, I only care about how it feels to ride his face.

Christian groans, his fingers pressing against a spot inside me that drives me wild.

My entire body shudders as he thrusts faster, pressing against that spot over and over again.

When he sucks on my clit, I crash over the edge of an orgasm, my back arching as I come.

As soon as the shaking stops, I move back into my own seat.

My cheeks feel like they're on fire, and I can't bring myself to look at Christian.

I shouldn't have done that. I should have just told him to take me home where I could have hidden in my room and pretended that everything was fine.

Going forward, I have to keep my distance from him.

He may be charming, but he is dangerous and threatening my family.

I would be a fool to forget that.

7

CHRISTIAN

The blaring of sirens has me jumping out of bed and grabbing my gun from my nightstand.

It takes only a second to pull on a pair of shorts before hurrying down the hall to Zoe's room.

As I get to the door, someone shouts and there's a crash.

I try the handle only to find it locked.

My heart hammers in my chest as I slam my shoulder against the door and tumble into the room.

Zoe is standing on her bed, a lamp in hand while a man stands on her balcony with the doors open.

There is shattered glass at his feet—a mix of the window he broke and whatever it was that she threw at him already.

I don't think twice, aiming the gun at the intruder's leg.

A gunshot rings through the room before the man drops to the ground, blood pouring from his leg.

Zoe screams before scrambling off the bed and out of the room.

I don't take my eyes off the man on the ground.

"You picked the wrong house to break into," I say, walking over to him.

I check him for a gun and come up empty. "Although, I'm sure that this was more than just an attempt to steal some money, isn't it?"

The man groans, holding his leg. "You're a fucking bastard."

'You've got that right." I crouch down beside his head, grinning as I look at him. "But you haven't seen anything yet. Just wait until I get you alone in a few minutes."

Ruben comes rushing into the room, his hair standing on end and his glasses off kilter. "I got the message about the alarm going off."

"Good." I set up the alarm system to alert his phone as well. "I've got to deal with this. Go find Zoe and take her to the library. Keep her in there until I come to get her."

"Who is this?" Ruben asks, pushing his glasses on top of his head and rubbing his eyes. "I should have put the damn contacts in before I rushed over here."

"Now you know for next time."

I stoop to search the man for weapons. When I find none, I punch his lights out and toss him over one shoulder. "Don't know who he is yet. But I'm going to know soon."

Ruben grins and nods, leading the way out of the room. He takes off in search of Zoe while I head to the hidden elevator that leads to the basement.

The man groans as I deposit him on the floor of the elevator and smash my finger against the button.

The ride down is quiet, but I can feel the tension building. I can almost smell the fear seeping off this man. I slap him awake.

"You know, you really shouldn't have broken into my home. I don't like intruders. Hell, I think they're the scum of the earth. You would rather profit off another person's hard work than to do anything for yourself."

The man groans and tries to pull himself into the corner of the elevator as the doors open, as if that is going to do anything to protect him.

"You don't have to make this harder than it needs to be." I grab the ankle of his injured leg and pull him out of the elevator.

His screams ring out as I drag him across the concrete floor to the middle of the soundproofed room.

The rest of the basement is through a door to my right. Out there, it looks like a normal basement stacked with boxes of things I don't need right now but might need in the future.

The door is hidden—a secret that only a few people know. It's the kind of place I take people to when I need answers.

"Now," I say as I go over to the row of knives hanging on the wall. "You can make this simple for yourself. You can either tell me what I want to know, or I turn you into a human quilt. It's not a pretty process either. I'm not the best at cutting even squares into skin yet, but I'm getting pretty good."

I try to disconnect from what I have to do as much as possible.

I hate this side of myself—the one that is capable of such brutality. It was beat into me at a young age and only continued to grow as I grew older.

My father used to claim that the leader of a cartel was nothing if he wasn't brutal.

It's something I've tried to change since I took over. I hope it's something that Camila continues to change once she is in power.

"We'll start with something simple." I grab some coiled rope off the wall. "I'm going to tie you to a chair so you won't squirm too much when I cut you. While I'm doing that, you can tell me your name and who sent you."

The man glares at me, his eyes narrowing as his teeth grind together. "Fuck you."

I chuckle and grab him by the arm, hauling him up and onto a chair.

He doesn't try to fight as I tie him up.

Smart man. I would only hurt him more if he tried to fight.

"Like I was saying, this can go one of two ways. The first is that you're going to tell me what I want to know, and I'll kill you quickly. The second is that you're going to want to play the big macho man and waste my time. If you choose option two, know that I'm going to take my time with you, so I would think about which option hurts you less before you make your decision."

I shrug. "Now, I don't care which one you pick. Just FYI, there is no option in which I don't hurt you or you live."

I finish tying him up and take a moment to stand behind him and still my shaking hands.

My entire body feels like it's at war with itself as I go back over to the wall of knives and pick a scalpel, perfect for precise cuts.

I hate what I have to do. I hate that I have to do it. But what I hate the most is knowing this fuckface was in Zoe's room.

He could have hurt her. Taken her.

I need to make my message crystal clear. Come for my wife, and you'll die.

"I'm not telling you shit."

Chuckling, I drag my scalpel down the side of his face just hard enough to leave a line from eyebrow to jaw. "Are you sure that is your choice? I want this to be easy between us, but if you aren't going to tell me anything, then we're going to have to go with option two. And option two kind of pisses me off even more."

Blood trickles down his face as he shakes his head.

Fear shines in his eyes as I give him a matching mark of the other side of the face.

"What were you here for?"

Before giving him a chance to answer, I cut off the tip of his finger.

He screams, the sound dying as soon as it hits the soundproofed walls.

"Scream all you want. There is nobody out there who can hear you."

"The woman." He gasps as he looks down at the blood.

"Pathetic." I drag another line down the side of his face. "All it took was losing the tip of a finger to get you to start talking. If my men were as weak as you, I would kill them for it."

The man whimpers as I drag the tip of the blade along the curve of his ear.

He tries to shrink back from the knife, but there is nowhere to go.

The muscles in my jaw flex as I consider killing him now.

I know who is trying to get to Zoe. There's only one person outside the people closest to me that knows she is here.

I have to make a point, though. I need to send a message. That's what any other leader would do in my position.

I have to make it clear that those who break into my home and try to take what's mine will pay for it.

"And who sent you after her?" I press the tip of the blade against his earlobe.

He shakes his head, the sharp point scraping against his skin,

Blood trickles down the side of his neck as he looks at the ground.

"Last chance before I cut off your ear." I position the knife at the top of his ear. "Who sent you here?"

"Jeremiah Redford."

I sigh, shaking my head as I crouch down in front of him. "That really wasn't so hard, was it? All you had to do was tell me the truth."

His eyes grow wide as I stand up and position the blade at his throat.

Tears roll down his cheeks as I drag the scalpel from one side to the other.

My stomach lurches as I take a step back and force myself to look at what I've done.

I stare at the body for only a few moments before leaving the bloody knife on the table at the side of the room.

I strip out of my shorts and step into the shower to wash away any blood splatter before heading to a little closet beside the door.

After pulling on my clothes, I head out of the room and message my cleaning crew.

They can handle the mess inside while I go deal with the man behind my most recent problems.

THE SUN IS JUST STARTING to rise when Jeremiah walks into his home office, wrapped in a black robe with a cup of coffee in his hand.

I stay still in his chair, the back turned to him so he can't see me.

It might be something straight out of a bad horror movie, but I need this man scared.

I've been waiting here for the last couple of hours, hoping he would stumble in here to call his man and ask about his daughter.

As his footsteps creak across the hardwood floors, I turn in the chair and look at him.

Jeremiah stills, his expression blank even though I'm sure he's fuming.

"I've been waiting to talk to you," I say as I lean back and cross my arms. "I thought that our little arrangement was going to work out. I really wanted to believe that you were a greasy politician with a heart made of something other than flaming dog shit, but I guess I was wrong."

"What the fuck are you doing in my house?" he asks, his voice tight with rage. "Get out of here, or I will be calling the police. I have some high-ranking friends who would love to get some time alone with you."

"Cute." I grin and kick my feet up on his desk, watching the way his gaze darts around the room.

He may play the tough guy, but we both know who is in control right now, and it isn't him.

"Sending a man to break into my house and try to get to Zoe was stupid. I should kill you for that, but then you'd stop being useful to me."

"You're a monster. Your kind deserves to rot in jail."

I roll my eyes and stand up, rounding the desk to stop in front of him. "What I can't figure out is why you are sending a man after your daughter. What was he supposed to do when he got to her? Do you really want me to have to kill her and you?"

"She would be better off dead than with you. She wouldn't have to pay for my sins that way. She would be free of this entire mess."

"What entire mess?" I loom over him, watching the way his jaw quivers. "What is going on here that I'm missing? I may be a monster, but I doubt that would be enough for you to think that Zoe would be better off dead."

"Keep her name out of your fucking mouth. My man was only supposed to take her and bring her back to me."

"And yet you think that she would be better off dead than with me. Why is that?"

"Get out of my house before I call the police."

I study him for a moment before looking down and seeing the small panic button in his hand. "You really are an idiot, aren't you?"

"They will be here in a few minutes. If you know what's good for you, you'll be gone before they get here." He gives me a smug smile and sips his coffee. "I will have my daughter back one way or another. She isn't going to spend her life with a monster like you if I have anything to say about it."

"You come for her again, and I will gut you where you stand."

I spin and take off, ducking through the window I broke to get in.

Sirens scream in the distance, red and blue lights illuminating the early morning sky.

I run across the property and disappear into the woods.

Now, to get home and make sure that Zoe is alright.

As I head toward my waiting car, I know that Jeremiah is too proud of a man to back off.

I'm going to have to keep a watchful eye over Zoe to make sure that he doesn't try anything stupid again. Even though the plan was to keep away from her as much as possible.

I groan and run my hands down my face the moment I get in my car.

This arranged marriage is turning into more of a pain in the ass than I ever thought it would be.

8

ZOE

"How are you feeling?" Ruben asks as he sits on the couch beside me in the library. "Christian should be on his way back soon."

"What happened to the man with the gun?" I ask, my voice faltering.

My heart is still racing, and my hands shake as I bring my mug of coffee to my mouth.

"Will all due respect, I don't think that you need to know. It's not going to be pretty and some things you will be better off remaining ignorant about."

My stomach lurches.

I don't know what to say or think.

One moment, I was asleep. The next I woke up with the distinct feeling of being watched.

I started screaming and throwing whatever I could reach as soon as I saw the man come through the balcony doors.

I was sure that I was going to die when he pointed a gun at me.

I hate this life. I just want to go home where it's safe.

I want to curl up with Ava and watch horrible rom-coms until I finally feel better about everything that's happened in the last few days.

There is a knock at the door before it opens and Christian walks inside.

Ruben gets up and nods to him before looking down at me.

"You have my number now," he says, reaching out to tug my blanket around my shoulders a little tighter. "I'm sorry that we had to meet under these circumstances, but if you ever need anything, please don't hesitate to reach out to me."

"Thank you," I say, my vision blurring as I look down at the coffee.

It's been a long night, and all I want to do is crawl back into bed and get some sleep. If sleep is even going to be possible at this point. I don't know what would have happened if Christian wasn't there to protect me.

Ruben says a few whispered words to Christian before leaving the room.

The door shuts behind him again, cutting off the light from the hallway.

I look around the room, not quite sure what to say to Christian first. It feels as if my entire body is frozen with fear right now.

I try to count the books lining the shelves that surround three sides of the room as a way to try and distract myself, but I lose count after the first couple.

The lamps cast dim light around the room while the sunrise filters through the window.

"How are you holding up?" Christian's voice is soft as he sits in one of the leather armchairs across from me. "I know that tonight has been a lot. I'm sorry for leaving you with Ruben, but I needed to handle the man who broke in. I wanted to make sure that everything was dealt with properly."

"It's okay." I try to swallow the lump in my throat. My hands are still shaking as I hold my mug a little tighter. "It's been a long night. Ruben is nice, though. He made me coffee and got me a blanket."

"Ruben is great. He's my right-hand man. If you ever need anything, and I'm not available, he is the person you should speak to."

A long silence stretches between us as the events from the last few hours keep racing through my mind.

All I can see is the man with the gun standing in front of me.

I was going to die tonight. It's a thought that chills me to the bone, but it's one I'm certain of.

God, what kind of life am I living right now? I married a man who kidnapped me. I just watched him shoot a man in the knee to protect me.

I just want to go back home.

"Zoe, you look like you're a million miles away right now. What's going on? You can talk about it with me. A man breaking into my house isn't normal, but I can't promise you that life is going to be as simple as the one you're used to."

I put my coffee mug on the table between us before sitting back on the couch.

Christian watches as I pull my knees to my chest. After nestling deeper in the blanket, I close my eyes for a moment.

My heart pounds against my ribcage as I think about the way the night could have gone differently.

When I open my eyes, not quite sure I'm ready to talk

about it, Christian is still watching me. There is a softness to his gaze that makes me think I can open up to him.

He's been nothing but kind to me, even though he is infuriating at times.

"Living with my family was simple. We knew there could be the threat of something happening to us at home, but the threat was unlikely. There were a lot of security agents around at all times. I didn't have to worry there because I knew that my dad and the people he paid were looking out for me."

Christian's jaw tenses, his hands curling into fists on the arms of the chair before relaxing. "I'm going to be increasing the security detail around the house. It's not going to happen again. I know you might not believe me, but I'm going to keep you safe while you're here. I don't want anything to happen to you."

"You're right." I play with one of the tassels on the end of the blanket. "I don't really believe you. I don't know why I should. I feel safe with you right now, but I don't know why someone came after me. It's like my worst fear coming true."

"I'm sorry," he says, his voice solemn. "I wish that I had seen this coming so I would have been able to better prepare the house. It's not going to happen again, though. You're going to be safe here, Zoe. This is your home."

"It doesn't feel much like a home." My voice cracks as I look at him. "I'm sorry. I know that you're doing your best to make me feel comfortable here, but I don't know if I ever will."

He nods, understanding flashing in his eyes. "I know. I wish that things didn't have to be this way."

"They don't have to. You're the one who made this

happen. You could divorce me and let me go home. Please. I miss my family. I want to see my sister."

Christian gets up and comes to sit beside me on the couch as tears start to cascade down my cheeks.

His hand touches my back before pulling away.

After another moment, his arm settles around me while I try to get the tears under control.

"I'm sorry." I wipe away my tears even as new ones fall. "It's the long night that's getting to me. I'll be alright if I can just get some sleep."

"Don't do that." Christian's hand drifts up and down my arm.

I lean into him, seeking comfort in the touch even though the little voice in the back of my head tells me that I should be running away from him.

"Don't do what?" I hiccup, my cheeks turning red.

I hate that I'm falling apart like this in front of a man I barely know.

My mom and dad would be ashamed of me if they saw it. They raised me to keep a cool head, even when times get tough. And now here I am, leaning on a stranger and crying on his shoulder.

"Don't diminish your feelings to make way for someone else's. If you want to cry, go ahead and cry. I might not be the best at comforting people, but I raised my younger sister. I can handle some tears."

I watch him for a moment, seeing only honesty shining in his eyes. "I want to go home. I miss my family. I wish that I was back there with them."

He sighs, his hand stilling on my arm. "I can't take you back to them right now. Believe me, I don't like this situation any more than you do. As soon as I can take you back to them, I promise I will."

"How do I know you're going to keep your promise?"

Christian shrugs. "I don't know. You're just going to have to make the decision to trust me or not."

He makes it seem so simple, as if there aren't a dozen other factors that go into whether or not I can trust him.

As I sit there, looking around the library, I try to come to a decision about Christian, but I can't.

He might have protected me tonight, and I will always be grateful for that, but he is still the man who forced me to marry him.

"Is there any way I could see my sister? Other than seeing her at a bar after a performance? Could I go out to visit her? I just want to talk."

He sighs and moves away from me, running his hand through his hair. "I can't let you leave the house yet. Not for the next few days until I get better security in and around the property, but she can come over to spend time with you, if you want."

"You really mean that? You'll let Ava come over to see me." Hope bursts through me.

"I might not be a good man, Zoe, but I'm not a monster. Your sister is welcome to come over here and see you whenever you like. She'll have to check in with the security team I'll be placing at the front gate, though."

I nod, knowing that this is the best deal I'm going to get.

Honestly, I'm shocked that he is allowing this much. I wouldn't think that a man who kidnaps someone is going to be open to requests.

I expected to be kept like a prisoner, but instead he is letting me have as much freedom as he feels like he can allow.

I don't know what to do or how to process any of that information.

My head aches as I stand up and head for the door. "I'm going to go to bed for a couple hours and try to get some sleep."

Christian follows behind me.

"Take one of the guest rooms for now," he says, his voice gruff as he holds open the door. "I'll have someone get your room cleaned up and put back together by the time you're awake."

"Thank you." My chest constricts as he stands in the doorway. "Thank you for saving me tonight, and thank you for letting me see my sister."

"I don't want you to be unhappy here, Zoe." He gives me a crooked smile. "Now, try to get some sleep. I'll be down here getting some work done if you need me."

With a nod, I head for the stairs and climb them, my palms sweaty and my heart pounding in my chest.

I don't know if I'm going to be able to sleep without nightmares.

"Zoe!"

I sit up in bed, sweat coating my skin.

My voice is hoarse from screaming, and the man with the gun is still standing in front of me even as Christian turns on the light.

His eyes are wild as he looks around the room before walking over to the bed.

My breathing comes in rapid bursts as I scramble backward on the bed, trying to make sense of everything going on around me.

"Zoe, it was just a dream. Everything is okay. It was just a dream." Christian sits on the edge of the bed and takes my hand. "Listen to me, okay? It was just a dream. You're safe and in bed. Just take some deep breaths and try to focus on the sound of my voice."

"He was here." My voice wavers. "He was here, and he was going to hurt me. You weren't there to stop him this time. I was going to die."

"You're okay now." He pulls me into his arms, holding me tight against his chest.

I should want to shove him away but instead, I cling to his shirt, trying to let the smell of his spicy-sweet cologne ground me. "It felt so real."

"I know it did. Everything is going to be okay. That man is never going to be able to hurt you again."

After a few minutes, I pull away from him, some of the fear fading from my body. I look around the room, noticing how dark it is despite the crack in the curtains.

"What time is it?" I ask, running my hand through my hair.

"Close to midnight. You slept through the entire day." The corner of his mouth twitches. "I'm going to head to bed soon. Is there anything you need from me before I go? I can make you something to eat if you're hungry."

"Please don't leave." My voice is barely more than a whisper as I lean back against the headboard. "I'm not hungry, but I don't want to be alone right now. Please don't leave."

He hesitates as he looks at me before stretching his legs out on the bed and leaning back against the pillows beside me. "I'll stay."

"Can you talk to me about something? Just distract me?"

He nods. "What do you want to talk about?"

"What did you spend your day doing?" I try my best to

relax even though my mind is racing with everything bad that could happen to me right now.

"Just work things. Not that exciting. I have a couple different businesses I run and a trainyard I own to keep up with."

"Tell me about that." I glance to the windows before looking at the bottom of the curtains, half-expecting to see a pair of feet sticking out beneath them. "I want to know what you do for a living."

As he begins to talk, I find myself melting back into the pillows.

I know that I'm safe with him, even if the rational part of my brain says I shouldn't be.

Christian isn't going to hurt me, that much I know is true.

It's just everything else about him and my new life that I'm questioning.

9

CHRISTIAN

Zoe is already out of bed when I wake up the next morning.

I don't remember falling asleep beside her, but I know I stayed up with her, talking about my various businesses until her soft snores filled the room.

Staying with her last night was a mistake. Staying with her in bed was an even bigger mistake.

I was sure that I would be able to keep my distance from her, but now I don't know how to do that.

Zoe was so scared last night. I couldn't just walk away and leave her to face more nightmares on her own.

I should have left as soon as she was asleep.

This isn't the way our marriage is supposed to go. I'm not going to let her get close to me, and I'm certainly not going to get close to her.

It's better if we don't. Safer. For her.

Groaning, I stretch and get out of bed.

The sun is streaming through cracks in the curtains while the scent of waffles wafts through the house.

I head to my room and take a long shower before getting dressed and heading downstairs.

Zoe is in the kitchen, flipping waffles out of the waffle maker and onto a plate. She hums to herself, the melody one that I don't recognize.

When she turns and sees me, her gaze drops to the band shirt I'm wearing and her nose wrinkles.

"Really?" she gestures to the shirt with the spatula in her hand. "*The Golden Haze*? You've got to have better taste in music than that. All they do is steal the hard work other artists have done and then try to pass it off as their own."

"Didn't know that." I look down at the shirt and shrug. "It's a comfortable shirt."

She rolls her eyes and pushes the plate of waffles across the kitchen island to me. "I made you these. Thank you for staying with me last night. I know that it was weird to ask, and I should have been fine on my own, but it was nice to have you there. It made me feel a bit better."

"Zoe, it's fine to ask for help when you need it."

She gives me a wry smile and turns off the waffle maker. "Not if you grew up in my family."

"Yeah, mine was the same way. I don't know about you, but I make it a point to be nothing like my parents."

It's more than I've said to anyone about my family life in a long time. It's also the most that I'm going to be telling her. The last thing I want to see is the horror in her eyes if she ever finds out about all the trouble in my family.

"I'm going to go get showered and dressed," she says, scurrying out of the kitchen.

I watch her go before digging into my breakfast.

As I pour syrup over the top of my waffles, Camila walks into the kitchen with a grin on her face. I groan and tilt my head back, looking at the ceiling and wondering what I did to deserve this.

"I should have taken away your key," I grumble as she snatches a waffle off my plate and takes a bite. "What are you doing here? Don't you have to study or something?"

"Don't have classes today, so I thought I would talk to you about whatever the hell that was at the airport and meet my new sister." Camila grins as she pulls herself up to sit on the edge of the counter. "Kill two birds with one stone."

"Camila, you don't have to do this right now. I'm sure that you have other things you could be doing."

"You only think that because you don't want to talk about why you got shot at when we were at the airport."

"I don't know what there is to talk about. Somebody tried to kill me, I killed them instead."

"And then after that, you ended up married." Camila crosses one leg over the other as she glares at me. "What I can't figure out is why I wasn't invited to my brother's wedding."

"It was a spur of the moment kind of decision." I shrug.

I do feel guilty for not asking her to be there. Even though I know she doesn't approve of the situation, I didn't think that I would ever get married without my sister there.

Hell, I didn't think I would get married period. Now that I am, I feel horrible for not asking Camila to be there.

"I thought that I would have been there to tell you what a horrible idea it was to kidnap a poor woman and perform the entire ceremony at gunpoint."

"First of all, no guns were pointed during the ceremony. And second, keep your voice down." I look to the door before finishing off my last waffle. "I don't need Zoe to hear this and get upset again. It's the first time that she's been in a seemingly good mood."

"Gee, I wonder why." Camila's voice drips with sarcasm.

She slides off the counter. "You should have done better, Christian. Kidnapping a woman to get married is stupid, even for you. Now look at what you have to deal with. If you had just let the deal fall through, you could have waited until you found someone that you would fall in love with."

I scowl and stand up, crossing my arms. "Falling in love is for people who want their lives to be ruined when they lose the people they care about. Families push each other to do horrible things that only pull them apart in the end. I don't want that."

Camila rolls her eyes. "You're so full of shit, Christian. If you really believed that, you wouldn't have spent years raising me and making sure that I was going to turn out fine. You wouldn't still be putting me through medical school."

"You're an exception to the rule."

Camila opens her mouth to reply, but it snaps shut when Zoe walks into the room with a towel wrapped tightly around her body.

Her eyes grow wide as she looks between me and Camila, clutching the towel a little closer.

"Sorry." She stammers over the word. "I was just going to go out for a swim instead of that shower. I didn't mean to interrupt."

Camila bounces forward with a bright smile. She throws open her arms and pulls Zoe into a hug. "Welcome to the family. I'm Camila, Christian's younger and far more brilliant sister. You must be Zoe."

"Yes." Zoe pulls out of the hug and looks over Camila's shoulder at me.

I shrug and sit back down, knowing there is nothing I'm going to do to stop my sister now.

Maybe Camila being herself is exactly what I need to scare Zoe into keeping her distance from me.

I love my little sister more than life itself, but she can be a lot to handle at times.

She doesn't trust people easily, which means those that she does trust are the only ones she truly spends time around.

She's always in my business, unless it's inappropriate in regard to the cartel, and won't settle for anything other than knowing what she wants to know.

"Why don't we both go for a swim together? We can crack into one of the nice bottles of wine Christian has and spend some time getting to know each other."

Camila is already opening my cupboards and rummaging around for wine and glasses while Zoe stands there looking stunned.

Camila isn't the kind of woman who is going to take no for an answer, and it's clear Zoe can see that by the way she nods and follows her out the door.

Hopefully, this doesn't blow up in my face. The last thing I need is for the two of them to become too attached to each other.

Even though I don't want them to bond too closely in case this marriage ever comes to an end, it will be good for Zoe to have someone in the cartel she can trust.

I was telling her the truth when I told her that I want her to be comfortable here.

Camila grins as she stirs the *Sudado de Pollo* on the stove, the scent of chicken wafting through the house.

Zoe sits at the kitchen island, folding *empanadas* with a glass of white wine beside her.

The two of them are laughing and talking with each other about some band I don't know while I go over quarterly reports for the trainyard.

Soft instrumental music is playing in the background while Camila cooks.

"So," Zoe says, her voice raising a little louder.

I look up from my paperwork to find her staring at me. "Do you know how to cook amazing food too, or is it just Camila?"

I chuckle and shrug, leaning back in my chair. "I'm better at cooking than she is. She used to burn the chicken all the time."

Camila sticks her tongue out. "I did not. He just liked to distract me and then the chicken would burn while he was doing something like pulling my hair."

Zoe grins and raises an eyebrow. "Were you a little terror as a child?"

I scoff. "I was an angel. Don't listen to anything that comes out of her mouth. I was the perfect child. Nobody could have asked for a better child."

Right now, this conversation is safe. As long as we talk about being kids and growing up together, we won't get into anything too deep.

There are things that Zoe doesn't need to know. Things I don't want to bring up with Camila either.

Our childhood wasn't all sunshine and rainbows.

How can it be when you're raised as children of a cartel leader? There are expectations to be kept and a brutal life to be lived.

It's not a part of my life that I want to sit here and talk about.

"I have a hard time believing you were an angel." Zoe looks to Camila for confirmation.

Camila nods. "He was a little shit as a child. Mom used to say that he was always into everything. If he could cause trouble, he did."

Zoe's smile widens, making a rush of warmth spread through my body.

I hate the way I feel when she turns that beautiful smile on me. It makes me feel horrible for what I'm doing to her, even though I know I have no other option.

I do have another option. I could find the rest of the bastards trying to ruin my life. I could commit more time to hunting them down and killing them.

Except I can't. Not now that Zoe is in my life, and I have to worry about her father coming after her.

"You're going to have to tell me more stories." Zoe takes a sip of her wine, glancing at me before turning her attention back to Camila. "If I'm part of the family now, I should know what I'm getting myself into."

Even though she tries to sound confident, her voice wavers just enough that I notice.

Sadness shines in her eyes while Camila launches into a story from our childhood.

The longer Camila talks, the more upset Zoe looks, and the more I hate myself for dragging her into this.

10

ZOE

For the last week, I've done nothing but spend my time wandering around the house and getting to know every corner while Christian goes to work.

I've been writing a couple songs, but most of them aren't anything I would ever want to record.

Even now, my guitar sits in the corner of my bedroom, mocking me.

God, I'm never going to be able to write a good song again. I'm going to be trapped in this house, and I won't be able to get my career off the ground.

I'm going to spend the rest of my life as nothing but a housewife.

I should have listened to my family. I should have had a backup plan in place or given up on music entirely.

My chest constricts as I look at the guitar, knowing that songwriting is the least of my problems.

I'm trapped in a house and unable to leave unless I have a performance. Which I haven't had in the last week.

Joe's bar flooded which means I got a call telling me that

the bar would be closed for a couple of weeks, leaving me without anything to do.

I sigh and stare up at the ceiling, wondering if today is going to be the same as all the others.

The early morning sunlight streams through the gauzy curtains, reminding me that there is an entire world out there that I don't get to experience right now.

All because of a protective man with a dark beard and a gaze that makes me feel like I'm coming undone at the seams.

I could go for a swim.

Except Christian watches me when I swim. I know he does, even if he is sitting in the library with the windows open and pretending that he can't see me.

Tension builds in my core as I think about the way he looked at me that night at the lake.

It was like I was the only person in the world who existed to him at that moment.

I felt wanted.

It was a dangerous feeling and one that I know I could get addicted to way too fast.

Before I know it, I could end up far deeper into this forced marriage with him than I ever planned to be.

I don't know if I could ever love a man like him, even though I want him.

Except the emotions are there. I can feel them lingering at the back of my mind when I catch him in the kitchen, singing along to songs in Spanish or talking with his sister when she comes over for dinner every other night.

I need to get him out of my system.

As I get up to make sure the door is locked, my heart is racing.

I keep thinking about the way his tongue felt as he

teased my clit until I came. Heat pools between my legs as I make my way to the ensuite bathroom.

The bathtub fills with steaming water.

I groan as I slide down into the water, feeling some of the tension ease from my muscles.

I close my eyes, imagining Christian hovering over me.

I picture his hands running over my body as I trace patterns on my skin. I can still feel his lips on my neck like that night at the bar.

My fingers dip between my legs, circling my clit as I arch my back.

I try to stifle a moan, thinking of the way Christian's fingers felt when he plunged them inside of me.

All I can think about is how it would feel for him to tease me again. To feel his fingers rocking inside my pussy while he licks my clit.

I tease my nipples with my other hand, rolling them until they're stiffened peaks.

My pussy pulses as I circle my clit faster.

I push two fingers into my pussy, moaning as I ride my hand.

When I move back to my clit, I'm teetering on the edge of an orgasm.

"Christian," I breathe as I come.

As I lean back against the tub, coming down from the high, I know I'm playing a dangerous game.

It starts with being attracted to Christian and ends with being in over my head.

I take another moment to relax before getting up and getting in the shower.

I take my time letting the steam permeate the room while I scrub the memory of Christian's hands from my skin.

By the time I finish and get dressed, I've almost forgotten about the way his body feels against mine. Almost.

"There you are," Christian says, grinning as I walk into the room. "I was going to get you sooner, but the walls are thin, and you sounded like you were busy."

My cheeks flame as I look up at him. "I was just having a shower."

"Sure. If that's what we want to pretend you were doing, that's what we'll pretend you were doing."

"What were you going to get me for?" I ignore his teasing the best I can.

If I could die right her, right now, just to avoid this conversation, I would consider it.

"I have a surprise waiting for you in the library. I know that it's been a long week, and you haven't been able to get up to much, but I thought this might make up for it."

My curiosity spikes as I head down the hall to the library.

When I open the door, Ava is standing in the middle of the room with her arms wide open. I laugh as I race toward her, my vision already blurring.

Ava stumbles as I launch myself at her.

We fall onto one of the couches, laughing and hugging each other. It takes a few minutes to sort ourselves out and stand up before heading for the door.

"Come on." I loop my arm through hers and pull her along with me. "You are going to die when you see the pool. It has to be one of the most beautiful pools I have ever seen. There's this waterfall with a bunch of pretty white stones behind it."

Ava hurries to keep up with me as we move through the halls and step into the backyard.

Her mouth drops open as she looks around at the

massive backyard that opens up to the woods beyond. She shakes her head and looks back at me.

"This is where you live?" She looks at the pool that stretches from one end of the house to the other, disappearing around one corner. "You have an entire outdoor kitchen set up."

There is a large rocky hill behind the pool that flattens out on top to an entire outdoor entertaining area.

I've spent most of the last several afternoons on the comfortable loungers up there, attempting to write music and playing some of my favorite songs.

"This is where I live." I let go of her arm and lead the way to the stairs that lead to the outdoor entertaining area.

Ava is silent while we climb the steps, but I know there is a lot on her mind.

Her eyes shine when I look back over my shoulder at her. She is struggling with this as much as I am.

"Alright, now that we're alone, why don't you tell me whatever is bothering you the most right now?" I fall back in the hammock, and she lands beside me.

We rock together, staring up at the sky and the fat clouds that drift across it.

Sitting here with her reminds me of the afternoons we spent together when we were younger.

We used to spread out a pile of blankets in the yard and spend the entire afternoon just staring at the sky and talking about our futures.

"What the hell is all of this? Why are you living with this man? He told me that you decided to go through with the arranged marriage after you and Dad sat down to talk with him."

I squeeze my eyes shut, hating for a moment that I have to lie to her. "Dad needs help, and getting married is what it took to help him. I know that it may not be the most ideal situation, but it's what works for now. Christian is a good man."

"And what's he do for work? How is he connected to Dad? How the hell can he afford this kind of lifestyle?"

I look at her and shrug. "He owns a trainyard, a few bars, and a couple other businesses."

She nods, taking it all in. "I still hate the thought of you being married to a man you don't love. Did you really think this through, Zoe? I know you want to help Dad, but there have to be other ways to help him."

"This was easy, Ava, and this fixed things fast." I smile and look back up at the clouds. "Christian may not be the man I always pictured marrying, but he is a good man, and I know that my life with him is going to be good."

"I still don't know about this, Zoe. I want you to want so much more for yourself than this."

"I'm still working on my music. Hell, I might have more time for it now than I did before. There won't be a ton of dinners to attend with stuffy politicians who want to kiss Dad's ass all evening."

Ava laughs. "Yeah, I guess you do get to avoid that now. I'm jealous. He hosted a dinner the other night. You should have seen the looks on their faces when they asked me what I did. Dad tried to play it off as if I was just a nurse. I think Mom nearly shit herself when I told them I was a nurse at the Ryderson Penitentiary."

"Of course." I smile, everything about my body feeling lighter with Ava here. "You know she is never going to let you forget that you embarrassed her in front of the people Dad wants to impress."

"He's the Head of State. I doubt he has to do much more than flaunt his title around to impress anyone."

We fall silent for a few minutes, rocking in the hammock and watching the clouds drift across the sky with the gentle breeze.

Ava hums one of my songs to herself, her eyes drifting shut.

I can't remember the last time I got to spend a day with my sister, relaxing and enjoying the day.

Even when I was at home, there was always something that we had to do to impress the politicians Dad was working with or help him get ahead in his career.

At Christian's house, there is none of that. I finally feel like I have the space I need to be who I want to be.

"Are you happy here, Zoe?" Ava asks, finally breaking the silence between us. "Are you really happy here, or is this all just an act because you're afraid to disappoint Dad?"

"I'm happy here," I say, and it feels like the truth.

Christian isn't the worst man to have as a husband, and Camila is a great sister-in-law, when she isn't bothering me about teaching me how to shoot a gun.

It isn't the life I pictured for myself, but it seems like what I need right now.

For the first time in my life, I feel free.

11

CHRISTIAN

The light in the office is only growing dimmer as the sky darkens outside. The low shuffling of trains echoes through the night as my general manager walks into the office with his dinner tucked under one arm.

"Evening, boss," Tomas says as he goes over to his desk and takes a seat. "So far, there is only a twenty-minute delay in the schedule for tonight. We should have everything cleared by the time the sun comes up."

"Good." I close the door to my office behind me. "See to it that the men are kept busy all night. I don't want to get any reports of trouble going on like I have the last few nights."

"Won't be happening on my watch."

"Good. Have a good night."

Rain is starting to drizzle as I step out of the office building and make my way to the parking lot.

I sigh and pull my coat closer to my body, trying not to get soaked as I walk around a couple of empty shipping containers.

A heavy weight collides with me as I round the last one.

I groan as we go sprawling to the ground.

Fists collide with my face as whoever jumped me manages to get on top of me.

I throw my forearms up to block the punches before driving my knee into the man's back.

As he rolls off me, he pulls out a knife.

I jump back as he swings the knife at my ankles.

It takes him only a second to get to his feet and come charging at me.

The black mask he wears slips but not enough for me to recognize the man trying to kill me.

"Fucker." I duck inside the man's reach as he swings again.

I slam my fist into his side, pain blossoming in my hand as he goes stumbling back.

Advancing on him before he has a chance to recover, I grab his wrist and force the knife out of it.

The man groans as I grab the back of his head and drag it down to knee him hard in the face.

Blood pours onto the cracked concrete as he stumbles to the ground.

As I pick up the knife from where it fell, my pulse is pounding.

To say I'm getting sick of the attempted assassinations is an understatement.

I stab the man in the chest, feeling the warm blood against my fingers.

He sputters, looking up at me with glassy eyes through the small hole in the mask.

"Fucking bastard." I pull off the mask.

My chest constricts as I stare down at the face of a man who used to be like an uncle to me. "It didn't have to be this way."

I throw the mask on the ground, my stomach lurching.

This is yet another reminder that getting close to someone is a bad idea that will get you hurt. It's also a reminder that all I'm ever going to be is the monster who kills people.

There is no hope for a man like me.

With a sigh, I run my hand down my face, considering what to do with the body. While I know that I should have my cleaning crew handle this, the darker part of me wants to show Zoe what this life is really like.

She's been too comfortable in the past week.

And though I want her to be comfortable in my home, I don't want her to be comfortable with me.

I hate the way the lingering glances and casual touches make me feel.

I know that she isn't doing it on purpose. She's a touchy person. I've seen as much from old interviews of her when her dad was rising to power.

There are some days when she looks at me like I'm not a monster.

Maybe Zoe needs a reminder.

I take off at a quick jog to my car before driving back over to the body.

It takes a few minutes to load the body into the car. I try not to look at his face as I do so, wanting to remain as detached as possible. There are no more old relationships.

He was like an uncle to me and then he tried to kill me.

I did what I had to do to survive. I can't blame myself for that.

I drag out the cleaning supplies I keep in my trunk.

In my mind, a silent little mantra keeps playing as I erase blood from concrete in the dark of night while the rest of the trainyard works.

It was kill or be killed. And I'm not ready to die just yet.

Once the blood is as cleaned up as it can be, I pack up the supplies and get in the car.

It's time to show Zoe what happens when I have to be the bad guy.

When I walk into the house an hour and a half later, Zoe is sitting on the couch.

She's got herself curled into one corner with a notebook in her lap. There's a pencil shoved through her messy bun and another one in her hand as she scribbles down music notes.

"You're home later than expected," Zoe says, looking up at me with that sweet smile of hers. "I made dinner. Yours is staying warm in the oven. I can heat it up for you if you'd like."

"That's not necessary."

Her eyes narrow as I step into the dim lamp light.

She springs to her feet and crosses the room, already reaching up to fuss over me. "Why is there blood on your face and clothes? Are you hurt?"

I take her hands and gently move them away from me before taking a step back.

Right now, I need to be cold and distant. I need to teach her what to expect in the cartel, and I can't do that with her so close to me.

"There are some things you need to know about what it means to be married to the head of the cartel." My tone is gruff as I turn and walk back out into the front hallway. "Come with me. I have some things to show you."

"What things?" She follows behind me.

I wait while she grabs her coat and slips on her shoes. "You'll see when we get where we're going."

"Anything to get out of the house." Her tone is cheerful.

More guilt rolls through me.

I hate keeping her locked up like this, but I still think her dad is going to come after her.

Time will come when I'm going to need to loosen up a little bit, but today is not that day.

Not when there are more important matters at hand.

I can't find anything to say to her on the way to the car. There is no way to explain what I'm about to do to lessen the hurt.

She is never going to look at me the same way. Not when she sees what I'm capable of doing with my bare hands.

Hell, *I* can't look at myself the same way after knowing what I'm capable of.

She is silent as we drive through the dark streets, heading away from the city.

I clench the wheel until my knuckles turn white, trying to remind myself that this is for the best.

"You need to see the truth about the world you're living in." I turn off the main road and onto a hidden one. "I have people who are coming after me. They try to kill me whenever they can."

Zoe bites her bottom lip as she looks at me. Her chest rises and falls with the shuddering breath she takes. "And what does that have to do with what's happening right now?"

"There's a body in the trunk of my car." I keep my eyes on the road, needing something to focus on while I talk to Zoe. "And we have to dispose of it."

To her credit, she doesn't react.

The car is silent as I pull up to a small cabin set deep in the woods.

Zoe stares at the cabin as she takes slow breaths. I know she is trying to keep herself from freaking out.

Anyone in their right mind would be freaking out right now.

Sooner or later, we would've had to get to this point. Without knowing about the monsters that lurk in the night, she is vulnerable in this life. She needs to know this is my life, and it isn't pretty.

People are coming for me. They might be coming after her too.

In a dog-eat-dog world, I need to be the alpha. The uber-predator. And I need her to stop looking at me like I'm not one of those monsters.

We need some distance from each other before we get too tangled up in the chemistry between us.

I can't get close to her and risk losing her.

As soon as the car is parked, Zoe gets out and hurries over to a bush.

She throws up as I open the trunk and look at the body there.

When she straightens up and wipes her mouth, I lift the man out.

Zoe looks like she is going to throw up again as she stares at the man I have draped over my shoulder.

"Come on." I head toward the house. "You need to see this."

She hugs herself, her eyes wide and shining with unshed tears.

My stomach lurches as I approach the retina scanner for the cabin and wait for the door to open.

Zoe enters behind me, though she looks like she is about to run.

The door slams shut behind us as lights come on, revealing stainless steel tables, white walls, and an assortment of saws and knives.

Zoe stands in the corner with her arms wrapped around her body. Her skin is pale, and she sways as she stands.

I'm not sure that she's going to be okay, but this is the reality of life in the cartel. One way or another, she is going to learn.

As I put the body on a table and step into a white jumpsuit, she lets out the first whimper.

"This is what has to be done, Zoe." I pick up a butcher's knife and one of the saws. "I want you to watch this. You need to understand that this is what happens to those that cross me."

Anger flashes in her eyes. Her jaw tightens and she gives a sharp nod.

"There's a suit over there." I point to another white jumpsuit. "Go put it on and then come over here. Do it fast. I don't want this to take all night."

Zoe looks at me, her bottom lip quivering. After a moment, she goes to grab the other jumpsuit.

I watch as she pulls it on with shaking hands.

Even though I wish I didn't have to be this man to her, I need a safeguard. If I go down because she decides to run to the cops, then she goes down with me.

As she walks over to the table, I begin to cut the man's arm off, knowing that my relationship with Zoe is never going to be the same.

12

ZOE

Camila sits beside me in the library early in the morning, her mouth pressed into a thin line.

"Ruben told me what happened last night. He had to go up there and burn the bush you threw up in after Christian brought you home. I'm sorry that he did that to you."

I stare at her, too numb to say anything right now.

Last night, I watched a man get cut into tiny pieces. I became an accomplice to a crime.

Christian dragged me deeper into his world than I ever wanted to be.

I still don't know what happened to those little pieces, but I can use my imagination.

I've lost track of how many times I've thrown up in the last twelve hours.

Though I knew that Christian kills people and has to get rid of the bodies, it's one thing to know it and another to see it.

I don't know how to look at him the same way.

"Zoe, I know that this is hard to deal with, but you need to pull it together." Camila reaches out to take my hand in hers. She holds it tight, her thumb rubbing circles into the back of it.

"How can you say that to me after I watched your brother cut someone he killed into pieces? He put me in a jumpsuit and made me stand right beside the table, Camila. How am I supposed to get over that?"

"You have to," she says, her tone stern. "The cartel is a hard place to be a woman. You have to get over it because there really isn't another choice. I know that this is hard. I cried for a week after I saw my first dead body. I'm still haunted by nightmares filled with the face of the man I had to kill."

"You had to deal with that, and you're still going to sit here and tell me to get over it?"

"It's get over it or become food for the wicked little games powerful men will try to play."

Camila lets go of my hand and leans back in her chair. "My brother is a good man when it comes down to it. Anyone with eyes can see that he cares about you. What he did last night was wrong, but he's trying to prepare you. It's better that you see the person this world has forced him to be in an environment he controls. He kept you from seeing the worst of him for as long as he could."

I want to argue with her, but there is a part of me that knows she's right.

This is a different world I'm living in. Letting the mutilation eat away at me day in and day out is only going to make life worse for me.

Other people are going to see weakness and exploit it. I saw it time and time again growing up.

"Don't let anyone publicly see how much it bothers you." Camila's voice is soft as she pulls my blanket a little higher. "When you're alone, feel as shitty about everything happening as you want, but you're in this life now. When you walk out of this room today, this needs to be behind you. It has to be."

"And if it's not?" My voice cracks.

"Then do your best to pretend that it is. You are a strong woman. You saw what happened last night, and you were able to keep yourself from fully falling apart. You can do this, Zoe. Just focus on the person that you know Christian is outside of what he has to do for the cartel."

"That seems impossible."

She shrugs. "Do people judge you on your worst days? Or do they accept those days as horrible days and judge you for who you really are?"

Camila makes a good point, though I hate it.

I'm not sure I'll be able to move forward, but I have to try.

There is no escaping from this life or the reality of who Christian has to be when he needs to.

I've seen both sides of him now. The protector and the monster.

He can turn the monster on, then turn it back off again. But which is the true Christian?

There is a knock at the door before Camila can say anything else.

My heart freezes in my chest.

For just a moment, I consider pretending that we're not in here. I don't know if I'm ready to face Christian after last night.

"Let him explain." Camila stands up and squeezes my shoulder. "Everything is going to be fine. If you need to talk to somebody later, you can always talk to me. Ruben is good to talk to if you can't find me, even if he can be an ass sometimes."

I chuckle but it feels hollow—like I'm just going through the motions and trying to survive.

I have to talk to Christian, though. I need to understand who is the real him. I need to see that there is still a good side of him.

"Come in." I pull my blanket tighter around my body.

Camila nods at me and stoops to give me a hug before pulling away and looking at her brother.

"We need to talk." Christian's voice is choked.

The last thing I want to do is talk to him. Not after what happened last night.

My hands shake as I try to force ice into my veins. I can't let him see how much this scares me. I need to stay strong.

"I'm going to leave the two of you alone to talk." Camila gets up and leaves the room.

I don't want her to go, but this isn't a conversation that can happen with her here either.

I glance over my shoulder at Christian and shake my head. "I think you said all you needed to say last night with that little show. Your message came through loud and clear. I don't know how there can be anything left to say after that."

I want to get as far away from him as possible.

My stomach turns just looking at him.

I knew Christian was a bad man, but I didn't know that he was capable of *that*.

How the hell can I stay in this life when I watched him cut a body to pieces? How can I look at him and try to see both sides to the same person with compassion?

As much as I want to get up and run, there is no point.

He would just hunt me down and kill my dad. That's even clearer now.

Christian crosses the room and takes a seat in the chair next to mine. "You haven't been to bed yet."

"You think that I'm going to be able to sleep after watching a body get cut into little pieces?" I scoff, even as my heart starts to race. "There is no way that anyone is going to sleep well after that."

"You're right," he murmurs.

He stares out at the yard, but it looks like he's a million miles away.

"I had to take you out there last night. There was no other choice. I know that you're aware that I have to kill people. You know that you're living in the cartel. It didn't seem like enough, though. Didn't seem like you quite understood the real risks of this life."

I don't speak for a moment, trying to figure out what there is to say to him. "You're right. You never should have done that to me last night. Not without warning. If you want to show me the horrors of this world, then fine. Do it. Maybe I *am* too innocent. However, I'm your wife. That means something to me, even if this is all just some sick game of yours to get back at my father."

"He owed me a debt. This is the collection."

I wave a hand. "It doesn't matter what this is. You owe me more than dragging me out at night to cut a body into pieces. You owe me a warning. If you want me to be aware of the dangers in this life, then I deserve to be warned of those demonstrations. I've done nothing wrong."

Christian hums, nodding as he continues to stare out the window.

His hands flex where they grip the arms of the chair. "I'll give you a warning next time. I understand that you weren't prepared to see any of that last night."

"I might be someone you forced to marry you, but I'm not a toy, Christian. I need to know you understand that."

This is going to have to be the way I lock away the damage he did last night.

I have to pull myself together. I have to make it clear to him that I will not accept this again.

I need to do one hell of a job pretending that I'm okay, even when I'm falling apart.

His Adam's apple bobs.

He looks at me for the first time since sitting down, and I can see the sorrow in his eyes.

I'm not sure that the sorrow has anything to do with what he did last night.

I think that there is far more going on beneath the surface than he is ever going to tell me.

What I need to do now is face the future. This is never going to be a normal marriage. It's clear that he doesn't want it to be either.

We are going to remain distant. Maybe friends if I'm lucky.

The thought of spending my life with someone who doesn't love me, who hurts me because they think I need a wakeup call, is horrifying.

Even the tender parts of Christian don't make up for the darker parts.

I'm going to have to learn how to live with both of them. Camila made that clear.

There is no choice in his life. Just the things that he has to do and the things that he cannot escape.

I don't need to be one more person adding stress to his life. I don't need to make it harder.

Maybe, if I'm the one person showing him kindness

despite what he is, the monster that lurks beneath the surface will start to fade.

At this point, I'm willing to try anything to make my life easier in the cartel. Even if that means pretending to move on from what happened last night.

"I do understand that." His voice is hollow. "You have a show tonight at the bar, don't you?"

"I'm allowed to go?" Hope fills my voice.

Performing is exactly what I need to distract myself tonight.

Stepping on that stage is the one thing that makes me feel complete. Everything else will fade away, and all I have to focus on is the music.

He nods. "Of course. Music is your career. Things might be rough right now, but I'm not going to keep you from that."

My heart plummets to my stomach.

Once again, I don't know what to think of the confusing man in front of me.

One moment, he is cutting up a body, and the next, he is supporting my dreams.

I put on my best fake smile.

This isn't the life I want for myself, even if it is the one I'm stuck with, so I need to make the most of it.

"Thank you. I think I might try to take a nap before I head to the bar tonight, then. Hopefully, I'll be able to get some sleep."

Christian nods as I get up. "Is there anything you want to do after your show?"

A million different things race through my mind.

I want to swim in the ocean. Ride a roller coaster until I can't think. I want to scream about what's happening in my life until my lungs give out. Curl in a ball and cry until I have no tears left.

Fall hopelessly in love.

Most of all, I want to bury the feelings I have for Christian as deep as I can.

"Can we go dancing?" I know that there is no way he will let me do that.

There are too many opportunities for things to go wrong. After all, the last time I went dancing was the night I got kidnapped.

Christian considers it for a moment. "Sure. Pick whatever club you want, and we can go dancing after."

He gets up and leaves the room.

I'm shocked that he would agree to let me anywhere near a club after the attack.

Maybe this is the first step to finding a functional relationship that works for us.

Maybe this marriage isn't entirely doomed.

THE BASS IS POUNDING as fog sweeps its way across the floor.

I run my hands along my body as my hips sway to the music.

Christian watches me from a few feet away at a table, the corner of his mouth twitching.

He sips on his drink as another man approaches the table and takes a seat.

I move toward my husband, but he gives a slight shake of his head and tips his drink toward me.

As I dance, I watch them talk, their heads bent close

together. They laugh together, whispering some more before the other man leaves.

Christian finishes his drink before joining me.

His hand presses against the middle of my back as he pulls my body close to his.

He sets the pace as I put my hands on his shoulders.

His hips sway, his forehead pressed against mine.

"Are you still mad at me?" His voice is deep. Low.

I run my hands up his shoulders, linking them together behind his neck. "It's not worth it."

He pulls back, a strange expression crossing his face. "I'm sorry, Zoe. I won't do that to you again."

"Good."

Christian spins me around before pulling me back to him.

His body presses against mine in all the right places.

Maybe it's the drink I had going to my head, or the high I get any time I perform, but I want him.

Even if our relationship is never going to be anything more than a casual friendship, I can't deny that I want him.

I try to push what I saw from Christian last night to the side.

All I want right now is to pretend that we're a normal married couple just out for a good night together. Tomorrow morning, I can go back to figuring out how to deal with all the different facets of Christian.

His hands slide up and down my curves before he dips me low.

When Christian pulls me back up to him, I feel the heat building between us.

He gives me a smile that makes my heart skip a beat.

"How much have you had to drink tonight?" His voice is throaty as he trails his nose along the side of my neck.

"Just a whiskey before I went on stage." I tilt my head back as his mouth starts to take the same path as his nose.

"Good." He pulls back to look at me for a moment, his heated gaze dropping to my mouth. "Me too."

His mouth captures mine, the taste of whiskey on his lips.

I moan as his tongue twines with mine.

Christian's grip on my hips tightens as he pulls me closer. His hardened cock presses against me through the thin layer of clothes separating us.

When his hand slides lower, moving beneath the slit in my short dress, heat builds in my veins.

His fingers drift across the slip of silk at my core, teasing me.

"People are going to see what you're doing." I tilt my head back as he kisses his way back down my neck.

"Don't care," he growls, before grazing my earlobe with his teeth. "You know the best part about fighting is the make-up sex afterward."

"Oh, is that true?" I keep my tone teasing as he nips at my neck. "What was your meeting about?"

"Doesn't matter." He flicks his tongue over the skin he was biting, soothing away the sting. "All that matters right now is seeing the face you make when you come. It's all I've been thinking about since you got yourself off in your room."

I stiffen, my core clenching as his fingers press against my clit. "We're in the middle of the club."

"And everyone else is too drunk to give a shit about my fingers in your pussy." He slides a finger into me as I grab his shoulders.

"Christian."

He kisses me again, nipping at my bottom lip while his thumb presses against my clit.

I moan as he teases me, pulling out his finger and sliding his hand out of my skirt.

We're breathless as he stops kissing me to take my hand and pull me to a dark corner of the club.

Wetness pools between my thighs as he spins me around, pinning me between his body and the wall.

I gasp as he picks me up, his hands sliding under my skirt to massage my ass.

"Christian, this is a bad idea. I'm not going to sleep with you in the middle of a club."

He chuckles and digs his fingers deeper into my flesh. "You know, you were soaked a couple minutes ago. I'm pretty sure that a part of you likes this."

My cheeks warm as I run my fingers through his hair. "I'm not going to answer that."

Christian smirks and presses his body harder against mine. "I'm going to take that as a yes."

His cock throbs against me as he leans into me.

Heat burns through my body as I lean in and kiss him.

Christian groans as I bite his bottom lip before smoothing my tongue over it.

My core clenches as he rolls his hips.

"Take me home," I breathe as he sets me on the ground.

"Planning on it." He loops his arm around my waist, his hand splayed against my lower back. "I'm going to be the only man who gets to see you come tonight."

I wonder how he'll feel when he finds out he in the only man who has ever made me come.

We stumble into Christian's bedroom, our bodies wrapped around each other.

I moan as his hands roam along my curves.

He cups my breasts, his thumbs drifting over my nipples through the thin material of my crop top.

"I have to tell you something." I pull away from Christian.

I take a couple steps back to put some distance between us.

He watches me as he takes off his shirt.

Every reasonable thought I've ever had leaves my body at the sight of his tattoos and muscled torso on full display.

It's hard to think that a man like him would want to be with me.

"What is it?" His voice is gentle as he grabs my hips and pulls me back to him.

"I never... I mean, this is..." I close my eyes.

"Whatever it is, you can tell me."

"Okay." I take a deep breath. My voice fails me when I confess, "I'm a virgin."

I wait for the look that crosses everybody's face when they hear that.

Most people think that it's odd to still be a virgin at twenty-four. The women I used to go out dancing with had all slept with someone by the time they were nineteen.

The one boyfriend I had after high school broke up with me when I said I was a virgin.

Christian grins and walks us back toward the wall, his fingers digging deeper into my hips. "Is that supposed to turn me off? Because you said it like you're expecting me not to want to bury my cock into you anymore."

My cheeks flame as I look up at him. "Men don't like virgins."

"Those men are fucking dumb."

He slides his hands beneath my shirt, pulling it over my head and tossing it to the side.

The wall is cool against my back as he cups my breasts again.

"If this is too much for you, let me know."

"No." I arch my back off the wall as he rolls my nipples between his fingers. "I want this. I want you."

Christian leans down, his mouth capturing mine in a searing kiss.

He groans as I slide a hand into the front of his jeans, palming his cock.

He throbs in my hand as we kiss.

Our tongues tangle together as I slide my hand up and down his cock.

I unbutton his pants and slide the rest of his clothing down his legs.

Christian gets to the ground in front of me, pulling my skirt down my legs.

He groans as he hooks his fingers into the sides of my thong, taking his sweet time.

As he pulls the fabric down my legs, he nips and sucks at my inner thighs.

"You're being a tease." I'm breathless as he slides his tongue along my wet slit.

"You're right." Christian looks up at me with a wicked smile.

He grabs one of my legs and pulls it over his shoulder.

I lean back against the wall, my back arching as I run my fingers through his soft hair.

Christian nips at my inner thighs until my core is aching.

His tongue circles my clit.

The slow strokes drive me wild. I need more of him.

Christian sucks on my clit as my hips rock forward.

His deep chuckle sends a shiver through my body.

He presses a finger into me as he flattens his tongue against the little bundle of nerves.

His finger moves, teasing me until he is buried deep.

"You're still teasing me." I roll my hips, trying to build the friction between us.

He circles my clit again.

His finger thrusts, stretching me before he adds a second.

"You're so fucking tight." His voice is raspy as he looks up at me.

There is something about having a powerful man on his knees for me that drives me wild.

Wetness drips down my thighs and my pussy clenches around his fingers.

I've never felt as wanted as I do with him.

"You're going to feel amazing wrapped around my cock."

Christian's fingers move faster, thrusting deeper as my leg tightens over his shoulder.

He groans, his tongue replacing his fingers in my pussy.

I moan, my core pulsating around him as he alternates between his tongue and fingers until I'm on the edge of an orgasm.

When he starts sucking on my clit again, the orgasm rushes through me.

My legs shake as I come.

He keeps pressing his fingers against my inner walls until I come down from the high of my orgasm.

Christian stands and licks his fingers clean before

pulling me closer to him. "Do you know how amazing your pussy tastes?"

I feel like my entire body is bright red as I shake my head.

He chuckles before kissing me, his tongue sliding against mine, making me taste myself for the first time.

I moan as his hand sinks into my hair, holding me in place.

When he pulls away from me, it's only long enough to guide me to the bed and lay me down on it.

His hands roam my body as he hovers above me.

His knees part my legs as he lines the head of his cock up with my core.

"I'm going to be gentle."

He groans as he inches his cock into me. "Shit, Zoe, you feel so fucking good. How are you?"

"I need more." I hook my legs around his waist and locking my ankles behind his back.

Christian exhales, like he is trying to keep himself in control.

He kisses me again, muffling my moans as his slow thrusts continue, burying himself to the hilt.

His weight settles above me as he gives me a minute to adjust.

I roll my hips, urging him to do more.

"Please," I say as he kisses his way down my neck.

My back arches off the bed as he pulls one of my nipples into his mouth.

His teeth graze the sensitive skin.

Christian starts to thrust, his hips rocking against mine.

I try to match his pace, my nails digging into his back.

He groans as he moves faster, thrusting harder into me.

Waves of pleasure start to roll through me as another orgasm builds.

"I want you to come for me," he growls low. "I want you to come all over my cock like the good girl you are."

My pussy pulses around him as he rolls his hips and grabs a pillow.

Christian lifts my hips long enough to place the pillow beneath him.

My nails rake down his back as the angle changes, and he thrusts deeper than before.

The new angle is enough to send an orgasm crashing through me.

I come on his cock, my wetness coating him as my back arches off the bed.

"Fuck." Christian rolls his hips, his cock throbbing as he comes. "You feel so fucking good."

He keeps thrusting until my pussy stops clamping down around him.

He pulls out of me and relaxes on the bed beside me.

I roll onto my side to look at him.

Christian tucks a strand of hair behind my ear as exhaustion starts to set in.

It's been a long couple of days, and all I want to do is relax.

"How are you doing?" His fingers run along my side, tracing over the curve of my hip and down my thigh. "Are you okay? Did I hurt you at all?"

"I'm great." I smile and reach out to press my hand against the side of his face.

My thumb drifts across his cheekbone as he watches me. "Just tired."

He smiles and turns his head to kiss my palm before

getting out of bed. He stoops down to scoop me up before turning and heading to the washroom.

"And what do you think you're doing?" I laugh as he sets me down on the counter.

"I'm going to get a bath going for us. It will help with any soreness."

As the tub starts to fill, I wonder how the hell I can see both sides of Christian and be okay with both of them.

Maybe one day, I'll find a way to accept both sides. Right now, though, there is no way that I can be okay with the monster. Not when I know what he is capable of.

Not when I've seen the blood on his hands.

I have to do what Camila says. I have to try to see the best parts of him for now and learn how to move past the rest.

The way Christian makes me feel is complicated and consuming.

I don't know what's going to happen in the future, but right now, I'm going to get in the bath with him and enjoy the night for what it is:

A moment in time that I might never get again.

13

CHRISTIAN

Zoe snores softly beside me as my phone vibrates on the bedside table.

I groan and roll over, running a hand down my face.

The last thing I want to deal with right now is another problem.

It's been a good night, despite what I did to Zoe yesterday.

I still can't believe that I could have been that cruel. I work so hard to not be that person, but when I'm trying to sabotage myself, the monster I try to hide comes rushing back.

I grab the phone and head into the bathroom, shutting the door behind me.

I want to crawl back into bed with Zoe even as I slide my thumb across the screen.

"Alessio, what's so important that you need to call me in the middle of the night?"

He chuckles as Billie shouts something in the background. "I was going to wait to tell you until the morning, but Billie said she would chop off my balls if I did."

I chuckle and flick on the bathroom light. "And what is she threatening you over this time?"

"I know who's after you."

As I lean against the counter, I roll my eyes. "I know who's after me too. The men who used to follow my father. This isn't new information."

"There's more!" Billie shouts in the background.

Alessio sighs. "Yeah. There is more. If she would let me tell you what I found, then she wouldn't have to shout over me."

"Billie is always going to be a brat. That's the woman you're choosing to spend the rest of your life with."

"I know." His voice is filled with love and admiration. "Back to your problem, though. You might know the men who keep trying to kill you, but you don't know who the person sending them is."

"Are we going to keep playing this guessing game, or are you going to tell me what's going on?" My tone is sharper than intended, but I just want to go back to bed.

Back to Zoe.

"Someone is cranky." Alessio laughs.

Billie starts shouting again. "Demarco Jones is the man behind the problem."

My blood freezes in my veins.

There is no way that Demarco is after me. Not a chance in hell.

"That's impossible." I grip the edge of the counter with my free hand. "He died seven years ago. I was at his funeral. So, unless you are suggesting the dead can walk the earth and make my life hell, I don't see how that's possible."

"He's alive."

Though I don't want to believe it, in some dark corner of my being, I do.

Alessio is my friend and ally. The relationship we have is built on trust. If he believes that Demarco is alive, then I have one more reason to watch my back.

Even if Demarco isn't alive, which I still need to verify for myself, if Alessio has enough reason to be suspicious, I should be too.

After everything that happened years ago, Demarco could still be out there.

Unlikely, but possible. He could be living in the shadows.

I'm going to have to send my people all over the state to start digging up information on his whereabouts.

I'll need to find the bastard and kill him before he gets to me.

Or Zoe.

If he knows that she is married to me, he is going to come after her.

"And to think, my own men have been trying to figure out who is after me for years and haven't been able to dig up anything." I run a hand down my face. "Thank you for finding this out. I will have it dealt with as soon as I can. How did you find this out?"

"Billie did some digging after she overheard a woman in a store talking about going to Tennessee with her old man sometime soon. Billie started talking a mile a minute as she does. Found out that this woman is Demarco's current girlfriend."

"Fuck. Alright. Thank you again. I have to get my people on this as soon as possible."

"Take care," Alessio says before the call ends.

I spend a couple more minutes in the bathroom, trying not to lose my temper.

People have been trying to kill me for years now. If I

hadn't hid in Columbia for the last few years, I would have been dead a long time ago.

Demarco is a man to be feared. He was my father's right-hand man for decades. He's the kind of person who won't hesitate to kill me when he finds me.

It's why I need to find him first.

Especially if he finds out about Zoe.

The moment he finds out that I'm married, I know his attention is going to shift to her.

Anyone would change their target if they thought it would hurt more. Going after her would be the way to get me to come to him.

I can't let anything happen to her. Not if I want her father to stay off my back.

Not if I want to see what else our chemistry leads to.

It's a scary thought, but I know that Zoe is slowly weaving her way deeper and deeper into my world. She proved that within the last day.

I did something horrible. I made her watch me cut up a body.

She still came back at the end of the day and was ready to move forward.

She was still able to look at me and see something other than the monster I know I am.

"Fuck."

I turn off the light before opening the door and heading straight for my closet.

It only takes a few minutes to get dressed before I walk back over to the bed.

Zoe nestles deeper into the blankets.

I lean over her, gently rubbing her shoulder until her eyes open.

"Is something wrong?" Her voice is soft and raspy with sleep.

"Nothing's wrong. Your security team is here. I'm going to be downstairs too, but I have to meet with Ruben."

Her eyes narrow. "If you have to meet with Ruben, then something happened."

I kiss her forehead.

I'm not going to stand here and tell her what's going on. It will only make her worry more.

"Nothing happened. I just have some things I need to address with him about the business. Get some rest. It's been a long couple of days, and I know that you have more shows coming up."

"I might be getting a permanent spot at another bar." Zoe yawns as she rolls onto her back.

She looks up at me through the darkness, a sleepy smile on her face. "Joe is talking to one of the other bar owners he knows."

I bite back my immediate response.

It's a horrible idea. She needs to stay home where she is safe right now.

Gulping down my fear, I say, "That's great, Zoe. You're going to have to tell me all about it in the morning, but right now you need to get some sleep."

She yawns again and closes her eyes.

I pull the blankets a little higher, tucking them around her body.

As I place another kiss on her forehead, I feel guilty for not telling her about what's going on.

She should know that there could be another person after her.

I'll tell her later. When the time is right.

As I leave the room, I send a message to Ruben. By the

time I get downstairs and make a massive pot of coffee, he is standing in my kitchen.

There are dark bags beneath his eyes, and he looks like he's had better days.

I pour him a cup of coffee before taking a seat at the island.

Ruben sits on one of the other stools and sips his coffee.

"Demarco Jones," I say, my voice tight.

Ruben looks at me like I have three heads. "What about Demarco? He's been dead for years."

"You would think, wouldn't you?" I chuckle and shake my head as Ruben's eyes widen. "It would seem like fate has a cruel sense of humor these days. I thought he was dead too. I thought that all the people trying to kill me were either being controlled by someone else or coming after me due to their own vendettas."

"How is Demarco alive?" Ruben downs his coffee and rubs his eyes. "There is no way. We were both at the funeral."

"But nobody saw the body. We were told that he died in a house fire, and his body was burned beyond recognition. Dental records were the only thing the police could go on. You and I both know that Demarco is a crazy bastard who would rip out his own teeth to play dead."

Ruben nods. "He would."

I drum my fingers on the counter. "Billie tracked him down through his new girlfriend. Apparently, this girlfriend wasn't taught to keep her mouth shut. I want you to see what you can find. Figure out where Demarco is now. If he knows he was made, he's on the move."

"I can do that. Do you want anyone else involved?"

For a few moments, I consider it.

There aren't many people I trust entirely in the cartel. I

don't want to have to worry about people Demarco has planted feeding information about my search back to him.

There is no doubt in my mind that he has at least one person in the cartel who feeds him information. People are easily bought when they think there is something better out there.

"No. Keep it to yourself for now. I don't want more people involved in this mess than there have to be."

"What other information do you want?"

I get up from the island and pour myself a cup of coffee.

Once Ruben leaves, I won't be able to go back to sleep. "Dig up everything you can. I want to know every single thing that has happened during his life. Anything could be relevant to how he is going to come after me. I need to be able to get inside his mind."

"I'll see what I can find on him, but if he's been able to hide for this long without us finding him, I doubt it is going to be easy to do so now."

I nod, taking a long sip of my coffee. "See what Billie knows. She might be able to go back to the woman and dig up some more information. I'm sure that she'd be more than happy to coordinate with you."

Ruben pulls out his phone and sends a message to Billie before looking back at me. "Demarco is going to be a problem. Now that you know he's alive, he's likely going to be planning a big move soon."

"I know. Make sure that the security detail with Zoe is made up of the best men we have. Between her father and now Demarco, there are going to be more people coming after her. I want to make sure that there isn't the slightest chance that any of them can get to her."

"I'll handle it."

"See that you do." I finish the cup of coffee and pour

another. "Make sure that Camila is protected too. Double her detail. If Demarco can't get to me, he might try to go after Camila."

"You're the one he has the problem with." Ruben gets up from his seat and yawns. "He used to have a soft spot for her when we were all growing up. If there is anyone you don't have to be worried about, I'm sure it's Camila."

"I'm still going to worry about her." I sigh and lean against the counter. "I want this all dealt with. I don't want to spend another year of my life worrying that I'm going to die or that Camila is. Track down Demarco as fast as possible and end this."

Ruden nods before heading for the door.

I watch him leave before dumping the rest of the coffee down the drain. My stomach ties itself into knots as I think about what's going to happen next.

I have to find Demarco before he finds me. Before he takes away the only people left in the world that I care about.

14

ZOE

"I still can't believe that Joe was able to hook me up with this job." I look over the contract again. "Performing at La Neige has been a dream of mine since I started singing in Nashville."

Christian nods and glances at my signature on the bottom of the paperwork. "I still wish that you would stick to one bar right now. I'm happy for you, but there is still the threat of whoever it was that broke into the house."

"And whatever else it is you're not telling me. Like who that man was you met in the bar the other night. Or why you got up in the middle of the night and had Ruben in the kitchen."

Christian's jaw clenches. "That was about the men who are after me. They're getting worse. There's more to be worried about. I want to see you succeed, but not if it puts you in more danger."

"This is a big chance for me," I say, taking a deep breath. "But if you really think that this is a terrible idea, I won't do it. I can tear up the paperwork, and we can leave right now."

If Christian really thinks that being at two bars a week

is that dangerous—even with the security detail—then I'll take a step back from performing. I'll stay home and work on writing more songs.

It will kill me inside, I won't lie, but truth is to perform, I need to be alive.

"I know it's a big chance for you." He sighs and runs his hand through his hair. "I want you to be able to achieve your dreams, but I'm worried. We have targets on our backs. I don't know if there is a way for me to be able to keep you safe."

I put the paperwork down the desk. "I'll be done with it. I can hold back on this for now. There will be other chances."

Christian pinches the bridge of his nose before looking back at me. "Zoe, the last thing I want is to hold you back."

He pulls out his phone and sends a message while I stand there with my heart pounding in my chest.

Our lives are dangerous right now. It feels like a knife is being driven through me as I think about putting my dreams on hold, but he knows the world of the cartel far better than I do.

If he says that it's too dangerous, then I have to trust him. He's kept me safe so far. I know that he's going to continue keeping me safe for as long as possible.

"The security team is going to walk about the venue. They're going to see if it will be possible for all of us to have a good sightline on you at all times. If they give it the green light, then you can perform here. No more bars, though. Two shows a week for now."

My heart skips a beat as I look at him. "Are you serious? I can do this?"

Hope flows through me as I look at him.

I know I shouldn't get excited yet, but I am. This is a massive opportunity, and he is trying to find a compromise.

Christian nods. "If the security team gets back to me in the next few minutes and say that it's safe enough, you can perform here. But I'm serious, Zoe. Two bars a week. That's it. I'm not willing to take more risks where your life is concerned. We have enough to worry about right now."

I pull him into a big hug, even though he is stiff in my embrace. "Thank you for even considering this. You don't know how much it means to me."

His phone starts buzzing as I pull back from him. His mouth sets in a grim line, and my heart starts to sink in my chest. There is no way that La Neige is going to be an option. I can see it based on his expression.

At least he was willing to try and work with me. He's not trying to hold me back. It just isn't safe right now.

Christian tucks his phone back into his pocket. "You're going to be performing here one night a week, so don't bother shredding that contract."

"You're kidding!" I leap at him again, laughing as he catches me around the waist and holds me for a moment. "Thank you! I can't believe this. Thank you so much. I promise, two bars a week. That's it."

"And if I tell you that we need to cut back more, then we need to cut back more. Got it?" His frown is deep, and I can still see the worry in his eyes.

"You say the word, and I'll be done."

He nods, sharp, before turning to the door and heading out into the hall. "I want to be happy for you right now, Zoe, but it's a little hard. I know how much this means to you, but it's scaring the hell out of me. We'll try to make it work for now, though."

I look at the contract on the desk.

If he thinks that this is such a bad idea, maybe I should just rip up the papers.

Christian is comfortable with me working at Joe's bar.

"Don't even think about shredding up the contact," Christian says, his tone hollow as he looks back inside the office. "Let's just go home so I can meet with the security team about the best way to protect you while you perform."

I nod and follow him, not wanting to create more tension between the two of us.

I don't know how I can thank him enough for finding a way to make performing at La Neige work.

This is a dream come true. One that I thought never would. Without him, it wouldn't be possible.

Christian is going to do everything he can to protect us while still letting me chase my dreams.

He's a better man than I deserve.

The car ride is silent as we head home.

Christian grips the wheel so hard his knuckles turn white. His jaw flexes like he has something to say but he doesn't.

When he parks the car in the garage, I hurry to get out and head inside.

Ava is standing in the kitchen as I enter the house.

Christian follows behind me, nodding to her before heading to the library.

I exhale slowly and take a seat at the kitchen island.

"What was that about?" Ava asks, her tone gentle as she opens up the fridge and grabs a bottle of white wine. "He called me and said that you signed the contract for La Neige. I thought that we would all be celebrating tonight."

"He called you?"

Ava nods as she rummages through his cupboards. When she turns around with two glasses in her hands, there is a small smile on her face. "He called me and asked me to come over to celebrate. Had Ruben let me into the house before you got here. I know I'm skeptical about him most of the time, but I think he really does care for you in his own way."

I stare down the hall in the direction Christian went.

He is a confusing man at the best of times. He doesn't want me to perform but he still calls my sister over to have a good time. It doesn't make sense.

"He has his moments," I say as I turn my attention back to her. "He thinks it's a bad idea, though. But he called the security team, and they're going to find a way to make it safe."

Ava bites her bottom lip. "I don't know how to feel about it either, if we're being honest. You're talented, and I want you to chase your dreams, but when you have so many new things going on in your life, do you really think it's the best time to chase down a career like that?"

I hold back the tears that threaten to fall.

I know that she doesn't mean anything by it.

Ava is practical. She's never been much of a dreamer. Our entire lives, she has been the one to evaluate situations before jumping into them.

She wants to know if the risks will outweigh the rewards. If they do, she is going to hold back.

Ava still wants to see me succeed, though. She's my sister. She supports me, she just has to act as the voice of reason.

I can appreciate that. Ava isn't one to hold back her thoughts, but at the end of the day all she wants is for me to be happy.

Between the support I get from her and Christian, I'm starting to see a life where I achieve all of my dreams.

Without them supporting me, I don't know where I would be right now.

I'm going to have to think of something special to thank the both of them.

"How is work going?" I want to catch up with her after days spent apart.

Ava shrugs and pours the glasses of wine. "It's alright. The inmates are a lot to handle, but they are not impossible. A few fights here and there, but nothing that really affects me. My peers respect me and so do the men doing time there, which is all I can really ask for."

"You know, sometimes I worry about you working there." I reach for my wine and swirl it around the glass. "Don't you think you would be better off in a more stable career? Something with a lot less criminals?"

Ava rolls her eyes and tips her glass toward me. "I see what you're doing here, and you're right, but it still doesn't change your situation. I could leave the prison tonight and find a job in the hospital. You don't have that same kind of plan in place."

"I have plenty of plans in place. They're just plans that you don't agree with."

She takes a sip of her wine. "I know that you're going to do great things with your life, Zoe. I just worry about you and whether or not you've really thought about what you're doing here and with your career."

"I'm here because Dad needs me."

"Is that really fair to you, though? You shouldn't have to be here because Dad needs you to be."

"I do a lot of things because Dad needs me to do them. Enough of that, though. It's just going to upset both of us. Tell me more about your job. How is working with hardened criminals all day?"

Ava takes her wine and makes her way over to the couch. She settles into the plush cushions as I get up and take one of the armchairs. "They're not all hardened criminals."

I give her a flat look. "I know that. But I also know that most of the ones who end up in the infirmary to see you are."

"There's one man that isn't so bad. But his baggage weighs a ton."

I point at her pink cheeks. "Alright, so even though it is incredibly wrong, how cute is this criminal? Based on the color of your cheeks right now, I would say he's pretty attractive."

Ava shrugs a shoulder. "I wouldn't say that he's hard on the eyes at all, but..." she shakes her head. "Besides, you know the rules. I don't get involved with the inmates."

"Be hot if you did."

She grabs a throw pillow and tosses it at my head.

I smack it out of the way, laughing as she downs her wine.

Ava's face is bright red. She tries to smother the smirk playing at the corner of her mouth, but she can't.

"Nothing is going to happen with him." Ava sips her wine and looks out the window at the backyard. "I have other things that I need to be doing with my time. Even thinking about what could happen is trouble."

"The entire job is trouble."

She waves a hand. "Enough about that. Why don't you go get your guitar and play some songs for me. I would love to hear what you're working on right now."

"Really?" I get up and head to the back door where I left my guitar when I came in this morning.

"Yeah." Ava smiles and pulls her knees to her chest. "I

know that I give you a hard time about your music sometimes, but you're the most talented person I know. If anyone is going to be able to make it in the music industry, it's you. Now, play me a song."

I laugh and bring the guitar back over to the living room, strumming a melody I keep dreaming about. Though I don't have the lyrics yet, when I close my eyes and focus on the music, all I can picture is Christian's gaze and the conflicted way he makes me feel.

15

CHRISTIAN

Zoe walks into the kitchen, her hair a wild mess and her eyes shining bright. Dark bags circle beneath her eyes.

She takes a seat and reaches for the cup of coffee I push her way.

A soft groan fills the room as she takes her first sip.

"I shouldn't have stayed up drinking and playing songs for Ava last night. It was a horrible decision. A smarter person would have gone to bed. I'm not a smarter person."

I smile as she drops her head to the counter. "Hangovers can be a bitch."

She groans again, covering her head with her arms. "Next time, remind me that going to bed is a good idea. Actually, scratch that. I'm still mad at you."

With a sigh, I lean back against the other counter. "I know. I shouldn't have reacted like that last night. I'm sorry."

Zoe looks up, her eyes narrowing. "Do you mean that, or is it just a tactic to get me to agree to stay home and slowly go insane looking at the same walls every single day?"

"I mean that. I still have my concerns, but there would've been a better time to talk about it."

Last night I was worried about her. I watched her sign those papers, and all I could think about was Demarco snatching her off stage and whisking her away.

I could picture her father waiting in the crowd to capture her and take her away from me.

When I saw that signature, all I could think about was losing her.

And the thought wasn't just jarring because I need her for her dad's help.

The idea of someone taking her, of losing her, made me lose my breath and my chest hurt.

"Thank you," she says, sitting upright and running her fingers through her wild hair. "I appreciate that. Thank you for calling Ava over. I know neither of you are the biggest fan of my music career right now, but it means a lot to me. I know I can do this, but it means that I have to take risks."

"If playing in a bar two nights a week is what it takes to make you happy, then I'm willing to go with you to every show. But you have to remember our deal. If I tell you that you have to pull back, then you have to pull back. I'm not fucking around with your safety."

Zoe's eyes grow wide as she meets my gaze. She pulls her bottom lip into her mouth as the blood rushes in my ears. I know that I should force her to stay home where it is safe, but I do want her to be happy. Even if I can never be the husband that she deserves, I can at least make sure that she is happy.

"You're going to go with me?" Her tone is skeptical.

She grabs her mug and holds it with both hands, drumming her fingers on the side. "You don't have to do that."

"Yeah. I do. You're my responsibility. Even though the

team is going with you, I need to be there to protect you. And I'm going to be there to support you, Zoe."

"You didn't seem like you liked that idea much last night."

I nod and round the kitchen island. "Come with me. I have something to show you. It's a little surprise that I've been working on for the last few days."

She raises an eyebrow but gets up and follows me out of the house and into the backyard.

We walk through the gate at the far end of the yard that leads to the rest of my property.

"What have you been working on?" I approach a small white building with her trailing behind.

"If I tell you right now, it's going to ruin the surprise." I move behind her and put my hands over her eyes. "I want you to feel like this is your home too, but I get the feeling that you don't, yet. I'm hoping that this shows you I'm serious about that."

Zoe puts her hands over mine. "Christian, this seems like a little much. You didn't have to get me anything. I know that this is my home now. It just doesn't feel like home all the time."

I keep one hand over her eyes while reaching around her to open the door to the little white building. The curtains are pulled across the windows right now, but when they're open, this part of the room will flood with light.

"Zoe, if it doesn't always feel like home, then it isn't your home. I want you to feel that way one day, though. I hope that this helps a little. I want you to know that I support your career, and I want you to do whatever you can to chase that dream." I take a deep breath and pull my hand away from her eyes.

Her soft gasp makes my heart skip a beat.

I move to open the curtains, letting light flood into the room.

In front of us is a soundboard and a wall made of glass. Just behind a little door to the right of the soundboard is the recording studio.

Zoe looks at me with tears shining in her eyes before making her way over to the computer on a desk in the corner. "This is amazing, Christian. You didn't have to do this. It's too much."

I shrug and tuck my hands in my pockets. "You want to be a musician, Zoe. All musicians need a space to practice and record their songs."

"Most of them don't have a recording studio at their home." She goes over and opens the door to the studio.

I follow her inside, watching the way she runs her fingers over a piano.

Her small smile is enough to send my stomach twisting into knots.

I was worried that she wouldn't like the surprise, but it's clear she does.

"This is your space. Do with it whatever you want. I mean that. If you don't like the color of the couch out in the main room, order a new one. Want a new instrument? Order one. I'm leaving you one of my credit cards. Get yourself whatever you need that I didn't think of."

She wanders around the room, taking in the instruments and equipment.

When she turns back to me, there are tears running down her cheeks. "Christian, this is too much. You didn't have to do this for me."

I reach out and pull her into a hug.

She buries her face in my shoulder, her tears soaking through my shirt.

The scent of her shampoo wafts up to me as she leans back to look at me.

"I know it's a lot," I say, running my hands up and down her back. "This recording studio is yours, but I would like to know when you're out here. Just for peace of mind. There's a security system set up, and your security detail will stay outside, but I would still like to know when you come down here."

Zoe nods. "I can manage that. This is still too much, though."

"I want you to be able to pursue your dreams. It seemed necessary."

She watches me for a moment, her hands running up my chest and linking together behind my neck. "You know, I keep thinking that I have you figured out and then you go and do something like this. It makes me rethink everything I know about you."

I chuckle and hold her a little tighter. "I'm a complex man. There's still a lot you don't know about me and some things that I may never tell you."

"And you expect me to be okay with that?" There's a hint of hurt in her tone.

I cup her face with both hands, wiping away the tear tracks. "If there's anyone I'm going to reveal those awful parts of myself to, it would be you. I just don't want you to have the same burdens that I have to bear."

"I don't know how to be okay with that. Or any of this. I keep trying, but it's hard, Christian. Our marriage is for show. Is telling me everything about you even what you want?"

My heart pounds against my ribs as I stare down at her.

Right now, I can't get into everything I want from her. But I can share my truth.

"I wouldn't say that the marriage is completely for show."

The corner of her mouth tilts upward.

I lean in and kiss her, reveling in the taste of coffee on her lips.

She smiles into the kiss, her fingers weaving through my hair.

I walk us backward as our tongues tangle, pulling her with me to the couch.

Zoe sighs as I pull out of the kiss and sit down on the couch, patting my lap.

She gives me a teasing smile as she spins around, her back to me.

My cock strains against my jeans as Zoe makes a show of swaying her hips.

She bends over slowly, her ass in the air as she works her tiny shorts down her long legs.

With a groan, I unbutton my pants and pull out my cock.

It throbs as I run my thumb over the head before stroking the length.

Zoe takes her time standing back up.

As she stands, she drags her hands up her legs and over her hips.

Those hands keep climbing, pulling her shirt up and off her body as she turns to face me.

Her nipples stiffen as she looks down at me with heat in her eyes.

Her gaze drops to my cock as she gets to her knees and crawls toward me.

My cock aches as I stroke it, needing to be buried inside of her.

"And here I thought you said you were a virgin before

me," I say, my tone teasing as I lift my hips and pull my pants and boxers off. "Now look at what a horny slut you are."

She smirks and kneels between my legs as I take off my shirt. "Oh, you thought you were going to get something? Maybe I was just getting a closer look at the floor."

My hips buck as her tongue darts out to lick the head of my cock. "You're fucking with me, Zoe. I'm not a man who likes to be fucked with."

"Well, in that case," she says, her tone teasing as she rocks back on her heels like she is going to stand.

I fist my hand in her hair and hold her in place. "Now who's being the tease?"

She wraps her hand around the base of my cock. "Seems like you like it. As for the virgin part, you know that you're the only man who's been buried in my pussy. I just might have read a couple scenes in smutty books and gotten some ideas. So much time alone at the house and all that."

"Fuck." My voice rasps as she takes my cock into her mouth.

Zoe teases the tip with her tongue and teeth.

With each pass of her teeth, she flattens her tongue against me, soothing away the painful pleasure.

I groan and keep my hand in her hair, guiding her head down my cock.

Her cheeks hollow as she sucks.

When her head starts to bob up and down, it takes everything in me not to start thrusting.

I want her to enjoy sucking my cock as much as I enjoy the sight of those full lips wrapped around me.

"Yes," I groan as I keep my eyes on her. "Just like that."

Zoe moans as she takes my cock deeper in her mouth, running her tongue along the underside from base to tip.

I pull her back, my cock throbbing as she sits back on her heels and looks up at me.

"Turn around and sit in my lap." I let go of her hair.

Zoe does as she's told, turning and sitting down.

I spread my legs, using them to keep hers apart while she leans back into me.

I kiss her neck, sucking on the sensitive skin while I run my hands up her thighs. She writhes in my lap as I ghost my fingers over her pussy before continuing up her torso.

She moans as I palm her breasts, massaging them.

Her hips buck as I pinch and roll her nipples between my fingers.

I switch to the other side of her neck as I run my hands lower down her body, teasing her.

My fingers trace patterns on her inner thighs as I suck on her neck until a dark mark is staring back at me.

"Did you just give me a hickey?" Amusement colors her voice. "I have to go on stage and sing in a couple days, and now I have this thing on my neck."

"Better to teach those assholes who you belong to from the beginning," I say as I run my fingers along her wet slit.

Her response is a breathy moan as I circle her clit.

Zoe's hips rock in time with my fingers.

I keep one hand cupping her breast, and my cock pressed into her back.

She tilts her hips as I tease the entrance of her tight little pussy.

"You want to come all over my hand, don't you? You want to soak it like the little slut we know you are deep inside, don't you?" I graze her ear lobe with my teeth as she tilts her head back.

"Yes. Please. I want to come on you."

"Good girl." I shove two fingers into her.

Zoe rocks her hips in time with my fingers, her wetness coating my hand and her thighs.

My cock aches as I thrust my fingers deeper into her.

Her pussy squeezes around me.

All I can think about is what her pussy is going to feel like when she comes on my hand.

I press my thumb against her clit as her pussy pulses around me.

Her inner walls clamp down as her legs start to shake on either side of mine.

As her orgasm crashes through her, I pinch her nipple harder and keep thrusting my fingers.

Her chest is heaving as she comes down from the high of her orgasm.

She moves quickly, turning around and straddling me.

As she sinks down onto my cock, I grab her hips.

I don't want to finish too soon, but I'm on the edge.

"Fuck, you're so fucking wet and tight." I use my grip on her hips to guide her.

Zoe's nails dig into my shoulders as she spreads her legs wider, taking me deeper.

I thrust up from below, setting the pace while she holds on.

I drive deeper into her as her inner walls clench around me.

Zoe dips her head to kiss me, our tongues tangling together as she moans.

She rocks her hips as I slip a hand between us.

My fingers circle her clit as I thrust faster.

I can't hold it anymore, so I give her my all.

My cock throbs inside her as I come.

Her pussy squeezes my cock, milking every last drop of it as her second orgasm takes over.

Zoe's body slumps against mine as she puts her head on my shoulder.

I wrap my arms around her waist, holding her close as I close my eyes.

Something about this moment feels different than all the others. Our relationship is shifting and morphing into something else. I don't know what to do about it.

Hell, I don't know if I even *want* to do anything about it.

"You know, you really aren't as horrible as you pretend to be all the time," Zoe says as she sits back to look at me. "I know you like to pretend to be the bad guy, but I don't think it's going to work on me."

As I hold her a little tighter, I know I don't want it to work on her anymore.

I'm tired of pretending to be a person I hate.

16

ZOE

As I stand in front of my closet, trying to figure out what to wear, I feel like I'm going to be sick.

It's been a long time since I last had dinner with my parents.

Though I want to see Dad, I don't know what Mom is going to say.

"You look like you're about to pass out," Christian says as he walks into the room and tightens his black tie.

I glance at him, taking in the way his black dress shirt and slacks hug his figure.

He looks like he stepped off the cover of a magazine while I'm standing in nothing but a towel.

My hair might be curled, and my makeup is done, but those are the only things about me that are ready for this dinner.

"I am freaking out. You don't know my parents. Well, I guess you know my dad, but you don't know them like I do. There is a certain expectation that they will have with this dinner, and I'm sure that I'm only going to disappoint them again."

Christian sits on the edge of my bed.

He leans back, bracing himself on his forearms. "I don't think that you're capable of disappointing anyone."

I scoff and sift through the dresses in front of me. "You would be wrong about that. My parents wish that I would go to school to become a lawyer or a doctor. Something that would make sense for the daughter of a politician. They think that music is a waste of time. Hell, my mother will say that to my face."

"Mild offense intended, but your mother sounds like a raging bitch. What kind of parent makes their child feel like they're anything less than amazing?"

I glance at him over my shoulder and shrug. "You'll see what they're really like tonight. They might not be happy with Ava's job, but at least she is working as a nurse. When songwriting comes up, which it always does, then it will become shit on Zoe hour."

His nose wrinkles. "That sounds disgusting."

Despite the nervous feeling coursing through my body, I laugh. "It is disgusting. You would have to wonder about what they do when I'm not around to criticize."

As I turn back to sorting through the dresses, I try to calm the anxiety.

I know that this dinner is going to be awful.

Going into the dinner as prepared as possible to be insulted and humiliated is the only way to handle things.

I love my parents, but they love their public image more. They want to look like the perfect family, and I don't fit into that idea for them.

"For what it's worth, I can start a distraction if you want to get out of there."

"I might take you up on that," I say as I pull out a mauve dress with long bell sleeves. "Do you think this is the kind of thing that the daughter of the Head of State would wear to dinner?"

The bed squeaks as I hold the dress in one hand and continue to search through my closet with the other.

Christian's hands settle on my hips.

I lean back into him for a moment.

In the week since he showed me the music studio, the energy between us has changed.

It feels more like we're a real couple and less like two people who were forced together.

It's easy to be with him, even on the days that he is driving me insane. Being with him gives me that warm and fuzzy feeling deep in my stomach.

It terrifies me.

"You would look amazing in your dress. Fuck what your father and the rest of the damn state thinks about it."

My cheeks warm as I turn to face him, holding the dress a little higher. "It's short, though. I don't know if I should go with something a little longer or not."

Christian rolls his eyes. "Wear what you feel comfortable and confident in, Zoe. Don't let these people make you feel like you're anything less than amazing."

"That's hard to do." I bite my bottom lip, rolling it between my teeth before sighing. "I've spent a lifetime with them trying to make me into the person that they think I should be. Do you think it would be better to skip this dinner completely?"

He chuckles, squeezing my hips lightly. "You won't be happy if you don't go to that dinner and hold your head high. Show them that you're more than they think you are. If you don't stand up to their shit now, you're going to live the rest of your life wishing you had."

I shed the towel and pull the dress on, grinning when

his hands only fall away from my body long enough to get the dress on. "I don't think that I would regret skipping the dinner. It would be a lot easier than trying to confront them."

"Zoe, it's okay to set boundaries with people. Hell, it's healthy to set boundaries with people. You're your own person. You might be their daughter, but you have a life of your own to live. They need to know what being in your life will look like."

"And what if they hate me for it?"

He shrugs and reaches up to cup my face with one hand. "I've spent a lot of time around Ava in the last couple weeks. There is no way that she could ever hate you. As for your parents, if they can't accept the boundaries that you set, then that's their problem."

I nod and take a deep breath. "We should get going. If we're late, there is going to be hell to pay."

He arches an eyebrow. "Then there is going to be hell to pay."

"Christian, it isn't worth it."

"I could make being late worth your while," he says, his voice raspy.

He leans down and grazes my earlobe with his teeth. "Especially if you don't plan on putting on anything under that dress."

My cheeks feel like they're on fire as I shake my head. "Not going to happen. The sooner we get to dinner, the sooner we're done with them for the night. I love my parents, but there is only so much of being around them that I can take."

He laughs and takes my hand, lacing his fingers through mine. "Fine. I won't lick your clit on the way to the restaurant."

"Not on the way home either." I grin as he rolls his eyes.

"You're going to be begging for it by the end of the night." He smirks as he turns to me. "You've been a fiend for my cock all week."

"You're full of shit." My cheeks ache from smiling as he walks with me to the garage.

I would be lying if I didn't say that part of what worries me about dinner is Christian and Dad spending time together.

Christian is a dangerous man, and while I'm still wrapping my head around that, I can't completely ignore the fact that he threatened to kill my father.

"Hey," Christian says as he opens my door. "What's going on? You just went from happy to completely out of it."

I shrug and get into the car. "You and my dad aren't exactly on the best terms. You threatened to kill him if I didn't do what you wanted. I don't know what I'm supposed to think or feel right now. It's hard to see both parts of you and try to fuse them into one person."

His expression goes blank for a moment before his gaze softens.

Christian leans down, the smell of his cologne wrapping around me as he invades my space. "I can't fix that for you, Zoe. You're either going to see me one way or another. I will not change who I've had to be or what I have to do for the couple hundred people who rely on me. It's up to you to either come to terms with that, or not."

"And what happens if I can't?" The lump in my throat threatens to choke me.

"Then I guess we have to find another way to make this marriage work." He brushes away a stray tear that escapes with his thumb. "Let's just try to make it out of this dinner alive."

I nod, knowing that I need to focus on something else right now.

Thinking too much about Christian and the cartel side of him is a lot.

I wish that I could tell Ava everything. She would be the one person who might be able to offer me solid advice.

Instead, I need to work through my feelings on my own.

I know that I'm falling for him, despite everything that's happened since we met. It feels like there's an attraction between us that I can't ignore.

Christian is also capable of horrible things. He's the kind of man who makes me witness the disposal of a body without a second thought.

Even though he apologized for it, I can't forget that he did it.

He might not know about my nightmares, but I do.

I take a deep breath and look out the window, watching the trees blur by.

There's the dark side to Christian, but there's the sweet side too. That's the one I see the most. It's the one that I'm falling for.

It's the side with the real power to hurt me.

I need to get myself together. Other people have to do horrible things too. He might be a murderer, but it's because he has to be.

Even as I try to rationalize it to myself, I'm having a hard time.

I want my family to like him and see the side of him that I see, but I doubt Dad will.

He's going to look at Christian and see the dark side I worry about. He's going to see his daughter sitting beside the leader of a cartel.

This is a mess. I don't know how I got here. Sometimes I wish that I never did.

Christian's hand lands on my thigh, his thumb rubbing slow circles as he drives.

His touch is grounding. It pulls me from the panic spiral that I've gotten myself into, reminding me of the dinner I really should be worrying about.

As we pull up to the restaurant, I turn to him and put my hand over his. "I don't know how this is going to go. They're not going to be happy with the marriage."

His eyebrows pull together. "The moment you want to leave, say the word. I'm going to be here with you through the entire dinner, okay?"

And there it is. The sweet side that makes me wonder who he would have been if he wasn't the leader of a cartel.

"Okay." I tuck a strand of hair behind my ear and stare at the building in front of us.

The valet opens my door and holds out a hand.

I take it and stand up, taking in the pristine white stone of the building.

Gilded lettering hangs above the door and expensive florals bracket either side of the double doors.

Christian gets out of the car and hands the keys to the valet.

When he joins me and wraps his arm around my waist, I start to feel hopeful.

Maybe tonight won't be as awful as I think it will. Maybe we'll get out completely unscathed.

The host smiles as we enter the restaurant, stepping out from behind the marble podium. "Miss Redford, it's good to see you again. Your family is already seated. If you would please follow me this way."

"Thank you." I smile as I follow behind him.

Christian moves so his hand is pressed against the small of my back.

His breath against the shell of my ear sends a shiver down my spine. "Should I be worried that the staff know who you are?"

"Dad loves this place. We used to come here at least once a month for dinner. And then there were all the business dinners that we all had to attend. He liked to show off his family to the other politicians."

Christian nods, his fingers flexing against my back. "Is the food any good?"

"Decent. You're a better cook, though." I smile up at him as my family's table comes into view.

Dad wears a big smile and Mom's face is pinched. Ava looks like she would rather be anywhere else.

"Get ready. The show is about to start."

"I can handle them," he says as we reach the table.

He pulls out the empty seat beside my sister and waits for me to sit.

Christian plants a kiss on top of my head and tucks the chair in before sitting beside me.

"It's good that the two of you could join us," Dad says, his voice warm as he looks at me with a smile. "I've missed you, Zoe. How is married life treating you? I wish that we could have been there. I never thought that I would miss your wedding."

"It was nice." I take my napkin and drape it over my lap. "It was small and quiet."

Dad's jaw clenches while Mom scoffs. "And that is what you really wanted? You know that you're welcome to come home at any time. We would be waiting for you with open arms. The last thing I want is my daughter trapped in a loveless marriage."

"You've got to be fucking kidding me," Ava says before she can stop herself.

I nudge her leg under the table, but she shakes her head and glares at our father. "You were going to marry her off to solve your problems and now you're sitting here talking about what a shame it is that she's in a loveless marriage?"

"Ava," Mom says, her tone sharp. "Lower your voice. What was to happen is none of your business. Zoe knew what she was going to be doing for her family. At least one of my daughters has a sense of duty."

I put my hands in my lap, my nails curling into my palms. "We don't need to do this right now. We could have a good time together without fighting. Dad, how is work?"

"Good evening." The waiter stops at the table beside my father's elbow. "I'm Shane, and I'll be your server tonight. Has everyone had a chance to look at the menu yet?"

"No need," Dad says, handing the stack of menus to the waiter. "We will have the lobster and steak. As well as your finest bottles of red and white wine."

Ava scowls. "I'm allergic to lobster. You know this. I'll have the truffle pasta please."

"No. She won't." Dad waves a dismissive hand at Ava. "You've been over your lobster allergy for years."

The waiter scurries away before he gets trapped in the fight.

I look over at Christian like a deer caught in the headlights.

I thought that dinner would go a little better than this. Most nights, my family can control themselves if we're out at a family dinner.

Mom looks between me and Christian. "Are the two of you planning on having children? I think it would be a mistake given the nature of his job. You don't want to have criminal children."

I see red as I look at her. I don't know what to say at first.

Mom has always been a difficult woman. I can't remember a single day where she went without talking down to at least one person.

This time feels different, though. I don't like the way not a single one of them has bothered to address Christian while talking.

They speak as if he isn't here. It bothers me far more than their rude behavior ever has.

Dad nods along. "Children is a bad idea. Especially where you don't have a real career lined up, and your husband is known to skirt the edges of the law. That's not the kind of environment you want to raise a child in."

Christian's jaw tightens, but he says nothing.

I feel as if I've been punched in the stomach. I don't know what to say about any of this. Even though we're seated at a private table in the back, I still can't believe that they would bring this up right now.

"You're a smart woman with a good head on your shoulders," Mom says, though it doesn't sound like she quite means it. "Can you really say that you want to have children with that man?"

"I think this dinner was a bad idea," I say instead of answering her question. "I don't think we're ready as a family to discuss what life looks like right now."

"You don't have to leave," Dad says, his tone stern.

It's not a suggestion. It's an order.

For the first time in a very long time, I don't think twice about disobeying him.

As I get up from the table, I feel the ties to my family

and what I feel I have to do for them start to sever.

Dad no longer has the hold over me that he once had.

I love him, but I don't know how to be the daughter he's always wanted anymore. I have to be the person that I am, and he is either going to accept that or he isn't.

Just like I have to accept the person that Christian is.

Ava grins at me and gets up, tossing her napkin on the table. "I've got to go too. There's some work at the prison that I need to catch up on."

Christian smiles at my parents. "It was nice to formally meet both of you."

As he stands and takes my hand, my heart starts to race.

I consider sitting back down and smoothing this over, but it's not going to happen.

This is the first step in showing them that while I may be part of this family, I'm also my own person.

I need to live life for myself.

Christian follows me out of the restaurant, grinning as we step outside into the cool night air. "That seemed like it went better than you thought it would."

I laugh as I look at him. "You think that leaving before the wine even got to the table means that dinner went better than I thought it would?"

He shrugs as the valet goes to get his car. "The night could have gone much worse."

"I don't think the night's over yet." I squeeze his hand as the car rolls to a stop in front of us. "I want to do something. Go somewhere. Order some greasy food that my mother would be ashamed of me for eating and then spend the night watching the stars."

Christian tips the valet and takes the keys from him. "And where do you want to go?"

"Take me to the beach."

17

CHRISTIAN

Zoe is quiet as we drive to the beach.

I don't bother to ask what's on her mind. I already know. She is worried about what a life with me will look like.

I would be worried about it too if I were her.

She doesn't know how to be with both sides of me.

To be honest, I don't know how to live with them most of the time either. When the monster comes out of me, I feel like I'm no better than my father.

I never wanted to be like him, but somehow, I ended up there anyway. Which is another reason that I want to get away from this life.

The monster is the top of the food chain. It is a necessity if I want to survive and protect my people.

But I'm so sick of him. So tired. I wish I could retire that side of me once and for all.

My eyes take Zoe in.

I hate that she has to live with him too now.

I don't like having to put her through that, even though it's necessary.

Zoe has been ignorant of the real world for too long.

Maybe it's a good thing, but it's not a peace of mind she can afford while married to me.

I dragged her down. Made her an accomplice. I did what I had to do to make sure there was no turning back for her.

The warm scent of burgers and fries wafts through the car as I pull onto the road that leads to the lake.

Zoe perks up a little, sitting taller in her seat as she stares out the window.

As I park the car at the edge of the lake, she kicks off her heels and unbuckles the seatbelt.

She sighs as if she's been holding back the weight of the world.

I leave the lights on, illuminating a path across the water.

"Do you want to talk about what happened back there?" My voice is soft as I slide my seat back and unbuckle, getting as comfortable as possible.

I don't know how long we're going to be out here, but for Zoe, I would stay here all night.

"Dad's a lot to deal with at times," she says as she sets the bag of food on the console.

She pulls out a burger and unwraps it with as much care as if it was a delicate flower. "Mom is even worse. I'm sorry about what they said back there."

I take out a container of fries and shrug. "Don't be. They both know what I am. Your father's job is to know about problems in the state. The Herrera cartel is a problem."

She takes a large bite of her burger and rolls her eyes. "I don't think that's the real problem, though. I mean sure, you are a criminal. There's no denying that. You made me into an accomplice, which I'm still pissed about, by the way. But

I don't think either of my parents have a right to talk about what we choose to do with our future."

I look away from her for a moment.

A future between us, something more than what our forced marriage entails, scares the hell out of me, even though I'm falling for her.

When I look at Billie and Alessio, I see a life I might want but don't know how to get. Alessio is a good man underneath it all. He's the kind of man who is going to make sure that Billie is always cared for and that no harm will come to her. They fought the odds to be together.

But I don't know if I'm capable of that kind of love.

I watched my father not love my mother for years.

I'm already too much like him. I would hate myself more than I already do if I strung Zoe along with the pretense of loving her one day.

More than anything, I don't want to be the person to break her heart.

"What do you think their problem with us is, then?" I ask, though I already know.

"They've lost control. The image of their perfect family is starting to shatter and neither of them knows how to deal with it."

She doesn't have a clue about who her father really is.

I've suspected as much for a long time, but after tonight, it's clear. Zoe doesn't know about all the damage that her father does. She doesn't know about the illegal life he lives behind the scenes.

I'm not going to be the one to tell her either. If she doesn't know who her father is, then I won't be the one giving her the rude awakening that will come with finding out. I want to protect her from that for as long as possible.

It's a hard world after you find out who your parents really are.

"And what do you think about no longer living that life with them?" I ask, finishing off my fries and reaching for my burger.

"That perfect family shit was all performative. They want me and Ava to fit into certain molds. I'm sure that they mean well, but they only care about my dad's career and how what we do propels that. If it wasn't for his career, the life we had wouldn't exist, so I guess there's that to be grateful for."

"Now that you're free, what are you going to do with your life?"

She hums for a moment, taking her time chewing the last bite of her burger. "I know that it's dangerous to be out and performing right now, but if you're okay with it, I would still like to do that every now and then. Just those two shows a week. I think I want to spend the rest of my time working on my music."

"I still don't like the thought of you going out and performing with the people looking for us," I say, my chest tightening. "But it's just two shows a week. I'll be able to keep making time in my schedule to be there, and the security team will be there too. We'll figure it out."

"Thank you." She gives me a smile that makes my heart skip a beat.

I would die a happy man if I got to see that smile for the rest of my life.

That scares the hell out of me.

"Working on your music sounds like a great idea." I twist in my seat to face her. "You're talented, Zoe. You're going to make it far as a musician. I have no doubt that you're going to be signed to a label before you know it."

"Are you alright with that?" Her voice is soft and shy, like she's not sure it's a question that she should be asking. "If I get signed to a label and start doing tours and things like that, what's it going to do to us?"

I swallow hard, trying to sort through the dozens of thoughts swirling through my mind. "I might be a horrible man a lot of the time, but I'm not going to hold you back from your dreams, Zoe. If you want to go on tour all over the world, I'm going to be right there with you when I can be."

The tension in the car grows thicker as she looks at me.

Her gaze flickers between my eyes and my mouth.

My heart pounds against my chest and my blood rushes in my ears.

"What do you want out of this marriage?" Her voice is a mere breath.

Her hands shake as she reaches out and takes my hand, lacing her fingers through mine.

"I don't know." I run my thumb over her knuckles. "I don't know if I could ever be the kind of man you should be with. The world I live in is not the kind of world you should be in."

"That sounds like there's a but coming." Her voice wavers.

My stomach ties itself into knots. "There is. I don't know how to be the man you should have in your life, *but* I'm too selfish to let you go. I want you too much to be able to sit back while you walk away from me."

She stares at me for too long.

It feels like she is stripping away the person I present to the world and trying to get to who is at the core.

I know that I should put some distance between us. I should keep myself from falling deeper for her.

But when it comes to Zoe, I don't know that I can.

"I know I told you earlier tonight that I don't really know what to do with both sides of you. I don't. But I think I would regret it forever if I didn't try to embrace both those sides. Despite the way you scare me sometimes, I think I'm falling for you too."

My breath hitches as I look at her.

The next moment is what makes or breaks us. I can feel it in the air, and I'm sure that she can too.

I don't have the words to say to her right now. Instead, I lean over and kiss her.

Zoe holds my hand tighter as I nip her bottom lip.

Her soft gasp breathes life into the car as I tease her tongue with mine.

Her lips are soft as I kiss her, leaning back as she follows me.

Zoe pulls away long enough to climb over the console before straddling my lap.

She looks down at me as she runs her fingers through my hair.

As I stare up at her, I can't help but wonder where we go from here.

I want her and I'm scared to have her.

I'm done fighting against the impossible, but I don't know if I can allow what I feel for her to flourish.

For now, all I want to do is get lost in the feeling of her body.

Figuring out where to go from here can come later.

I slide my hands up her waist, trying to memorize her curves.

I sink one hand into her hair, gently holding the back of her head as I bring her mouth back to mine.

She rolls her hips, grinding against my cock as her hands leave my hair and move down my chest.

I groan as her mouth makes its way over my cheek and down my neck.

She nips at the skin while she unbuttons my shirt.

Her nails rake down my skin, her hands traveling lower and lower until she reaches my pants.

"Patience," I say, pulling her hair and forcing her head away from my neck. "I want you to come for me first. I want to feel that tight pussy wrapped around my fingers as you ride my hand."

Fire burns in her eyes as I slide my hand up her thigh and beneath the hem of her dress.

She arches her back as I drag the neckline of her dress down, exposing her breasts.

Zoe inhales sharply as I lean forward and suck hard on her nipple.

My cock aches as I slide my fingers along her wet slit.

As I tease her nipple with my tongue and teeth, I press my thumb against her clit.

She writhes against me, trying to build friction between us.

"Tease," she says, her voice breathy as I switch to her other nipple. "I thought you wanted me to come on your hand?"

"Oh, I do." I pull back to look up at her.

She arches her back, rocking her hips forward. "But not until you're begging for it. I thought we already talked about that."

I plunge two fingers into her, pushing against her inner walls.

As my hand stays still, she lets out a small whimper and rolls her hips.

I grin and wrap my other hand around her neck,

keeping the pressure just enough to be pleasurable without hurting her.

"Don't move." I pull my fingers out, inching them back in. Torturing. Teasing. "If you start to ride my hand, I'm not going to let you come."

Her eyes grow wide, her tongue darting out to lick her bottom lip.

I start thrusting faster, driving deeper and harder into Zoe as her pussy starts to pulse around me.

Her core clamps down on my fingers as I dip my head to take her nipple back into my mouth.

I groan and bite down, pulling her nipple into a stiffened peak between my teeth.

"Please." She moves, gripping my shoulders as her hips twitch. "Please make me come, Christian."

"You want to come?" I lean forward and graze her earlobe with my teeth. "Come for me, Zoe. Soak my fucking hand."

Her nails dig into my shoulders as she starts rocking her hips in time with my fingers plunging into her.

I keep one hand on her throat, pinning her into the angle I want.

Zoe's entire body starts to quiver as her orgasm rocks through her.

I unbutton my pants and take out my cock as Zoe pants.

She grins before leaning in and kissing me, lowering herself onto my cock.

With a groan, I lift my hips, pushing deeper into her.

"Holy shit," Zoe says as she leans back. "Your cock feels so good."

I grab her hips and use my grip on her to set the pace.

Zoe runs her hands along her body, teasing her nipples as I drive deeper into her.

My cock throbs as she slides one hand between us, toying with her clit.

I moan as she starts to rock her hips, meeting me thrust for thrust.

"Fuck yes, Zoe. Keep doing that. Fuck me."

I tilt my head back against the seat, watching as she rides my cock while playing with herself.

Her pussy milks my cock as I come, clamping down around me with her own orgasm.

I keep thrusting until her entire body relaxes.

My cock is still throbbing as I pull it out of her.

"Fuck," I say, leaning forward to kiss her shoulder. "Maybe next time I should fuck you against the hood of the car."

Her eyes light up as she moves into the passenger seat. "That might have to wait for another night. I don't know if I can stand right now. My legs feel like jelly."

I grin and find some napkins to clean up. "Just wait until I get you alone back at home tonight."

She laughs and shakes her head. "You're insatiable."

"When it comes to you, you're fucking right I am."

A comfortable silence falls between us for a few minutes as we stare out at the stars and the water.

I take a deep breath before looking over at her.

I can't fall in love with her, but I don't want to lose her either.

"What do you think about going out on a date? Starting this relationship over?" My words rush out as my heart pounds.

I'm not used to being nervous, but when it comes to what exists between me and Zoe, I'm terrified of fucking it up. "We could start with being friends."

Zoe rolls her bottom lip into her mouth for a moment before nodding. "I would like that."

We settle back into that comfortable silence, both of us lost in our own thoughts.

It feels natural to sit here with her, though. There is no need to say something or keep the conversation moving.

With Zoe, I'm able to relax.

Until I start thinking about planning the perfect date for her.

I'm not the kind of man who goes on dates. I have no clue how I'm going to pull this off for her.

18

ZOE

Ava's thumbs fly over her screen, typing out a massive message while I toss the potential outfit options for the night onto my bed.

She looks lost in thought as she continues to type away.

"Talking to someone special?" I ask, my tone teasing as I tie the belt of my silk robe a little tighter around my waist.

Ava shrugs one shoulder. "Nothing too important. I just have a lot going on right now at the prison. There was a fight last night and we have a few people staying the night. Just making sure everyone is behaving and healing."

"I'm really scared of your work sometimes." I sit at the vanity by the windows and rummage through my makeup. "You're an attractive woman all alone in the middle of all those criminals."

"Says the woman *married* to a criminal," Ava teases. "Speaking of Christian, do you know where he's taking you tonight?"

I don't miss the way she changes the topic away from the prison. Even though I want to, I'm not going to press her.

Ava is free to live her own life just like I'm free to live mine.

I just wish that I knew more of what was going on in hers.

"He asked me what I wanted to do a couple of nights ago after we got back from that awful dinner with Mom and Dad."

Ava chuckles. "I don't know if you can call it dinner when half the people there leave before food shows up."

"I know. I thought that dinner was going to be bad, I just didn't think it would be *that* bad. Either way, he asked me where I wanted to go and when I told him that I wanted to go to the amusement park, his eyes nearly popped out of his head."

Although, I don't know if it was because he doesn't want to go to such a crowded public place right now, or if it's because I want to ride roller coasters until I feel sick.

Ava looks at the pile of clothing on the foot of the bed. "You really think that he's going to get on a roller coaster with you?"

I shrug and put on my eyeliner. "He agreed to go with me, so I'm sure that he's fine with it."

"There's something about Christian that doesn't exactly scream the amusement park type." Ava sighs and adjusts her position on the bed, crossing her legs beneath her. "When are you going to tell me the truth about what's going on here?"

A lump in my throat threatens to choke me. "How much do you already know?"

"I know he's the leader of the Herrera cartel." Ava leans forward. "He's killed people, though none of those murders have ever been proven."

I put down the eyeliner.

There's no way to avoid telling her the truth anymore. It's clear that she's been talking to some of the men in the prison about Christian. Though I don't know where to start, I have to tell her everything.

Losing my sister because I keep lying to her isn't an option.

"He kidnapped me. Dad owed him a debt, and he decided that was the way he was going to collect. I got married because he threatened to kill Dad. I've seen things I never thought that I would ever have to see. Bad things."

"What things?" Her voice trembles.

I shake my head. "Ava, I can't tell you more than that. There are things that I'm never going to be able to tell you."

"You would give your loyalty to a man who kidnapped you? Just like that?"

I run a hand through my hair, the guilt gnawing at me. "I wish that I could tell you more, but it isn't safe, Ava. You have to understand that."

"And how the hell am I supposed to just let you go out with this man, knowing these things? How the hell am I supposed to walk out of here tonight and just leave you with him?"

"He's not a bad man when it comes down to it, Aves. He takes care of me. He takes care of his people. That person who comes out when he has to take care of business isn't who I think he really is."

"You're honestly going to sit there and defend him?" She shakes her head. "I'm sorry if I find it hard to understand that. I know that there is always more to a story than people think, but this is a lot to process, Zoe. Aren't you scared?"

"He scares me sometimes. Knowing what he's capable of scares me. But I know he wouldn't hurt me. I've seen him around his people. He's kind to them. He makes sure that they're taken care of. The only time something bad has happened is when it has to happen."

Ava gets up and walks over to me, wrapping her arms around my shoulders and hugging me tight. "I'm worried about you, Zoe. I can imagine what you've gotten hauled into, and I don't like it. I want you to be happy."

"I am happy." I pull back to look at her, my vision blurring.

I hate that she's worried for me. "Believe me, Aves. The man I see most of the time is the one I'm happy with."

"That's all I want for you." She lets me go and takes a couple steps back. "I still worry about you, though. This life isn't easy. I see what the men I work with have to go through. Are you sure that this is what you want?"

"I doubt that this kind of life is what most people want." I keep applying makeup, trying to distract myself from my deepest fears. "There are days when he walks out the door, and I wonder if he's going to come back alive. I know that this marriage isn't traditional, but there's a part of me that's grown to care for him."

"Caring for him is one thing. Spending the rest of your life with him is another." Ava turns her back to me and starts to look through the outfits on the bed. "If you ever change your mind, you know that you can call me, right? I'll be here to get you."

"I'm not going to leave, Aves. Regardless of how this started, I want to be with Christian. There's something between us. I don't know if it's the worst heartbreak of my life waiting or my greatest love, but there's something there."

She turns around holding up a pair of ripped black jeans and a white bustier top. "Wear this when you go out tonight. He's not going to be able to keep his hands off you."

I smile and finish up my makeup. "Thank you, Aves. You might be the one person in the world who makes me feel close to normal about this relationship."

"If he makes you happy, then I'm going to be happy for you." She puts the outfit down and comes back over to tug on a strand of my hair. "Let's finish getting you ready for this strange friend date of yours."

Christian holds out his hand for the colorful stamp at the ticket booth. "This is the first time that I've been to an amusement park in a long time."

I grin and wait for my own stamp. "It's going to be a great time."

"I still wish that we were doing something a little less in the open." He looks at me as the cold stamp is put on the back of my hand. "Although, nobody is going to start anything with a bunch of children around."

We walk through the gate together, the sounds of children laughing filling the air.

The scent of funnel cake and corndogs wafts on the breeze.

My stomach rumbles as I take Christian's hand and pull him toward the first roller coaster I see.

"It's the perfect spot. The men who are after you aren't going to risk an amusement park in the middle of the day. It's too open." I squeeze his hand as we join the back of the line. "Thank you for agreeing to this, though. I know it wasn't your favorite idea for a date."

He chuckles and leans over to kiss my bare shoulder.

"The security team is here too. It makes me feel a little better."

"Well, get ready. By the time we get off that roller coaster, you're going to be done worrying about everything else going on. We're going to have a good time and if anything does happen, the security team is going to take care of it."

Christian lets go of my hand as we shuffle forward in line. "As long as you don't make me eat one of those disgusting corndogs, then everything will be fine."

"Corndogs are a delicacy."

He pretends to gag as we get closer to the front of the line. "Corndogs are *not* a delicacy. It's lips and assholes ground up and wrapped in corn bread."

People turn around and give Christian a dirty glare.

He nods to them before turning his attention back to me.

I burst out laughing as he rolls his eyes.

If this is a sign for how the rest of the day is going to go, we might get kicked out of the amusement park.

Christian hums to himself as we get on the roller coaster.

The bar comes down across our laps once the ride is full.

I'm nearly bouncing in my seat as the roller coaster starts to move.

It's been a long time since I went to the amusement park. I think I was still in high school the last time I got to spend a day on rides and pretending that I don't have a care in the world.

The roller coaster starts to climb the massive incline near the start of the track. It's slow, but the tension starts to build the closer we get to the top.

Fat white clouds drift across the blue sky. Children are already starting to shriek as we hit the top of the slope.

Christian reaches out and takes my hand, squeezing as the roller coaster crests over the top and plummets toward the bottom.

I scream, throwing our hands up in the air as the roller coaster whips around the track.

Christian grips my hand tighter, his jaw set in a hard line as we go around the final sharp curve in the track and start to slow to a stop.

"You looked like you were going to shit yourself." I grin wide as I pull him to the next ride.

"I hate roller coasters," he groans as we stop in front of another ride.

I look at the loops that will put us upside down before glancing back at him.

He sighs. "You love this shit, don't you?"

"I can go on this one on my own if you would rather sit it out."

Christian shakes his head. "I said that I hate them, Zoe, not that I'm not going to do something with you that you obviously love."

Butterflies erupt in my stomach as we join the line for the next ride.

As we wait, I don't miss the looks that people give him.

I have to be honest; he does look terrifying. The lack of smiles, groomed beard, and tattoos covering his arms make him look like the kind of man most people would avoid.

He's also the kind of man that I'm starting to see a future with, even though the way we got together is less than ideal.

The only part I still get hung up on is his job.

Christian does what he has to. He protects the people

who rely on him, and I can't fault him too much for that. Although, I wish that he didn't have to kill people to make that happen.

However, I know if I love the man, I'm also going to have to learn to love the monster.

19

CHRISTIAN

The corner of La Neige is dark as I sit at a booth between the stage and the bar, watching my wife enchant the crowd around her.

She stands beneath the bright stage lights, holding the microphone and belting out the song she spent all of last week writing.

I barely saw her. If she wasn't sleeping, she was locked away in her studio and working.

Not that I mind. If she stays in that studio, it means that she's safe. I know where she is, and her security detail has her surrounded. There is no way that Demarco or her father are getting to her.

In the bar, everything is out in the open.

From where I sit, I can see the bar. I watch the people who enter, waiting for the next person who wants to kill me.

I still think that her performing right now is a bad idea, but I can't be another person who holds her back.

As the song finishes, I start clapping along with the crowd.

Zoe looks around the bar before her gaze lands on me.

She waves to the crowd before the band starts playing another song. This one is more upbeat.

Zoe dances around, her hips swaying as she sings.

If it's possible, the crowd falls even more in love with her.

I tap my foot to the beat of the song as I glance around the bar again.

Ava weaves through the people dancing, heading straight for me. Her hands are in her pockets and her shoulders are rolled back.

She looks like a woman ready for battle.

"Evening," she says as she slides into the other side of the booth, her back to the room. "I think that it's time you and I had a chat about my baby sister."

I arch an eyebrow as she leans back in the seat and crosses her arms.

She glances at Zoe and sticks her tongue out at her before turning her attention back to me.

I swivel, going from sitting sideways in the seat to facing Ava.

"You seem like there's something you want to say to me." I keep my tone neutral. "Are you sure that right here and right now is where you want to say it?"

Ava leans forward, placing her crossed arms on the table. "Don't try the intimidating shit with me. I know that you could make me disappear in the blink of an eye if you wanted to. But I also spend my days meeting with men who are far worse than you."

I chuckle and shake my head. "You really don't know who you're dealing with, then."

"I know exactly who I'm dealing with. You would be amazed at how willing some people are to talk while you're stitching up their wounds."

The fierce look she gives me is impressive.

She might walk in the shadow of her family most of the time, but she's got the balls to sit here without flinching. Hell, Ava doesn't look scared at all.

"And why is this coming up now? You spend at least one day a week at my home."

Ava nods toward Zoe. "You think that I want her to overhear this? I don't want to hurt her. For whatever reason, my sister seems to be falling in love with you. She wants to protect you. What I want is to make sure that she isn't going to be hurt by you."

I look over my shoulder as Zoe leans against the guitarist, their backs pressed together as she tilts her head back and sings.

There is no denying the glow and energy that radiates from her every time she steps onto the stage.

"I have no intention of hurting Zoe."

Ava's eyes narrow. "But you're not falling in love with her. Not the way that she is falling in love with you. My sister has a big heart. She might not see the dark side of your life yet. Not in full. But one day she is going to wake up and see everything for what it is."

"Don't tell me how I feel about Zoe." My tone is low and dangerous as I lean toward her. "Never make the mistake of thinking you know exactly what I feel for your sister. "

"I don't think you even know how you feel about Zoe."

I'm not about to sit here and prove to Ava that I care for her sister. She's just going to have to learn that over time. "If you're done sitting in here and trying to figure out the intricacies of my marriage, you can go."

Ava shakes her head. "Not yet. You might scare other people, but you should know that there's going to be hell to pay if you ever hurt my sister. You're not the only one with the ability to make people disappear."

The corner of my mouth twitches upward. "And you're going to be the one to make me disappear? I have a hard time believing that."

Ava grins, making my stomach lurch.

There is something cold and dangerous in that smile. "I like you right now, Christian. If you hurt my sister, I'm not going to like you very much. I can and *will* make you disappear. The men I take care of at the prison are loyal to a fault. More than one of them owe me favors."

Her smile brightens as the song comes to an end. She stands up on the seat whistling and cheering for Zoe before hopping out of the booth. As she leans close to me, I tense.

"Don't fuck this up, Christian. Zoe is the best thing to ever happen to you."

Ava straightens up and walks away, disappearing into the crowd.

I wait until she's left the bar before turning to look at Zoe.

She smiles and hops off the stage, stopping to talk to people on her way over to me.

Zoe slides into the booth beside me, leaning her head on my shoulder for a moment.

I kiss her forehead before she sits up and reaches for my glass of water.

"I think that's the first time I've ever seen you talk to Ava without me there," she says.

Zoe takes another sip of water before setting the glass to the side. "Did you have a good conversation?"

I chuckle and shrug. "Your sister is a terrifying person, but I like her."

And it's true.

While I don't appreciate the fact that she is comfortable enough to threaten me, I like that Zoe has someone like Ava in her corner. Zoe needs someone fierce like that in her life, and it's entertaining to have someone not give a shit about the power I have in this state.

Zoe smiles and gets up from the seat, taking my hand. "I'm glad you got along. Now come on, I could use a nap."

"I was thinking of taking you for dessert and a drink to celebrate." I loop an arm around her waist and walk with her to the door. "If you want to."

"Please tell me that we're going to find the biggest piece of peach cobbler that we can." Zoe is almost bouncing on the balls of her feet as we step into the cool night air.

"There's a place around the corner from here that has *the best* peach cobbler ever."

Zoe hums a melody to herself as we walk, lost in whatever song she's trying to work through.

I've gotten used to her wandering through the house and singing. It's not unusual to hear a random line or two of a song before she moves onto something else.

If I'm being honest, I love the life that she's brought into my home. There used to be so much silence, but since she moved in, it feels like I'm not as alone.

As we approach the peach cobbler place, I pull out my phone and look up a recipe for it.

If this is the way she wants to celebrate a good show, then I'm going to need to figure out how to get her a good peach cobbler when we're out on the road together.

Making it seems like the easiest option.

The thought of making cobbler for her is enough to freeze me in my tracks while she walks into the dessert bar.

I could spend the rest of our lives together following her around the world and listening to her sing. I would get to listen to her perform and after every show, we would have our own little tradition.

It scares the hell out of me to think that way. To crave that. To feel happy at the thought of it happening someday.

A future with Zoe is terrifying. It makes me think that there could be more to life than the cartel.

Camila isn't ready to take over the cartel yet, but she will be one day.

When that day comes, I could be free to travel the world with Zoe. I could spend the rest of my life wrapped up in her.

And then I could lose her and watch it destroy the rest of my life. I could watch loving her set my world on fire and burn it to a crisp when she's gone.

If she could ever bring herself to fully love me as I am.

I try to shake the thoughts from my mind as I put away my phone and enter the dessert bar.

Zoe follows the host to a small table in the back.

The dim room is lit with warm toned lights. The cozy atmosphere makes it easy to settle into the seat across from her and let go of everything else on my mind.

A few minutes after sitting down and placing our order, two slices of cobbler and two whiskey sours appear.

Zoe sips her drink before digging into the dessert.

"This is the best peach cobbler I've had in a long time," she says, closing her eyes before taking another bite. "I think I've died and gone to heaven."

I chuckle and sip my drink. "There is no way that the pie is that good."

Zoe's eyes fly open, and she stabs her fork in the direction of my cobbler. "Try the pie before you diss the pie."

I take a piece and shove it in my mouth, flavors bursting on my tongue. "You're right. It's amazing. I wouldn't say that it's died and gone to heaven worthy, but it's a pretty good pie."

She scoffs, amusement dancing in her eyes. "You wouldn't know a good dessert if it bit you in the ass."

"Now we're going to be rude?" I take another sip of my drink. "You had a great show tonight."

"Even though you're still worried about taking me out to perform?"

I nod. "Even though I'm terrified that taking you out to the bars is going to get us in trouble. I don't want to lose you, Zoe."

The smile on her face drops as she reaches out and takes my hand. "I'm not going anywhere. You don't have to worry about losing me."

Except if I consider the lifetime we're going to have together, all I can do is worry about her.

20

ZOE

Christian's arms wrap tighter around me as I start to wake up.

I open my eyes and stare at the shadows cast on his face from the dim light streaming through the cracks in the curtains.

He sighs in his sleep, his hand sliding along my hip.

I smile as I reach up to trace one of the shadows on his cheek.

His eyes flutter open as he yawns.

My heart pounds as I look at him, heat racing to my core.

Last night was fun, but I'm still not satisfied. After we got home from dessert, we lost ourselves in each other. I can still taste the whiskey on my lips as I wet my bottom lip.

"It's too early," Christian says, his voice husky. "Go back to sleep."

Grinning, I reach between us where his hardened cock is pressing against my thigh. "It doesn't really seem like you think it's too early to be awake."

He smirks and tilts his hips forward, pressing his cock harder into my hand.

I squeeze it, taking my time sliding my hand up and down his length.

His silky skin is hot in my palm as I run my thumb over the head.

"You should be tired right now." he watches me through hooded eyes as I continue to stroke his cock. "I kept you up most of the night."

"Maybe you weren't as good as you thought you were." My tone is teasing as I trail my hand lower, wrapping it around his balls.

He groans as I squeeze before working my way back up his cock.

Christian rolls us over, laying on his back while I straddle his hips.

His hardened cock brushes against the curve of my ass as I plant my hands on his chest.

"And just what do you think you're doing?" I ask as he tries to cup my breasts.

I swat his hands away, giving him a wicked grin.

As I sit up straighter, his eyes widen. "No touching."

Christian smirks and tucks his hands behind his head. "Carry on."

Even though I feel awkward at first, I want to please him. I want to make him feel as good as he makes me feel.

At times, I feel insecure, like I might not be enough for a man like him.

"Where did you just go?" Christian's tone is soft as he runs his hand up my thigh. "Zoe, you don't have to do this, you know that, right?"

"Who said that you could touch me?" I try to rebuild some of the confidence I felt a few minutes ago. If Christian didn't want me, his cock wouldn't be rock hard and pressed against my ass right now.

As soon as he pulls his hand away from my body, I rake my nails down his chest.

Christian shudders, his gaze trailing along my body.

A shiver runs down my spine at the look in his eyes when his gaze finally meets mine.

"Fuck," he says, his voice raspy. "You do not know how fucking amazing you look. I could devour you. I'd die a happy man if I spent the rest of my life just like this."

I smirk down at him, my confidence building.

Even though I didn't voice my insecurities out loud, he is getting good at reading my moods. The more time we spend together, the closer we seem to get.

Which is why I roll my hips, rewarding him for not touching me by rubbing against his cock.

He groans as I run my hands through my hair, pushing it back.

I slide them down my body, cupping my breasts.

His gaze follows the movement as I massage my breasts.

I pinch my nipples, moaning as I tease them into stiffened peaks.

Christian moans, lifting his hips beneath me. His cock brushes against my pussy again.

I move higher on his body, wetness between my legs and spreading across his lower abs.

"You're already soaked, and you haven't even played with your clit yet," he says, glancing up at me. "You're always so wet for me. Does the thought of teasing me turn you on? Are you thinking about how great it's going to feel to ride my cock when you're finally done with your little game?"

"I might be." I trail my fingers down to my clit. "Maybe

I'm thinking about the way your cock feels when you're buried inside me. Or the way it throbs when you're about to come. Fuck, I love that feeling."

Christian snaps, surging upward and grabbing me by the hips.

I squeal, grinning as he shifts me down onto his cock.

I moan as I take him deep, rolling my hips until he's buried to the hilt.

"Fucking tease." He smirks as he lifts his hips, thrusting from below. "We both know you love the feeling of my cock buried in you when you come. I want you to come all over my cock now. I want to know exactly how wet you are for me."

I place my palms on his chest, rocking my hips in time with his thrusts.

Tension starts to build in my core as I take him deeper.

Christian thrusts harder, his fingers digging into my hips.

My pussy pulsates around him as I come.

As my pussy clenches down around his cock, my back arches deep.

"Get on your hands and knees," he says as he pulls out of me.

I move to the bed beside him, hurrying to obey.

Wetness drips down my thighs as he moves to kneel behind me.

Christian drags his cock along my wet slit before pressing the head against my entrance.

When he plunges inside me, I fist the sheets.

Christian takes my hair in one hand, using it to pull my head back and arch my back.

He slams into me hard, making me cry out.

His hand comes down on my ass before his hips start rocking faster.

I push back, trying to take him as deep as I can.

Christian moans as his cock throbs inside me.

He wraps one arm around my torso and pulls me upright.

Holding me in place, he slams into me, keeping my back pressed against his chest.

"You feel so good wrapped around me," he rasps as he kisses my shoulder. "Come for me, Zoe."

His other hand leaves my hair and runs down my body.

His fingers tease my clit, circling it as if in slow motion while his thrusts plunge deeper.

I hold onto his arm, my nails digging into his skin as I come again.

Christian groans, his thrusts slowing as he reaches his own orgasm.

He holds me to him, showering kisses over my neck and shoulders.

We collapse on the bed together, our limbs tangling as he kisses me. Our tongues tangle together as his hands run along my body.

"What do you say we go for a shower and then I make you some breakfast?" he asks a few moments later.

I yawn and grab the sheets, pulling them around my body. "I need another nap. You've been keeping me awake."

He laughs and shakes his head. "I'm not the one who woke us up early."

I arch an eyebrow. "So, you don't want me to do that again?"

Christian leans over the bed, his face close to mine. "You can wake me up by playing with yourself anytime you want."

He pecks me in the mouth before heading out of the room.

I tuck my arm beneath his pillow, nestling deeper into the bed and drifting off to sleep.

CHRISTIAN WALKS into the studio with a grim look on his face.

My stomach lurches at the cold look in his eyes. It's one that I haven't seen since the night he cut up the body.

The memories of that night come rushing back. The rusty smell, the grating sound of the saw grinding bone.

It's hard to look at him as he stands in front of the couch and looks down at me.

"I have to go out for a little bit. I'll probably be gone until later this evening. Camila is on her way over. She said something about wanting to spend some time with you this afternoon."

I nod, trying to slow my racing pulse. "What do you have to do?"

His gaze softens. "Zoe, don't ask me that unless you want to know the answer, alright? I'm not going to lie to you."

I swallow hard and nod. "Okay. Stay safe."

Christian stoops to kiss me. A caress, but no more. "I will be. Call me if you need anything."

"I will."

He walks out the door, shutting it behind him as I set my guitar to the side.

As I pull my knees to my chest, the panic starts to bubble.

For the last couple of weeks, I've been able to put the

thought of what he does for a living mostly out of my mind. He goes to work at the trainyard every morning and then he comes home at night.

I don't think about what he does between those hours.

But there're times like right now when it's hard to pretend that I don't know what he does for a living.

There're times when I can't ignore the fact that he kills people.

My stomach tosses and turns. Bile rises in my throat.

I don't want to know what he's doing today, even though I asked.

I still haven't figured out how to mesh the two sides of Christian together in my mind.

Some days I think that I will never be able to.

How can I fall in love with a man who kills people with no remorse?

They might not be good people, but I've seen the coldness in him. It's like Christian shuts parts of himself off when he has to take lives.

The door to the studio opens, light flooding the space before I can go down the spiral.

Camila walks into the room, her maxi skirt swirling around her legs.

She takes one look at me before sitting down on the couch beside me and looping an arm over my shoulders.

"You look like you're going to be sick," she murmurs. "Tell me what's bothering you right now. And don't try to start that don't worry about me thing. We're sisters now. I'm here to support you."

I look at her as my vision starts to blur. "Does it ever get easier?"

"You're going to have to be a little more specific than that."

"Does looking at someone and knowing they kill people get easier? Does trying to figure out how a person can be a murderer and one of the best people you've ever known ever start to make sense? Because it doesn't for me, and I don't know if it ever will."

Camila bites her bottom lip. "I wish that I had the answer you're looking for, but I don't. The truth is that it never becomes easier. Christian isn't the kind of man who gets a thrill out of taking care of business, but he does what he has to. A lot of stuff happened when we were younger, and he swore that he would protect the people who follow him with all he has to offer."

"And what about the people he drags into his life just because he can?" I hate the way my voice breaks.

I don't want to cry in front of Camila. There is no way that she won't tell Christian how much this bothers me.

Camila turns to face me, crossing her legs beneath her. "Christian is a good man. I know you see that. He brought you into this life to protect the people he swore he would protect, but he's giving you a good life. And I see the way he looks at you. There is no way that he doesn't spend time doting on you."

"He does." I sigh and wipe away the few tears that fall. "And I don't know what that means either. We're supposed to be starting this relationship over as friends but neither of us seems to be able to do that. It keeps seeming like more, even though it feels like that could be a bad idea sometimes."

"Have you talked to him about this?"

I shake my head. "I don't want to hurt him."

"I think you need to talk to him. Christian is a grown man. He can deal with being a little hurt. He needs to know that you're struggling with this."

My chest constricts at the thought of trying to have that conversation with him.

Even though Christian is nothing but understanding most of the time, this feels like something that will hurt him.

He's doing his best to make this feel like home. But there's still a part of me that feels distant from this life.

"Keeping this secret and dealing with this life is only going to get harder when you become a famous musician and put yourself in the public eye. You need to figure out if this is something that you can do."

I nod, knowing she's right. "You make it sound so much simpler than it is."

Camila chuckles and reaches out to squeeze my knee. "You're going to get through this, but you and Christian need to have an honest conversation with each other. No more sweeping things under the rug and pretending that it doesn't exist."

"When did you get so wise?" My tone is teasing as I try to lighten the mood.

Camila laughs and shrugs. "I fell in love with one of the guys in the cartel. Things didn't work. There were a lot of things standing in the way for us. I don't want to see some of those same things stand in your way when I know you could be happy with my brother."

"I'll talk to him about everything going on," I say, stretching out my legs in front of me. "I don't think I can focus on writing music anymore today, though. Not while knowing what he's out there doing."

"What do you say we go inside and watch a movie for a bit? After that, we can get ready for the party tonight."

I raise an eyebrow as she gets up and leads the way to the door. "There's a party tonight?"

"At the trainyard. It's one we have every year to celebrate being together as a cartel. You're one of us now. You have to come."

"Alright," I say as we leave the studio and head to the main house. "Movie and a party it is."

As we head back to the house, I try to let go of everything worrying me for just one night, even though it seems like an impossible task.

21

CHRISTIAN

Zoe tucks her hands into the back pockets of her painted-on jeans while she stands beside Camila at the entrance to the trainyard. There's a smile on her face, but it doesn't meet her eyes.

I know I shouldn't have told her that I had to leave earlier. I should have come up with some excuse for why I had to leave in the middle of the day when I was supposed to be off and relaxing with her.

Except I won't lie to her. I won't be like her father and conceal the world we live in with a shroud of lies.

I have to be transparent with her because I get the feeling that very few people are.

I weave through the crowd to get to them, grinning as I nod hello to several people.

The music blares as people dance. The scent of spices and cooking meat wafts through the air.

I dodge several of the children as they run by, almost stumbling into a row of garbage cans.

Zoe's gaze lands on me and her smile lights up her entire face.

Just as quick as that smile appears, it's gone, and she's looking at me like she's seen a ghost.

"I didn't know if you were going to be here tonight," Camila says, looking up at me as she crosses her arms over her chest. She cuts her gaze toward Zoe, a subtle sign that something is wrong.

"I finished work quicker than I thought I would." I watch Zoe as her mouth presses into a thin line.

She takes a deep breath before smiling again.

"I'm going to go find some food," Zoe says before disappearing into the crowd.

Two of the men I have stationed as her security detail take off after her while I turn to my sister.

"What's going on?" I ask, my tone sharper than intended. "Why does she look like I've kicked a puppy?"

Camila looks around before walking over to a secluded corner away from the rest of the party. I still have a good line of sight in the direction Zoe went, but the rest of the cartel isn't going to be able to hear us speak.

"You killed a guy. That might have something to do with it. Or how about the way you took her to that damn cabin and cut up a body in front of her?"

I sigh. "I thought we had moved past that."

"Maybe you had, but whatever happened today brought her back to that frame of mind." She shakes her head. "The girl looks like she is in love with you most of the time. But every now and then, she looks like she's next on the murder list."

"This is the reality of this world," I say as I glare down at my sister. "You know that as well as I do."

"And she was not raised in this world. She is a normal person who isn't nearly as fucked in the head as we are. You need to talk to her and sort this shit out before you lose the best thing that's ever happened to you." The last few words are punctuated by a finger hammering my chest.

My sister sighs. "She's scared, Christian. She hides it well, but this life is scary and she's new to it. Do fucking better."

Camila takes off into the party, leaving me to stand there and think about everything.

I showed Zoe what I had to. Every exposure she's had to the monster who lurks in the dark has been calculated but necessary.

I've kept her from everything else that she doesn't need to see.

Camila might be right that she is new to this world, but that shouldn't mean I have to shield her from it.

The way I introduced her to it was wrong. I can see that now. But the danger is real. People are coming for us. For her.

I've been trying to protect her from the worst of this world since that night.

Maybe I should stop sheltering her. Maybe it's time to make her see that this is her world now too.

I won't be as harsh or as brutal as I was that night, but it's time to drop the curtains on her new reality and let her come face to face with the creatures that lurk in the dark.

When it comes down to it, Zoe might surprise me.

I take a deep breath and run my hand through my hair.

I hate that there is no clear answer to this problem. I want to fix everything and make her feel comfortable, but I don't know how to do that if I keep hiding parts of my life from her.

After another moment alone, I weave through the crowd to go find Zoe.

She stands in a corner, sipping a beer and talking to Ruben.

As I approach them, Ruben nods to me before taking off.

"How're you doing?" I ask Zoe as I stand in front of her with my hands in my pockets. "With this. Me. All of it."

"I'm fine," Zoe says, plastering on a fake smile. "We should go dance. I love this song."

She takes me by the hand and leads me into the center of the party where people are dancing.

I spin her beneath my arm before pulling her to me.

Zoe laughs, some of the tension fading from her as we move our hips to the music.

"What's bothering you, Zoe?" My voice is soft as I look down at her. "If there's a problem, and it's in my power to do so, I want to fix it."

Zoe shrugs. "And what if the problem is something that can't be fixed?"

I press my forehead against hers, inhaling the sweet scent of her perfume. "I don't know."

She nods and cups the back of my neck with one hand. "Then I would rather not talk about it right now. I need time to think it over before we talk. I want to gather my thoughts because to be honest, I don't know how to talk about any of this right now."

Even though I want to keep pressing her, I don't. There is no point in starting a fight when she needs time to think about it.

I can't shake the feeling that I'm going to lose her, though. And it scares me more than I'd like to admit.

"Okay," I say softly, kissing her forehead before standing up straight. "We can talk about it later."

Zoe smiles and nods, but the look doesn't reach her eyes. There is a sadness there that still lingers.

I can see it in the way the corners of her mouth twitch, like she is trying to have a good time, but she doesn't know how.

I hold her a little tighter, wishing there was more I could do.

With each breath, Zoe's chest brushes against mine. I'm sure that if I put my hand on her chest right now, I would be able to feel her racing heart.

"You know that I want you to be happy with your life with me, right?" I swallow hard, the music pounding around us.

My stomach turns as I try to find the right words to say to her. "If there is a part of this life that you're still struggling with, it's normal. Most of us still have a hard time wrapping our heads around everything we have to become."

Zoe's eyes shine with tears as she bites her full bottom lip.

I reach up and run my thumb along it, pulling it out of her mouth.

Her glance cuts away from me, looking at the people around us dancing and having a good time.

"Christian, there is a lot that's going through my head right now. I told you that I don't want to talk about this right now. Can you please respect that tonight?"

"I'm trying, Zoe, but I can see how much this is bothering you. You want me to let you just cave in on yourself and go through everything on your own? You're my wife."

"Through no choice of my own," she says, her voice breaking.

Zoe takes a deep breath and puts her hands on my chest, nudging me back a step.

I look at her, wondering what I'm supposed to do right now.

She wants space and I can understand that, but I also need to know that she isn't going to try to run away from this life. From me.

She means too much to me to let her go.

Though I don't know how or when, she wormed her way into my life. I don't think there is another day that I can spend without her by my side.

If she has worries about this life, then I want to erase them.

I look around the party, watching my people smiling and laughing.

Children race between the adults, laughing and shouting at each other as they head for the waiting food trucks.

One day, it could be our child racing through the crowds.

The second the thought comes to my head, terror grips my chest.

I don't know that we're going to have kids in the future. I don't know that Zoe is going to come around to the cartel life. While I'm sure that she can put on a good show, it's not an easy life.

Part of me wants to tell her everything I've been through. I want to tell her the things that I've had to do in this life to survive and how it still shakes me to my core.

If I tell her the darkest parts of my life, there is still a chance that she's going to close herself off to me.

Hell, if I told her everything that I've done, and I was in her position, I would find a way to leave me, and I would never look back.

The fact that she's still standing here after everything she's seen is enough to give me a small shred of hope.

I know it's foolish to think that the little bit of hope is enough to get us through this massive hurdle, but I have to believe.

"What do you need from me?" I ask, my chest constricting as I look down at her.

If I could go back in time and erase the last couple minutes of our lives, I would.

"Time to think. The space to consider what is going on in our lives. I need to figure out if there is a way to love both halves of you at the same time. Trying to figure that out all in a short amount of time is making me feel sick."

Her arms wrap around herself as if she is hugging herself. Or stopping from falling apart.

The pain inside my chest intensifies at how powerless I am to help her.

For being the cause of her hurt.

She sighs. "I don't know what to do about any of this. I need to know what keeping your massive mountain of secrets is going to look like when I finally start performing around the world. So, right now, I need time and I need space, Christian. Please."

It feels like she's rammed a knife through my gut and twisted it.

I inhale a jagged breath, looking around to make sure that nobody is listening to us. I don't want to have to scold her in public for the way she is talking to me right now. Not when she is clearly panicking, and there is nothing I can do to fix it.

I couldn't be more thankful that the people around us are all involved in their own lives.

A new song starts to play, the music pounding through the speakers. Strobe lights circle, shining off the shipping containers spread throughout the trainyard.

"I'll give you all the time and space you need," I say, my voice soft. "This is a lot. I know that it's a lot. Everything is going to be fine. We're going to figure it out when you're ready to figure it out."

Unable to hold back anymore, I pull her back into my arms. "It's not a conversation that we need to have right now. I'm sorry that I tried to push you too soon, but we're going to have to talk about this eventually."

Zoe melts into me as if the fight has gone out of her.

Her body moves against mine as she lets the last few minutes fade away and blend into the music. Her hands raise to my shoulders, her fingertips brushing against my neck.

I run my hands up and down her waist, my cock stiffening because every touch from her awakens every primal instinct within me.

She smirks as she presses her body closer to mine, making my cock throb while my hands skim along the sides of her breasts.

This is what we're good at. This back and forth. Our physical attraction to each other seems like the only thing that's simple between us.

When we're together, it's like nothing in the world can touch us.

It's when we have to step out of the bedroom and talk to each other that things get hard.

Her smile comes back in stages as one song blends into the next.

We dance together, our hands roaming each other's bodies beneath the shining lights and the stars.

The rest of the world fades away as I lose myself in the feeling of her body pressed against mine.

I could spend the rest of the night with her here like

this.

If we could only spend the rest of our lives doing this, I know that we would be perfect together.

My body jerks and tenses as a gunshot rings out through the crowd.

I hold Zoe tight as I pull the gun from my waistband and duck with her behind one of the food trucks near us.

She looks at me with wide eyes as I hold a finger to my lips and peek out around the truck.

People are scooping up their children and running behind whatever they can find to hide.

More gunshots ring out and people fall to ground.

I feel like I'm going to throw up as I look around and see a man I don't recognize standing on one of the shipping containers.

He hides behind a crate up there, pointing his gun into the crowd.

I level my gun at him and flick off the safety.

As I wrap my finger around the trigger, more people stream into the trainyard with guns.

I shoot the man down before turning to the next.

After I kill another man, I duck back behind the truck and turn to Zoe. "Did you bring a gun with you?"

Zoe shakes her head, her bottom lip quivering. "I didn't think I needed to. I'm not going to stand here and kill people."

I kneel down and pull another gun from the holster on my ankle.

After checking it quickly, I hand it to her. "You don't get a fucking choice anymore, Zoe. If someone comes at you, then you have to kill them. If they point a gun at you, you kill them. If you want to survive, you're going to have to kill people eventually. Do you hear me?"

She swallows hard and nods, tears shining in her eyes.

A pit opens in the bottom of my stomach.

I know that this is only going to shove her further away from me, but it has to be done. She needs to be able to kill people if it comes down to it.

I don't have time to fuck around with her fear of what she could become. Not when her life is on the line.

Ruben and Camila race over to us from behind the stage where the speakers were set up.

Ruben shoots two more people down before crouching beside us.

"What the fuck is going on?" I lean around the truck, taking aim at a man with a black bandana wrapped around the lower half of his face.

The bullet whizzes through his chest before he drops to the ground.

"Don't know. Security was supposed to have this place shut down, but I haven't been able to get in contact with any of them." Ruben's eyebrows furrow as he looks at Camila and Zoe. "Demarco could be behind it, but I don't recognize any of the men here. If it were him, I would recognize somebody, I'm sure of it."

He's right. The men running with Demarco were close to my father. At least, the ones I know about. It's possible that there could be others now.

However, the attack could be coming from Zoe's father. It seems like more of his style. There is nothing well-thought out about the attack.

"Get Zoe and Camila out of here. Get them to the house. I'll follow you when I can. Make sure that the pair of them are safe and locked away. If anything happens to either of them, I won't hesitate to kill you."

Camila glares at me but gives a sharp nod.

I know that she wants to stay and help, but she is the heir. She has to get to safety in case anything happens to me.

Our people are going to look to her for what to do.

Ruben looks at Zoe and Camila, his mouth set in a grim line. "My car isn't far from here. We're going to run for it. Camila, take the lead. I'll provide cover. Zoe, you stay in between me and Camila at all times."

Zoe's eyes look like they're going to bulge out of her head as she nods.

The three of them get ready on Ruben's signal.

She looks to me again, the shine in her eyes gone.

I don't know where she goes in her own mind, but she looks fierce and ready to do what she has to.

The three of them take off running as I race to a spot behind the stage.

I use one of the speakers for cover as I shoot more people trying to race for the parking lot.

More of my people flood into the tight quarters, their guns raised as they shoot the attackers.

More people start to fall, blood coating the cement and dirt.

Such a waste of good lives.

The shooting starts to slow until it comes to a stop.

I look around at the carnage, counting how many of my people have fallen.

I hold back the tears that threaten to fall, knowing that I can't show weakness right now.

I need to be the strength that my people need, even if it's the hardest part of my job.

It's going to be a long night, and it's clear that this is just the beginning.

MARRIAGE AND MALICE   199

By the time I get home, the sun is high in the sky, and I'm ready for a nap, even though I know I'm not getting any sleep for a while.

Zoe is awake and sitting in the kitchen with Ruben when I walk in.

Dark circles are beneath her red-rimmed eyes. She looks like she hasn't slept in days even though it's only been a few hours since I left her.

"How did it go?" Ruben asks as I head over to the fresh pot of coffee on the counter and pour myself a mug. "How many dead?"

I take a long sip of the coffee, trying to use it to wash away some of the guilt rolling through me in waves.

Even after seeing how many of the attackers my people were able to take down, it still feels like I could have done more to prevent the loss of life there was tonight.

"I doubt that we got everyone that was there tonight, but whoever sent those people after us is weakened. I saw a couple of men we used to know. The attack was Demarco's."

Ruben nods, his face solemn. "Are there many funerals to arrange?"

I'm going to throw up if I have to think about how many people I lost tonight. I don't want to have to think about it at all. I want to move on from here and never have to look back. This has all been one nightmare of a night.

And yet, this is all on me, so I have to endure, even if just for a little while longer. Until I can hide I the shower and let the tears fall.

"I'll deal with the funerals on my own. We lost nearly a dozen. Thankfully, none of the children were lost."

I down the rest of the coffee and put the mug on the counter. "I'm going to spend the rest of the day in the office arranging the funerals. I need you to make sure that Camila gets home safely."

"Will do, when she wakes up." Ruben gets up and stretches, his joints cracking. "Last night was rough for her. She's in one of the guest rooms right now."

I nod. "Get some rest yourself."

Glancing at Zoe, I watch as she seems to draw in on herself more than ever.

I look back at Ruben. "It's been a long night for all of us. You're going to need your rest. I need everybody at the top of their game. Once you've made sure Camila is home and safe with her security team, I want you to start digging for more information on Demarco."

Ruben faces pinches as he nods. "I don't know how possible that is going to be. Even though I've been coordinating with Billie, we don't know anything more than we did before."

"There has to be more out there." I open the fridge and grab the plate of leftover fried chicken. "Zoe, we need to speak."

Ruben looks between the two of us, his gaze landing on Zoe.

The corner of her mouth tips up as she gives a slight nod.

I don't know what bond the two of them have formed, but at least she seems to be making more friends in the cartel. Maybe that will make life here easier for her.

Out of all the people she could befriend, Ruben is a good one. I know that he will put her life above his own when it comes down to it.

When I glance at Ruben, he clearly wavers between

whether or not to leave the room.

I arch an eyebrow and clear my throat as I take a seat at the kitchen island.

Ruben sighs and dips his head, leaving the room.

"What is going on?" Zoe's voice wavers.

She balls her hands into fists, digging her nails into her palms. "Why were we attacked at a party? Who is after you, Christian? Please. I need to know. Why do they want to kill you? Why do we keep getting attacked?"

I sigh and unwrap the plastic from the plate before pulling off a piece of the once crispy chicken skin. "Zoe, it's not as simple as you're making it seem."

"Please." She looks at me with those big green eyes, and I feel myself start to melt. "I don't want to know everything, but it might help if I know why I keep almost dying."

It's on the tip of my tongue to tell her about her father, even though he has nothing to do with tonight.

I don't want to hurt her, though. Not more than I already have.

It's best that she learns the truth about him on her own. That way she really believes what she sees.

"Very well. Demarco Jones used to be my father's right hand. Years ago, a lot of bad things went down. He faked his own death, and now he's trying to kill me. I don't know much more than that. It's not the first time that someone has something to gain from my death, and I doubt it will be the last. It's the nature of the job."

I pop a piece of chicken in my mouth as Zoe nods.

It's clear that she's trying to take it all in.

Her hands relax as she shifts in her seat and takes a deep breath. As her shoulders roll back, I get the distinct feeling that I'm not about to like what she says.

"I know you've done a lot to protect me and help me

build my career. I appreciate that. I really do. But you also scare the hell out of me, and I don't know if I can keep living like this. Christian, I don't know if I can do this."

I swallow the anger, the hurt, that bubbles to the surface.

Zoe might be scared, but right now, she is making a choice. One that means she wants me as distant from her life as possible.

"Too fucking bad," I say as I lean closer to her, the plate of leftovers in my hand. "You don't get a choice. This is the life. You married into it, and you're going to die in it. Just like the rest of us. Get your shit together and start acting like a cartel wife, Zoe."

As I leave the room, I can only imagine the look she's giving me.

Guilt claws at me.

Though I know I'm lashing out at her, it doesn't change the fact that I'm doing my best to keep her safe. She doesn't know the entire truth of the situation yet, and I want to do everything I can to keep her in the dark for as long as possible.

There was a better way to handle tonight, though.

I let the lives lost get to me, and I took it out on her.

But I don't have it in me to pretend that everything is alright when I know it's not. Not around Zoe.

I can only hope she forgives me, though I don't know if I will forgive myself.

I hate the part of myself that's capable of saying things like that to her, but it's time that she gets it together.

This is the life that we're both stuck with. It's time that she embraces it because there is no other choice.

Not with her father and Demarco breathing down our necks.

22

ZOE

I can't remember the last time I slept through the night. It had to be while I was still living at home. Back when everything was safe and calm.

Before I had to worry about people sneaking through my window and standing over me in my sleep. I didn't have to think about the possibility that I would die every single day.

Those were before the days of seeing people die or a body cut into pieces.

As much as I'm falling for the Christian I see ninety-nine percent of the time, there is that other side to him. The one that's harder to fall for.

Although, the other day, the afternoon after the shooting at the party, I could see the scared little boy hiding behind the monster he keeps pretending to be.

There is more to that darker side of Christian than I ever thought there was. I don't know what fuels the beast, and I have a gut feeling that tells me I need to find out if I ever want to come to peace with the way I feel for him.

What a giant mess.

I was never supposed to start falling for him. I wasn't supposed to like the passion and the tension between us when we argue.

I certainly wasn't supposed to consider what it would mean to get it together and become a proper cartel wife.

What does that even look like? Will I have to be brutal and vicious like my mother when it's time to take down Christian's enemies?

As I get out of bed after another sleepless night and look in the mirror, I think I could be.

I see parts of my mother in myself. There is a world in which I could be the partner Christian needs.

I look at the gun sitting on my bathroom counter.

Camila has spent more time teaching me to shoot in the last couple of days than she has in several weeks.

I'm confident in my ability to hit a target, though I may not kill it on the first shot. Not yet.

I have to get to that point if I decide to dive into this life. I have to be ready to do what it takes to protect myself and the people below me in the cartel.

Though, I don't know if when the time comes, I'm going to be able to pull the trigger.

"Morning," Christian says as he appears in the doorway to the bathroom.

I glance over at him, trying to prepare myself for the conversation I know we need to have.

"Morning." I brush past him and into the bedroom, pulling on my silk robe before perching on the edge of my bed.

Christian takes one of the chairs from the other side of the room and pulls it over to the foot of the bed. "It's time that we got whatever is going on out in the open. You said that you needed some time to think about things. Is that time over?"

I nod and cross my legs, picking at a loose thread on the duvet cover. "What do you want from this marriage?"

His eyebrows knit together.

Christian leans into the chair, crossing his legs at the ankle as he thinks about the question. He looks around the room, his gaze distant.

I don't know where his mind is at with any of this, but I doubt that we're thinking the same thing.

It seems like no matter how often we talk, we're rarely on the same page even if I want us to be.

I'm hoping that this conversation finally aligns us, but my stomach twists and turns. I don't know what to expect.

This is a conversation I've never had to have with anyone else.

"I never wanted a marriage," Christian says, his voice gravelly as he finally looks back at me. He pins me in place with a stare that seems to see right through me. "I haven't had the best track record with any relationship, so I've never given marriage much thought."

"That's the difference between us, then."

I sit a little taller, trying to make it seem like I have myself together. "I thought that the person I married would love me. I thought that there would be a mutual sense of respect, and we would build a life together. When I think about marriage, I don't think about being kidnapped and forced into it. You might have had your reasons, and I understand that they were good reasons, but I was still kidnapped."

Christian cocks an eyebrow. "Do you really think that I don't care about you at all? Are you going to sit here and really try to say that?"

My pulse pounds as I look out the window.

People patrol the property, guns in their hands and fierce looks on their faces. Since the attack at the party, there have been more people than ever around.

"*Do* you really care about me?" I ask, hating the way my voice wavers.

I'm not an insecure woman at all, but I'm not sure that his answer is going to be yes. "Because I keep feeling like I'm falling for you, and there's nothing but hurt waiting for me at the end of it."

Christian sucks in a sharp breath. "If I didn't care for you, I wouldn't have built you a studio. I wouldn't spend two nights a week in a bar to watch you perform. I certainly wouldn't tell you to start acting like a cartel wife. *My* wife. So, yes, Zoe, I do care for you."

My heart skips a beat as I stare at him. I don't know how to react.

In my wildest dreams, I didn't think that Christian would ever admit that he cares for me.

Warmth spreads through me, and for a moment, I don't know what to say. My mouth goes dry as I exhale slowly.

Caring about me is amazing, but what about the monster? Can this be enough for me to be able to live with it?

"I don't think there's a world in which this marriage is going to survive. I don't know how to mesh the two parts of you together when they are both very different people. I don't know how to be the cartel wife and the singer. How am I supposed to go on tour and have my personal life invaded when there is all of this that I have to keep a secret?"

Christian leans forward, bracing his forearms on his knees. "We can figure that out together. This marriage isn't going to end just because things are hard. I have to be two different people at times, Zoe. It is what life is. I have to be the man I am to protect the people who look to me for protection."

A lump rises in my throat as I twist to grab a pillow from the bed behind me. I hold it close to my chest, stuffing my hands deep into it and trying to hide the way they shake. "And what if I can't be the perfect cartel wife? I'm not going to run around killing people for the hell of it. That's not me. I don't even know if I'm capable of killing anyone."

Christian shrugs. "Won't know until it happens."

"And that's the problem!"

I toss the pillow to the side and stand up, pacing back and forth. "You think that I can just step into this life and start killing people. Hell, you demand it of me. You want me to be the perfect cartel wife, and I want to be a musician. I want to be able to tour without worrying about going to jail for killing someone. I want to tour around the world with a husband who can actually get on the fucking plane without a warrant for their arrest."

Christian rolls his eyes, and it only pisses me off more.

He watches me as I pace, his mouth folding into a thin line. "I can get on a plane, Zoe. There are no current warrants for my arrest, just a bunch of shit that nobody can prove I did."

I toss my hands up in the air before sinking back down on the bed. "Don't you think that's part of the fucking problem? What if someone finds out about the things that you've done? Then my husband gets locked away, and I have to figure out where to go from there. I have to visit you behind bars because we both know that if you go in, you're never coming out. Not with the things that you've done."

The corner of his mouth turns up in a smirk. "You would come visit me in prison?"

"Hell, Christian, stop being amused by this. I'm trying to talk to you about all the things that have been going through my head, and you're acting like an ass. I need you here with me to actually talk about what's going on. I don't need the person you have to pretend to be for the cartel."

"And how do you know who I really am?" He scoffs and leans back in his chair. "You keep talking about the two sides of me as if they're that easy to differentiate. You don't know the things that I've had to do to survive."

He runs his hand through his hair and shakes his head. "It's a tough world, Zoe, and you have to decide whether you can deal with it or not. There is no government money to protect you anymore. What you give into the cartel, you get back. I'm a monster, Zoe, because that's what the cartel needs. There is no changing that, even if you think you can."

"I don't want to change you. I just want to figure out how I'm supposed to continue on with both sides of you."

Christian crosses his arms, the movement of his muscles making his tattoos pop. "That's on you to figure out, Zoe. I don't hide things from you. Not about my life. I don't know what you think I can do to make this easier for you."

"And yet, you call yourself a monster."

"I know what I am. You know what I am. I don't see a point in hiding that from you."

I sigh and run my hand through my hair. "I don't think you're a monster. Not anymore. The more I think about it, the more I think that you're just trying to make everyone think you're a monster. You're not a bad man, even if you aren't about to win an award for sainthood."

The corner of his mouth twitches. "Then why do we keep going around in circles like this?"

My chest constricts, the answer on the tip of my tongue.

Taking time to think has made things clear for me.

I might not be at peace with both sides of Christian yet, but I know what I want. "I need to know that you're worth it."

"If you don't have that figured out yet, then that's your fucking problem." He stands up and puts the chair back before heading for the door. "I'm not going to keep playing these games while you try to figure out what the fuck you want, Zoe. You know what you need to do. If you want me outside of that, figure it the fuck out."

"I worded that wrong." I hug myself, my cheeks flaming as the lump in my throat threatens to choke me. "I know you're worth the relationship. What I don't know is worth it is the heartache I'm going to go through when this blows up my face."

"Why do you think that this is going to blow up?" His tone is sharp as he walks back across the room and looms over me. "Why is it that your only constant thought about this marriage is that it's going to fail?"

"We want different things out of life. We have very different lifestyles. I don't know if I can be the person you think I need to be to fit into the cartel."

He sighs and stretches, locking his hands behind his head.

I pick at the loose thread in the duvet again, needing something to do with the nervous energy rolling through my body.

"We'll figure out a way to make this work," he says, his voice softer than before. "You're going to be able to be a musician without having to worry about how the cartel is going to affect your career."

"You can't be sure that we can figure it out." I drop the thread and look up at him. "Would you ever consider walking away from the cartel? I know that Camila is the heir. You can't tell me that this is what you want to do with the rest of your life."

Christian glares at me, and I know I've overstepped.

Guilt claws at me.

I've done the same thing to him that everybody has done to me my entire life. I told him that he should walk away from his job because it doesn't fit into the plan I have for life.

The hypocrisy isn't lost on me as Christian drops his hands and crosses his arms.

He stands in the middle of the room, taking up more space than any person should.

It feels like the room is getting smaller and the air is getting hotter.

"You really just said that to me? After everything that I've been told your family put you through over a job? Do I want to spend the rest of my life doing this shit? No. I hate the things I have to do, but you would know that if you had asked. I will not be stepping away from the cartel when Camila is not ready to take over. That is a burden that I would never place on her."

"I'm sorry. I should have thought about that." I run my hands down my face.

I don't know where to go from here. This conversation has been less than productive.

"Whatever," Christian says as he heads for the door. "I have business I need to take care of."

He walks out of the room and slams the door behind him.

Though we weren't yelling at each other, it feels like our worst argument yet.

I don't know where we go from here or what I'm supposed to do with the way I feel for him.

This was supposed to clear everything up. We were supposed to be able to move forward after we spoke.

I need to get out of this house for a little bit.

Christian said that I could go shopping with Ava a few days ago as long as I took the security detail with me. Maybe it's time that I take him up on that offer.

I could use some sisterly advice.

Mom purses her lips and shakes her head when I pull a pair of jeans off the rack.

I need some more outfits for performing, but Mom is disagreeing with everything I try to buy. I don't know why her opinion matters to me still.

With Mom here, I can't talk to Ava about Christian.

It's probably a good thing. I could use a little time to not think about him and the cartel, even though there are several men following us around.

"I don't know why you continue to pick up clothing that does not suit you, Zoe. You know that you are supposed to dress appropriately, and yet you keep selecting shirts that don't cover anything."

Mom sniffs as I run my fingers along a suede bustier. "You are not going to purchase that."

Ava glares at our mother as she digs through the rack and finds my size in the bustier. "She can buy whatever she likes. Not only does she not live at home anymore, but she's her own person."

I give Ava a warning look as she shoves the bustier into my hands.

The last thing I want is to fight with Mom in the middle of a store. She would insist that I'm going to bring bad press to the family and she's right.

With who my husband is, it's best to lay low. Even the security detail does their best to blend in whenever we go out.

"I don't want this outing to turn into a mess," I say, keeping my voice quiet as one of the saleswomen looks over at us. "I don't have to buy this today. I just need something nice to wear to La Neige next week for my performance."

Mom rolls her eyes. "I still can't believe that you are chasing after this silly little dream of yours. Have you even thought about what people will say to your father? Do you think that you're making it easy for him to be in the public when you want to spend your days parading around naked on stage?"

Anger bubbles up, but I try to stuff it down.

Mom is always going to be who she is. I learned a long time ago that I was going to be a disappointment in her eyes.

It doesn't make it sting any less, but as I get older, I start to move on faster.

"Dad is perfectly capable of managing his public image." I hold the top a little tighter and start looking for some flared leather pants to go with it. "There is no need for me to pull back on my career when he has an entire team of people to help him with his."

Mom rolls her eyes and tries to take the bustier from me.

I scowl and hold onto it a little tighter, my heart pounding in my chest.

After all our years of shopping together, I know that she has no issue making a scene in a store if I don't do what she wants.

I'm tired of being that person, though.

The cartel has given me a freedom I never thought I would have. I'm not about to let my mother take that from me just because she doesn't like what I want to wear.

"I don't know who you've become," Mom says, letting go of the bustier and taking a step back.

She crosses her arms and glares at me. "Do you think now that you're running with that criminal bastard that you can have everything that you want? Open your eyes, Zoe. A man like him is only going to use you for what you have between your legs. He is going to grow tired of you and move onto the next best thing, leaving you home alone while he runs around with his mistress."

Ava's mouth drops open as I stand there, completely speechless.

The tight hold I have on my anger snaps as I shove the shirt at my sister.

Mom smirks as I approach her.

"You know I'm right, Zoe. A man like that is only going to bring trouble into your life."

"Fuck you." Venom is in my voice as I stand inches from her.

My blood is boiling inside my veins and the steam needs to be released. Now.

"Fuck you and fuck this shit. I'm tired of dealing with it. You think that you can control my life, but that's over. I'm moving on with everything. You've made it clear that you don't want to be part of my life and that's fine. You're not going to stand here and insult my marriage or my husband. Not when has shown me more kindness and compassion and love than I have seen in an entire lifetime from you."

As the words leave my mouth, I know they're true. The relationship I have with Christian might not be the best, but it could be if I get out of my own way.

I spin on my heel and stride out of the store.

Ava jogs to catch up with me, a grin stretching from one side of her face to the other.

We say nothing as we make our way through the mall and back to the parking lot.

"I'm so proud of you," Ava says as she pulls me into a hug. "I know how hard that must have been for you. What do you say we go back to your place for celebratory drinks and a swim in the pool?"

I laugh and hug her back before pulling away and heading to the car. "Sounds like a great idea."

As we get in the car and leave my mother behind, I take a deep breath.

I owe Christian one hell of an apology.

23

CHRISTIAN

Zoe stands in the doorway of my office shortly after her sister left. She gives me a small smile before coming in and perching herself on the edge of my desk.

My gaze drags down her body, taking in every inch of exposed skin before I look back up at her.

"Couldn't have bothered getting changed before dripping water all over the office?" I ask, my tone sharp as I look at the wet hair hanging down her back.

Her bikini strings cling to her body, begging to be pulled, but I resist the urge.

After our conversation this morning, I'm not in the mood to play nice. Not when a thousand different feelings have been coursing through me since then.

She's falling for me.

I'm falling for her.

She doesn't think it can work.

I don't see how it can't work.

We're opposites in almost every sense of the word, but I know that this thing between us is built to last. It has to be. I wouldn't consider changing my entire life if it wasn't.

And since our talk, it's all I've been thinking about.

The need to change, to get out of this life has consumed me even more.

I hate the life. I hate the monster. I hate that I am so committed to the people who depend on this cartel. Because even if I want to leave more than anything, to get away, I can't.

Camila isn't ready yet.

"I'm sorry," Zoe says, ignoring my question. "I'm scared of the way I feel for you. I want this to work between us, but instead of supporting your position in life right now, I was unfair and asked you to give up your life."

I sigh and run my hand through my hair.

Though I appreciate the apology, I still hate that she asked. Especially when she knows that Camila is still in school and working toward a career before she takes over.

She put me between a rock and a hard place. Wanting to be with her and needing to be with my people.

"Yes. You did. I think you also questioned whether or not I care for you."

"I never claimed to be a smart woman. Hell, I don't think that I think at all when it comes to you."

Zoe cracks a small smile. "Or maybe the problem is that I think too much. I go around in circles and try to convince myself that things could never work because I don't know how they could. Except you see a way forward."

"I think we could work on it. But I don't know if that's what you want."

My chair creaks as I lean back in it. "You don't seem to. You seem like you're looking for any excuse you can to make sure that our marriage won't work."

She crosses one leg over the other. "I didn't know better.

I kept going back and forth with myself, but I had an enlightening conversation with my mother today."

I arch an eyebrow, preparing for what could be another fight.

There is no telling what her mother may have told her. Either that, or she could burst into tears. Her mother isn't a kind woman.

"And what was that conversation?"

She smiles and nudges my knee with her foot. "You may not be perfect, and I sure as hell am not, but nobody has ever cared about me the way you do."

My heart races as I look up at her.

The conversation from this morning falls away as I consider the possibilities going forward.

If she really is prepared to give this relationship the chance it deserves, then I don't want to dwell on the past.

All I want is to move forward with her and know that there are better days waiting for us.

Sure, there may be mountains of bullshit standing in our way and more problems than I can count from outside factors, but we can figure it out. Together.

"Come here," I murmur, grabbing her by the hips and dragging her into my lap.

I run my hands through her wet hair, clutching the back of her head.

She sighs softly as I pull her down for a kiss. Her lips are soft and demanding against mine as she grips my shoulders.

The sound of my phone ringing pulls us apart.

Zoe stays in my lap, giving a teasing roll of her hips against my cock.

I glower up at her as my cock swells, knowing that we don't have time for this today.

However, I'll be making plenty of time for make-up sex later tonight.

I grab the phone and hold it to my ear as Zoe winks at me. "What is it?"

"Boss, someone broke into Camila's dorm while she was out."

Zoe stiffens in my lap, her eyes growing wide.

I hold a finger to my lips as her mouth starts to open.

I blow out a slow breath, needing a moment to process before I ask whoever is calling me what the hell is going on. This shouldn't have happened.

"What do you mean? Someone is supposed to be watching her dorm at all times. What's your name?"

"Jeff Ward, sir." His voice wavers, and I'm sure that he's seconds away from pissing himself. "Cooper was supposed to be stationed at the door, but when we got back from one of Camila's classes, he wasn't here. Logan is hunting him down, and he will be brought to you immediately."

"Send him to Ruben. I'm on my way down there now. Nobody is to go in or out of that dorm until I get there, are we understood?"

"Yes, sir."

I hang up and slide the phone into my pocket as Zoe springs up from my lap. Worry shines in her eyes as I stand and grab my car keys from where I tossed them on my desk earlier.

"What happened with Camila? Is she alright?" Zoe follows me to the door. "She wasn't in there when somebody broke into her dorm, was she? I couldn't hear everything that was said."

I shake my head and stop in front of the bookshelf near the doors, opening up a small panel and taking out a gun. "She wasn't there when it happened. She's fine."

I check the Glock before I holster it. "I'm going to get the keys to the emergency apartment I keep, and she's going to move in there. I told her that the dorms were a bad idea when she said she wanted to move in there."

"Christian, you can't go in there with guns ablazin' and not expect the cops to show up." Zoe puts her hands on her hips and watches as I take the apartment key out of the secret compartment. "It's a school. If they see you with a gun, then there's going to be a big problem."

I sigh and put the gun back.

She's right and I know it.

Camila's university has metal detectors all over the place.

Fine. My men have guns they smuggled in if I need one.

"You need to stay here," I say as I close the compartment and lock it. "Your security team will be here if anything happens."

Zoe crosses her arms. "Like hell. I'm going to go put on some clothes and then I'm coming with you. I want to make sure that she's alright."

The corner of my mouth twitches as I hold back a smile.

Whether Zoe knows it or not, she is more suited to this life than she thinks. She's not hesitant about rushing into what could be a dangerous situation if someone she cares about is involved.

"Zoe, I don't want to have to worry about you too."

Her eyes narrow as she looks up at me before heading for her room. "Wait for me. I'm going to get changed and then I'm going to come with you to make sure that she's alright. She's my sister too, Christian."

With that statement, I know that there is no refusing her. Not when she considers my sister hers. If I try to stop her, there is a look in her eyes that tells me she will find her own way there.

"Fine." I smile as I shake my head. "Be quick about it, though. We need to get to the dorms as soon as possible."

Zoe takes off as I head into the garage and get one of the cars started.

Zoe appears a moment later, pulling her shirt over her head as she hurries to the car.

As soon as she slides in, we take off.

Camila is sitting on the floor outside her dorm when we get there. She looks furious as she gets to her feet and walks over to me.

I can already see that a fight is coming as her security detail moves farther down the hall, giving us a bit of privacy.

"What do you think you're doing?" Camila's voice is venomous as she crosses her arms. Her foot taps against the ugly blue carpet as she raises an eyebrow. "Someone broke into my dorm. That doesn't mean you need to rush over here and have a guy on a break hauled away."

"I'm so glad you're okay!" Zoe pulls her into a tight hug and whispers something in her ear that I don't catch. When Zoe pulls back, Camila's glare is a little less deadly. "It was a good thing you were at class."

"Camila, it's time to move into the apartment. You know that the dorms aren't safe, and this just proves it. Anyone can get in here if they want to. All it took was getting a visitor's pass to be able to roam through the campus." I open the door to her dorm and look around.

The dorm isn't large, but there is a lot crammed into that small space.

Her desk has been overturned and pens are scattered everywhere. Sheets of paper are ripped in half and clothes have been thrown all around the room. Her sheets are in a pile near the mini fridge, and something is spilled all over them.

I take one good look at the dorm before turning to look at her. "Do you really think that I'm going to let you live here when one person was able to get inside and make your room look like this? Do you even know what they were looking for?"

"It's likely just some drunk idiots who decided to trash the room." Camila shrugs and looks to Zoe for help.

Zoe gives a slight shake of her head and looks at me. Her bottom lip twitches, and I can see the gears in her head turning.

"The lock isn't broken and none of your roommate's stuff is touched."

Camila sighs. "Sometimes she forgets to lock the door behind her. I've tried talking to her about it, but she doesn't really think it's much of an issue. It's not that bad. I don't keep anything important here."

I pinch the bridge of my nose, trying to keep my temper in check.

I know that this isn't Camila's fault, but she should have been more careful.

She knows what we're dealing with. She knows that there are people out there who would love to get to her to hurt me.

"You're going to the apartment, Camila. I'm not going to have you living in this place when you have an idiot roommate who seems to want to make it impossible to keep you safe. You're going to be getting a new man to watch your home too. Cooper is done."

Camila throws her hands up in the air, looking to Zoe again. "Please tell him that this is part of a normal university experience. He might actually listen to you!"

"I listened to you for years." My tone sharpens as I gesture to the room. "All the damage done in there is the result of listening to you. There is no way that this is going to happen again. You're moving to an apartment. No roommates to fuck things up."

Zoe sighs and steps between the two of us.

Putting her hand on my chest, she pushes me back a step. "Why don't you think about a private dorm here? I'm sure that you would be able to work something out with the dean. She would still be able to live at school, but you wouldn't have to worry about other people risking her safety."

"I'll agree to that," Camila says, raising an eyebrow at me.

She shakes her head and sighs. "Look, you can't lock me up in an ivory tower until the day that salvation comes, Christian. I can take care of myself, and I know that you have people looking out for me. Everything is going to be fine, but you have to trust that I can do this."

"You know it isn't that easy," I say, though I know this is a losing battle.

"It *is* that easy. You taught me how to handle myself. Everything is going to be fine. A private dorm is a good compromise."

She comes closer and grabs my hands. "Please, Christian. Once I leave school, I'm going to be entirely consumed with training to take over the cartel. Please just let me have this."

I can't take that away from her. She is right that once she is done here, she'll be consumed by the cartel.

Doesn't mean I don't hate it.

I sigh and nod.

Camila squeals and tosses her arms around me, pulling me into a tight hug. As she squeezes, she forces the air from my lungs.

I chuckle and hug her back for a moment.

When she steps away, there is a wide smile on her face.

Zoe looks at me and winks before looping her arm through Camila's and pulling her off to the side.

I watch the two of them as they whisper together before pulling out my phone and sending a message to Ruben.

He'll get in contact with the dean about the room switch and then I'll start moving her things today.

A few minutes later, as I'm busy searching through her room for anything the intruder might have left, Camila enters the room. She smiles at me and shakes her head.

"You love her, don't you?" she asks, her voice soft as she takes a seat on the bed. "I didn't think that you would ever get to that point with any woman, but I'm glad it's with her."

I stiffen before tossing more of her clothing to the side. "I never said that I loved Zoe."

"Please. You don't have to tell me." Camila kicks her legs out in front of her as she looks around the room. "I know that you never would've agreed to a private dorm if she didn't suggest it. She soothes out some of your rough edges, Christian. It's not a bad thing."

I stoop to grab some of the ripped pieces of paper off the floor. "Don't go getting ahead of yourself. We might be working things out right now, but we still have our problems. I don't know where this is going to go."

"You know exactly where this is going to go. You're going to want to be with her forever."

Camila rolls her eyes and takes the papers from me, stuffing them into a wire trash can. "When she starts touring the world, you're going to be going insane as you sit at home and worry about her."

Even though I know Camila's right, I'm not going to admit to it. If I do, my sister is going to think that it means she should drop out of school.

She's going to see the confirmation as a request for her to take over the cartel early when it's not.

"You've sacrificed a lot for me over the years." She gets up to help me pack her clothing into an open suitcase tossed in the corner.

"I know where this is going and don't even bother bringing it up. You're going to get your medical degree and become the best doctor in the world. There is no way that anything is going to ruin that for you."

Camila sighs. "Do you know where your wife is right now?"

"She popped her head in to say that she was going downstairs with your security to get some food."

Camila chuckles and shakes her head. "She went to go sweet talk the dean into giving me the caretaker's cottage. She knows that it's empty, and her father is one of the alumni here."

My chest feels tight as my heart swells.

Zoe is everything that I could want from a partner and more. She loves my sister just as much as I do, and she openly shows it.

Somedays, I worry about how that open show of love could be turned against her.

Every single day, I'm glad that Camila has Zoe in her

corner.

"She's too good for you," Camila teases as she bumps her hip against mine. "She's too good for everyone in this world, but out of the billions of people that exist, I think you're the one that comes closest to being enough for her."

I laugh and roll my eyes. "I know that she's too good for me, but thanks for the reminder."

"It should make you feel good. Your wife could have a life without you. She's a smart woman. Even with the threat of collecting the debt from her father another way, she could find a way to leave if she really wanted to."

Camila rolls up a sweater and shoves it into the suitcase. Zoe chooses to stay. She wants you, even though the two of you are constantly bickering."

As I look at my sister, I see the hope in her eyes.

She wants my life with Zoe to work out. Through the years, she's said countless times that all she wants is for me to be happy.

"I'm going to make it work with Zoe." I stand up and look around the room, taking in what we still have to pack.

My heart beats a little faster. "I don't know what happens tomorrow or the day after that, but I know that I want my future to be with her, even when we do annoy the shit out of each other."

"Aw," Zoe says as she walks into the room with a stack of empty boxes. "That was almost sweet until you had to go and ruin it. Now, what do you say we get the rest of this place packed up and get Camila settled into the caretaker's cottage? Then, one of you can take me to dinner."

Camila squeals and launches herself at Zoe, the boxes falling to the ground.

"Thank you. You are the best sister to ever exist. You

just tell me where you want to go tonight, and I'll take you there."

Zoe laughs as she pries herself away from Camila. "We better hurry up. I'm starving."

Camila gets to work, moving around the room with the force of a small hurricane.

Though I didn't find anything to tell me who might have been in here, I know it's Demarco and his men. They're making a point.

Demarco wants me to know that he can get to her if he really wants to.

Zoe joins in on the packing, laughing and talking with my sister as if they've been friends for years.

I don't understand half of their inside jokes, but that's fine. I'm too busy worrying about what happens when Demarco finally makes his big move.

How long is it before he goes after Zoe?

24

ZOE

The scent of Christian's cologne wraps around me as I nestle down deeper into his sheets.

Now that I've spent the past week sleeping in his bed, I don't think that I'm ever going to leave. There's something about the spicy and sweet smell that lures me in and makes me think I could live in this bed forever.

With a yawn I roll over and grab the remote to open the curtains.

Even if my plan for my twenty-fifth birthday is to stay in bed all day, I can at least get some sunlight while doing it.

The door swings open, and Christian comes in wearing nothing but a party hat and a pair of black boxers.

He holds a cake with two forks stabbed in the top as he makes his way across the room and to the edge of the bed.

"Happy birthday," he says as he sets the cake on the bedside table. "How does it feel to be a quarter of a century old?"

I grin and loop my finger in the elastic of the hat, pulling him down for a kiss. "I feel ancient. I also never want to leave your bed. Do you know how comfortable this thing is?"

He chuckles and sits on the edge of the bed, running his hand up and down my thigh.

Sparks rush through my body, a promise of what's to come later. "You don't have to leave my bed if you don't want to. In fact, we could finally move your things into my room, and we could stop pretending that you don't love sleeping with me."

My cheeks warm as I roll my eyes. "I definitely don't. You're a bed hog who steals the blankets. I swear, getting into bed with you at night is like preparing to step into a wrestling ring. One of these days I'm sure that you're going to jump from the top ropes and just slam me through the floor."

Christian laughs and pounces on top of me, straddling my hips and using his weight to keep me pinned down.

He peppers kisses all over my face and neck until I'm laughing so hard tears are in my eyes.

"What was that about jumping from the top ropes?" he asks as he pins my hands above my head. "Because I could do a lot more than just that. We could have you screaming my name in minutes if you like."

"I don't know if only lasting a few minutes is something to brag about." I stick my tongue out at him, laughing when he nips at it.

"You know damn well I can go all night long if I'm properly motivated."

I writhe around beneath him, grinning as his cock presses against the thin fabric of his boxers. "We don't have all day for you to be properly motivated."

He snorts and gets out of bed. "I'm going to make you beg for it all day long. But first, there's another surprise for you. After that, then you can eat cake off my body all you want."

I scoff and shift back to lean against the headboard. Wriggling around, I get the pillows in a comfortable position behind my back to watch as he leaves the room.

When Christian comes back in, he's holding a pale-yellow electric guitar with a signature scrawled across the bottom in gold.

My mouth drops open as he comes back to the bed and hands the guitar over to me. "There is no way that you got me Ivy Faison's signed guitar. You did *not*. Christian, this must have cost a small fortune."

"Say thank you and then stop worrying about how much I paid for it." He sits on the edge of the bed and leans over to swipe his fingertip through the icing.

He licks the icing from his finger before leaning back in bed. "You're going to have to play me a song later."

"Later? We could go out to the studio, and I could play one right now. Or a million."

Christian chuckles and lays back in bed. "And here I thought you said that you never wanted to leave my bed."

I gently put the guitar to the side, leaning it against the bedside table before moving to hover over him. "Thank you for the guitar. It's the best gift that anyone has ever gotten me."

"You're welcome." He tilts his head up to kiss me, his lips soft as they move against mine.

I lose myself in the feeling for a few minutes before my growling stomach breaks us apart. Christian laughs and grabs the cake before settling back against the headboard. "You sound like you could use some food."

Taking one of the forks out of the cake, I use it to carve a piece coated in icing.

I moan as the taste of chocolate and cherries hits my tongue. "This is an amazing cake. You're going to have to start keeping one of these in the freezer so I can have it whenever I want."

He smiles and puts the cake on his lap before taking his fork and trying a piece. "You're right. How about we spend the morning in bed eating cake and watching a couple movies?"

I give him a wicked grin as I stick my finger in the icing before drawing a chocolate path down his toned stomach. "I don't know about that. Eating cake off your body sounded like a pretty good idea to me."

Christian's gaze burns through me as he shuffles down the bed and gestures to his stomach. "Eat away."

As I draw more icing patterns on him, I think that this might be the best birthday ever.

Ava grins as Christian and I hurry down the street to the club.

She pulls me into a tight hug, rocking us back and forth. "I can't believe that my baby sister is finally twenty-five. Tonight will be amazing. We're going to get loaded on alcohol and have a great time."

Ruben and Christian roll their eyes.

Ava smirks and takes me by the hand before reaching back for Camila. Together, the three of us walk past the bouncer and into the club Ruben owns.

The men trail behind, muttering to themselves about having to carry us home later.

I don't bother to listen to anyone as the smell of alcohol and a pounding bass invade my senses.

When Ava called and asked what I wanted to do tonight, I knew that I wanted to spend time at the most exclusive club in the city. I doubted that she could make it happen until I found out that Ruben owns the club.

Now, we're beneath the strobing lights as bodies writhe to the music.

Liquor sloshes in cups and to the floor where staff hurry to clean it up.

To the right there's a sleek black bar with bartenders tossing the shakers high in the air. One of the bartenders juggles several bottles before catching them all and pouring a line of shots.

"Who knew that Ruben could actually put together a cool club?" Camila teases, her voice loud enough for Ruben to hear over the music.

Ruben rolls his eyes. "I can still have you kicked out if you're not going to behave. Don't think that I won't."

Camila flips him off before heading up the stairs to the VIP lounge.

We follow behind her, dodging women in short dresses and men in dress shirts and slacks.

Camila leads the way to a large booth in the corner that overlooks the rest of the club.

I pull down the hem of my black dress before sliding into the booth opposite Camila. Christian sits beside me, and Ava slides in beside him while Ruben opts to sit with Camila.

It's a daring choice, based on how often the pair of them argue.

"Hundred dollars says he's going to end the night wearing the drink she dumps on him," Christian says, his voice a whisper in my ear.

He grazes my earlobe with his teeth, sending a shiver down my spine.

"You're on." Ava looks across Christian at me with a grin. "They're grown adults. There is no way that Camila is going to dump a drink on him."

"You might be surprised." I grin as I look at the pair on the other side of the table.

They're already arguing with each other as the bottle service girl drops off the complimentary bottle of champagne.

I smile at my sister. "The pair of them have a hard time getting along for more than an hour at a time. I doubt tonight is going to be any different."

"Maybe betting against you was a bad idea," Ava says as she looks at Christian.

Christian smirks and shrugs one shoulder. "Could be. Going to have to wait until later in the night to find out."

As it turns out, later in the night comes much sooner than anyone expects.

Within an hour, alcohol is soaking through Ruben's shirt and onto the black leather seat.

He scowls as he slips out of the booth and goes to his office to get cleaned up.

Ava glares at Christian as she opens her clutch and pulls out a hundred-dollar bill. "I'm never betting against you again. Zoe, next time you need to give me a little warning."

I grin as Christian hands me the hundred dollars. "Come on, I'll give it back to you if you agree to go buy us an emergency round of shots."

Ava lights up and takes the bill.

Camila is out of her seat in the blink of an eye, following Ava over to the private bartender for the lounge.

As the pair of them leave, Christian settles in beside me, draping his arm over the back of the booth.

"Are you alright if I have a few more drinks?" I lean into Christian's side and glance around the room, watching the security team as they move around the perimeter, blending in with the rest of the crowd.

Christian kisses my temple. "Go for it. Have a good birthday. I'll even hold your hair back when you vomit up the copious amounts of tequila you've consumed."

I throw my elbow into him, my gaze still bouncing around the room and taking it all in.

One day, I'm going to walk into a club and a remix of one of my songs is going to be playing.

Out of the corner of my eye, I see a familiar face.

My brows knit together as I see my dad standing with another man in a dim hallway just to the left of the VIP bar.

Dad holds something out and the man gives him something before taking what's in his hand.

A pit opens in the bottom of my stomach as I look to Christian.

His jaw clenches.

"Did you see that? What do you think that was about?" My voice wavers.

Christian shrugs. "See what? Maybe they're just friends meeting up."

Dad takes his friends to nice restaurants. Not clubs.

I don't know why my father would be in a club like this. Although, there are people near him that I recognize. Maybe he is starting to branch out.

"Yeah, that's probably it."

When I glance back at the hallway, Dad is still standing there with a drink in his hand and talking to some of the younger people from his office.

"I'm sure it was. Those people are photographed with him at conferences all the time."

"You're right. He would try to keep up with the younger people at work. Especially if he is trying to keep his poll numbers up." I laugh and lean against him. "If it was anyone else, I might have thought that it was a drug deal. But nope, it's just Dad trying to be cool." I shake my head.

Christian's fingers drift along my shoulder. "We could go over there and ask him if you want to. Maybe offer to show him a few dance moves so he can keep up with the kids these days."

I grin and elbow him in the side gently. "I don't want to sound like a bitch, but this is the first birthday in a long time where I haven't been photographed with my father to show to the public how much he loves his children. It's a lot, and just once, I want to spend a birthday without having to cater to his needs."

Christian slides out of the booth and holds his hand out to me. "That doesn't make you sound like a bitch. It makes you sound like a woman who has been through a lot at the hands of her family and wants more for her life."

I roll my bottom lip between my teeth as I look back at where my dad was.

He's no longer there, his back disappearing down the stairs as Ava and Camila start to weave their way back through the lounge.

It's my birthday, and all I want is to have a good time.

Christian clears his throat and makes a show of holding out his hand again. "Come on, Zoe, don't keep me waiting all night."

"And what do you think we're doing right now?" I put my hand in his.

He pulls me up and out of the booth.

"I think I'm going to dance with you until you're begging me to take you home."

Christian laces his fingers through mine and pulls me toward the stairs, leading the way onto the dance floor.

He spins me beneath his arm before pulling me against his body.

His hands are warm as they press against my back, holding me close while our hips roll to the music.

Christian dips me low before pulling me up and capturing my mouth in a searing kiss.

My fingers run through his soft hair, our bodies still swaying to the music as the rest of the club fades away.

I think this is the best birthday that I've had in a long time. Maybe even ever.

25

CHRISTIAN

Zoe sits on the diving board, strumming an acoustic guitar beneath the stars.

Long and low clouds drift across the sky as her sweet voice carries across the open space.

Her toes dangle in the water as she leans over to write something down in her notebook before continuing to strum.

Nights like these are becoming my favorite.

Although, as I sit here tonight, listening to her write another song, I know that sooner or later I have to tell her the truth about her father. I was able to cover for him a few nights ago, but I'm not going to do it again.

I didn't want to ruin her birthday. She deserved to have a good night.

I'm going to make sure that every single one of her birthdays for the rest of our lives are good.

She doesn't need to know what her father was really doing at that club. Who that man was. It doesn't matter in the long run. But the rest of his shady dealings do.

One day, she is going to find out, but it should be him that tells her.

There is no way that will happen, though. Her father is a coward.

Zoe looks up at me with a smile and tucks her pencil back into the messy bun on top of her head. "You're staring at me."

"You're a hard person not to stare at."

I lean back against the cushioned lounger and raise my glass to her.

The amber liquid sloshes around inside before I take a sip.

Zoe rolls her eyes at me before beginning to strum one of my favorite songs. She hums as she plays, her fingers moving over the frets and sliding down the strings.

"Well, now you're just showing off," I tease as she switches back to the song she was working on. "You really are talented, Zoe. You're going to make it in music. I bet you're going to be going on your world tour in no time."

The smile curving her full lips drops. "You won't be going on that trip with me, though."

"I will fly out as much as I can." Guilt claws at me, shredding apart the broken heart that's finally starting to piece itself back together. "I'll be there for you as much as I can."

The corner of her mouth twitches. "I know you will. I just wish that it would be something we could do together. Although, by the time I finally get signed to a label and start touring, you could be done with this all."

"I could be."

Loud cracks like fireworks shatter the peace around us.

Gunshots. From behind the pool house.

Zoe dives into the dark water, abandoning her guitar on the pool deck as I drop to the ground.

I pull the gun from my waistband before looking up.

A tall person dressed in black stalks across the far end of the pool, looking down into the water.

I aim and shoot, hitting the person in the thigh. A deep voice swears, and the man aims his gun at me and fires. He moves closer as I crawl back behind the side table to take cover.

Zoe stays beneath the water, hiding in the dark.

My heart pounds as the man looks back down at the water before circling the far edge of the pool.

Even though Zoe is out here, it's now clear that the man is here for me.

He stalks closer to my hiding spot.

I glance over at the pool as Zoe surfaces slowly, her nose just barely peeking above the water.

The man turns his back to me to look at her.

I take my chance and stand, my finger wrapping around the trigger and pulling.

The bullet burrows into the man's back, just behind where his heart should be. He stumbles and looks over his shoulder before dropping to his knees as blood runs down to the pool deck.

Zoe scrambles out of the water and races over to me. She is dripping wet, her eyes wide as she glances over at the body.

She squeezes her eyes shut and rubs them with the heels of her palms.

"I'm so tired of this," she says as she opens her eyes. Her hands drop to her side, her eyes shining with tears. "Don't you ever get tired of watching people die all the time? Of having to kill people?"

"I thought we talked about this." My voice is tight as we dance around the same conversation we've been having. "I have to do this until Camila is ready to take over."

"I know you do." Zoe takes off her shirt and wrings it out, water pooling on the ground. "That's not what I asked, though. I'm not asking you to walk away. I know this is important to you. I'm asking if you ever get tired of it all."

I sigh. If only she knew how exhausted I am of all of this.

"Of course, I do." I reach out to tuck a strand of her wet hair behind her ear. My heart pounds in my chest as she looks away from me. "I'm tired of having to kill people all the time, but this is the way that it is right now. I don't have another choice. Not yet."

She nods. "I know. It's only going to be a matter of time, but I needed to know that this bothers you as much as it bothers me. I need to know that there's still a human heart beating in there."

The words cut deep, but I understand where she is coming from.

To the rest of the cartel, I have to be the heartless killer. The man who will do whatever it takes to protect everyone around him.

And I am that man at the end of the day, but those deaths still weigh on me.

"I am the monster I am because that's what I need to be. As my wife, you need to learn to be just as ruthless because time will come when you have to choose between your life and someone else's."

Zoe says nothing, her eyes narrowing before she lunges forward, dropping her shirt and ripping the gun from my hands.

She raises it, points it at my head, her finger curling around the trigger as my blood freezes in my veins.

I went too far. She is done with this life. With me.

This is all my fault.

Blood rushes in my ears as I stare at her with wide eyes, unable to move.

This is me and my dad all over again. Except this time, the outcome won't be the same.

I can't hurt her.

I won't.

Bile rises in my throat as I look at her, my chest caving in at the betrayal.

I close my eyes.

Maybe this is a good thing. Maybe now I'll be free from the monster.

If my own father tried to kill me, why did I think that she would be different?

He saw me as weak. She sees me as a monster. There's nothing I can do about it.

The only regret I have is that right here, right now, she is losing her innocence. Her soul will forever be tainted by the life she is taking.

At least for a little moment in time, I was happy. I knew love. I saw a part of myself I thought I'd never experience.

I just wish I could have always been that man to her.

Now it won't matter anymore.

We can both be free.

Peace settles over me as I wait for the hit. The piercing hit of the bullet shredding my flesh.

The gunshot cracks through the air, but I feel no pain.

There is no blood dripping down my clothing. No wound where the bullet lodged. Just a groan and a thud.

When I open my eyes, Zoe is standing in front of me

with the gun still raised and tears rolling down her cheeks. Her bottom lip quivers as she keeps the gun at the ready.

I approach her, careful not to startle her.

I place one hand on the gun and lower it down.

When she doesn't resist me, I take it from her, checking it over before flicking on the safety.

I turn around.

The guy on the ground isn't wearing a mask.

My breath hitches as I look down at the man who used to be like a second father to me.

Blood trickles out of Demarco's head and onto the ground.

More lines crease his face than I remember, and his eyes are faded. Scars cover his cheeks, and in his hand there is a gun.

I kick the gun away from him before crouching down and feeling for a pulse.

No more blood seeps from the bullet wound between his eyes.

I choke back a sob, stuffing it down as far as I can.

I kneel beside the body, looking at the man I thought was dead for years.

He *should* have been dead.

If he were dead like I believed him to be, then none of this would have happened.

I wouldn't have been killing people who wanted to kill me for the last few years.

There was no way that I would have entertained the deal with Zoe's father.

Hell, I might not have even gone to Colombia with the cartel for years. We wouldn't have had to go into hiding.

I would have never married Zoe.

And now it's all over.

Demarco Jones is dead.

Zoe's strangled cry breaks through the thoughts swirling through my mind.

I turn to face her, not sure what to do.

She sinks to the ground, staring at the man she just killed.

Tears continue to stream down her cheeks. Her eyes shine as she stares at Demarco like she's seeing a ghost.

I don't know what to say to make this better. I never wanted her to have to do that.

The reality of our situation dawns on me.

She went against her own principles. She fired a gun and killed a man to protect me.

She never should have had to kill for me.

I move to kneel in front of her, cupping her face in both my hands.

I block the view of the body as I gently urge her to look up at me.

"Hey, it's going to be okay. He would have killed us. You did what you had to do. He can't hurt us anymore."

Zoe takes a shaken breath and presses her face into my chest.

I hold her tight, pulling her in as close as I can.

She clutches my shirt and holds onto me.

As I run my hands up and down her back, I can't shake the knowledge that Demarco has been trying to kill me this entire time.

I thought that he died years ago. Even with the information Alessio gave me, I didn't want to believe that he was still alive.

It had been a mistake.

"Can we get out of here?" Zoe asks, her tone soft and hollow. "I can't be here right now. I just need to get away from this. I need to be away from here. Please take me somewhere else." Panic colors her voice as I stand up and pull her to her feet.

"I'll take you away from here. Don't worry. Everything is going to be alright. I just need to call Ruben to come deal with this and then we can go."

Zoe nods, her eyes still wide as she wipes away the tears.

I kiss her forehead, doing what little I can to console her while I pull out my phone and send a quick message to Ruben.

The moment the message is sent, I take Zoe to the car, eager to get her out of here.

As we walk, I stuff down everything I'm feeling. I can deal with that later.

Right now, Zoe needs me.

The night sky is starting to fade as we set in the bed of my truck at the edge of the lake.

I have pillows and blankets spread out through the bed, creating a nest to keep us warm while Zoe stares out at the water.

"You did what you had to do," I murmur, leaning forward to grab her and pull her back to me.

My legs bracket her body as she leans back against my chest. "He would have killed us if you hadn't taken the shot, Zoe. I know that this is difficult, but you had to do it."

She nods, looking back at me with red-rimmed eyes. No more tears stream down her face, but she looks like the dams could break at any moment.

Not that I blame her in the slightest.

It's not easy to have to kill your first person. Not when you never knew that you were capable of doing that.

"Who was he?" Zoe asks, looking back out at the water as I loop my arms around her torso.

"Demarco Jones." I swallow hard, trying to find the words to tell her about my past. "He was my father's right hand. He was like a second father to me."

Zoe laces her fingers through mine. "Why did he want to kill you?"

This is the part of my life that I hoped I would never have to talk about again.

"Years ago, I had to take control of the cartel. My father wasn't a good man. More and more of our people were dying every single day."

I look off to the line that breaks the two separate pieces of the horizon. Breaking the lake away from the sky. The same way that moment broke me into two different sides that make a whole.

"He was killing innocent people. He was going to kill me for speaking out against him. He saw me as a threat and said that I would be better off dead."

I was twenty back then and was put in an impossible position.

So much hurt could have been avoided.

"I shot him first."

Zoe spins around and kneels between my legs, throwing her arms around me.

The scent of her perfume wraps around me, soothing away the panic currently constricting my chest.

I take a deep breath, hugging her back.

"I'm sorry that you had to do that." She toys with the hair at the nape of my neck. Her mouth presses against my throat in a soft kiss. "I'm so sorry that you had to do that."

"A lot of people were upset after that. Most of them left. I thought Demarco died years ago. I was at his funeral."

I'm still having trouble believing that the man I mourned, cried over, was the one trying to kill me.

"People who used to follow my father started trying to kill me shortly after his death. I moved the cartel to Colombia for a long time to protect us. When I came back, the assassination attempts started again."

"Do you think Demarco was behind it all?" Zoe pulls back to look at me, warmth in those bright green eyes.

I could spend the rest of the night sitting here like this and counting the freckles on her face.

"I know he was. The other men wouldn't have been organized or motivated enough to do it on their own. Not once they got news that I was killing the people after me."

"You think that they're done coming after you now?"

I comb my fingers through her soft hair to cup the back of her head. "I hope so. What happened tonight will serve as a warning for the few men that are left. But if they do, I'll take care of it. I don't want you to have to kill anyone ever again."

Zoe gives me a sad smile and runs her fingers along my jawline. "I don't think we're going to be able to avoid that. You're the leader of the cartel. You're also my husband, and I'll do whatever I have to do to protect you."

My chest constricts as I look at her, and my stomach ties itself into knots. "Zoe, I didn't think that this was going to happen when I forced you into this marriage. I had made up my mind to never love anybody because love hurts. What my dad did to me..."

I can't think about how much that cut into my soul. This moment isn't about that.

I take a deep breath. "I saw what losing my father did to my mother. I saw how much it hurt her, and I didn't ever want to feel that."

My eyes find hers for a second.

Her smile warms me up inside.

I smile back. "Then I married you and started spending more time with you and everything changed. I fell for you. I didn't even know what was happening until one morning I woke up and knew that you were it for me."

She turns those beautiful eyes I call home to me, and I can't help kissing her. Just a caress of lips.

"I love you, Zoe, and I'm going to do everything I can to protect you. Even if that means you want to leave me to go live a life outside of the cartel."

Zoe's eyes water as she cups my face with her hands.

Her thumbs drift across my cheekbones as she shakes her head.

My heart pounds against my ribs. I gave her freedom back to her.

She is the most important person in my life, along with my sister. I can't hold her against her will anymore.

I wait for her to tell me that she's leaving. That she never wanted this life either, and now that I've offered her an out, she's going to take it.

"I couldn't live life without you." Her voice wavers as the corner of her mouth turns upward.

Her eyes are looking so deep inside me. I'd be surprised if she isn't looking right into my soul.

She shakes her head. "Not anymore. Not when I'm head over heels in love with you. I didn't think that it would happen either, but it did. We're better together, Christian."

I can't breathe. I can't talk. All I can do is listen as Zoe continues to seal my fate to hers.

She smiles. "I love you, and I'm not going anywhere. We're in this together until we die. You understand me? I love you, and I'm staying."

The constricted feeling around my chest snaps like a rubber band, all the fear and tension easing.

I crush her to me, capturing her mouth in a searing kiss.

Zoe straddles my lap, her hands sinking into my hair as I try to pull her closer.

I can taste her tears mingling with our kiss as I slide my tongue against hers.

Zoe moans and rolls her hips, grinding her core against me.

With a groan, I slide my hands down her body. Feeling the curves of her breasts and hips beneath my hands has my cock throbbing.

She pulls out of the kiss long enough to whip her shirt over her head and toss it to the other end of the truck bed.

I lean back against the pillows as she leans down and grazes my neck with her teeth.

I run my hands up the planes of her stomach as she sucks on my neck, marking me as hers.

She can mark every inch of my body if she wants to. I'm hers until the day we die.

Zoe sits back and pulls at the hem of my shirt.

I sit up and pull it off before she continues kissing her way down my torso.

As I fist her hair in my hand, she slides my sweatpants down.

Her tongue darts out to lick her bottom lip as my cock bobs free.

"Fucking hell, Zoe. You need to wrap that pretty little mouth around my cock right now."

Zoe's gaze burns as she swirls her tongue around the head of my cock.

I groan, holding her hair tighter as she takes the tip into

her mouth. She smirks around my cock before hollowing her cheeks and gripping the base.

Her head bobs as she takes more of my cock into her mouth, sucking hard.

She drags her tongue along my length.

I moan, guiding her head faster as she sucks my cock.

When I hit the back of her throat, I pull out and force her to look up at me.

"Take off the rest of your clothes and ride my cock like a good girl, Zoe."

She smirks and stands up, turning her back to me as she makes a show of taking off her pants.

When she bends over, I grip my cock and slide my thumb over the head.

She slides the fabric down her legs inch by inch before letting it pool at her feet.

"If you don't take off that fucking thong right now, I'm going to rip if off you with my teeth."

Zoe laughs and hooks her fingers into the sides of her thong before working it down her long legs. When she turns back around, she reaches between her breasts for her bra clasp.

It pops open with a squeeze, and she tosses the lacy material to the pile of clothing.

She cups her breasts as she looks down at me, rolling her nipples between her fingers.

"I can see your soaking wet pussy from here. Are you really going to stand there and play with yourself or are you going to ride me?"

She smirks and shrugs a shoulder, her gaze dropping to my cock. "I don't know. You look pretty happy with your hand."

"Get on my fucking cock and make yourself come, Zoey."

Zoe obeys, getting on her knees and straddling my hips.

Her wet pussy brushes against the head of my cock.

I move my hand to her clit, circling it as she sinks down onto me.

"Good girl. Ride my cock. Make yourself come."

Zoe rolls her hips and spreads her legs wider, taking me deeper. "Like this?"

I tilt my head back, lifting my hips and burying myself into her as I circle her clit faster. "Fuck yes, Zoe. Just like that."

"Please don't stop." Her voice is breathy as she leans back and braces herself with her hands on my thighs.

Her hips rock faster, her pussy pulsating around my cock.

When her nails dig into my thighs, pleasure rolls through my body.

My cock is throbbing with the feeling of her tight inner walls milking me.

"Your cock feels so good," she moans as her grip tightens.

Zoe's back arches as she comes, her wetness coating my cock as her pussy squeezes around me.

I grab her hips and thrust into her as my cock stiffens.

Her inner walls clench around me as I come, filling her.

Her smile as she slumps against my chest makes my heart skip a beat. I wrap my arms around her waist, holding her close. I kiss her shoulder, trailing my fingers up and down her back as I go soft inside her and slide out.

"So," Zoe says, sitting up with a teasing smile on her face. "What do you think about skinny dipping?"

"Last one in the water has to fuck the other person until the sun comes up."

Zoey raises an eyebrow before wriggling away from me and jumping out of the truck bed.

Despite what happened tonight, she laughs and races to the water.

I grin as I get up and follow her, slowing to let her get into the water first.

When I finally catch up to her, I pick her up and slide back into her pussy.

She moans and grips my shoulders, looking down at me with lust-filled eyes.

"I love you," I say, my voice soft as I look up at her.

Zoe locks her legs around my waist, rocking her hips. "I love you too."

I'm going to spend the rest of my life showing her how much I love her.

26

ZOE

I don't know how I'm going to be able to fall asleep at night without Christian.

In the two weeks that have passed since I've shot Demarco, I haven't slept on my own often.

If I try to nap in the middle of the day while Christian is working, I wake up screaming. All I can see when I close my eyes is the man I shot in the head.

Even though I know he would have killed us, the guilt is still eating me alive.

The dead look in his eyes keeps haunting me.

But if I had to do it again, I would.

Sleeping in Christian's arms at night is the only thing that keeps the nightmares away. With him, I know that I'm safe. He isn't going to let anything happen to me.

But now that he's going away, I'm going to have to try to sleep on my own. Demarco's face is going to star in my nightmares every night.

I already know that I'm going to be counting down the days until Christian comes home.

It's going to be a long couple of nights.

I sit on the edge of the bed, watching as he packs his bag for the next few days. Christian smiles at me, tugging on a strand of my hair.

"Stop looking so sad," he says as he turns back to the dresser and pulls out a couple of his faded band tees. "Everything is going to be fine, and I'll be back before you know it."

"If I keep looking sad, is it going to stop you from leaving?" I pull my knees to my chest and wrap my arms around them. "I know everything is going to be fine. I'm just going to miss you. I wish that there was some way I could have changed the performance schedule around so I could be there with you."

Now that Demarco is dead, Christian's been allowing a third night of performances a week.

He's been there for every single show over the last two weeks, sitting near the stage and cheering the loudest.

I've got two performances while he's gone, and Ruben is going to be escorting me to both of them. Camila and Ava are going to be there as well, along with the entire security team that follows me around.

It feels good to know that he is confident enough to let me go without him now, but I still wish that he was going to be there.

Christian smiles and drops a kiss to my forehead. "We talked about the performances, Zoe. You love performing. You're not going to miss doing what you love to come sit around and wait for me every day. Especially not when there are going to be agents at those performances."

"What?" My mouth drops open as I stare at him. "What do you mean? I didn't hear anything about agents being there."

Christian shrugs and packs the last shirt into his bag

before zipping it up. "Joe told me the other day after one of your shows. He was talking to some of his industry friends and invited a few of them."

My heart races, and my pulse pounds in my ears.

I grin and squeal, leaping up from the bed to hug Christian.

He laughs as he catches me and spins me around.

His mouth finds mine, our lips moving together softly as he sets me down on the ground.

"There will be no rearranging your performance schedule when this is your big chance," Christian's voice is soft as he smiles down at me. "You're going to go and play your songs and sing your heart out, and I'm sure that one of those agents is going to sign you."

"How do you know that?" My stomach twists and turns as all the ways that this could go wrong circle through my mind.

I could lose my voice in the middle of a song. I could forget how to play one of my songs. I may forget the words. The agents might not like me. They might leave the bars and tell their record labels that I'm not good enough to work with them.

"Zoe, you are the most talented person that I've ever met. The shows are going to go great and I'm going to call you after each one and ask you how they went. Then you're going to tell me that the agents loved you, and they're fighting over you for their record labels."

"I swear, you have more faith in me than I have in myself."

He chuckles and hoists his bag over his shoulder. "Isn't that part of being your husband? I know you're going to do great things. Zoe."

My vision blurs with tears as I walk with Christian

through the house and to the garage. "I hope you're right. I don't know how I'm going to deal with the nerves, but I'm going to get through it."

"You're going to be amazing." He opens the door to the garage and holds it open for me.

"Thank you." I walk by the trucks and simple sedans to one of the flashing sports cars on the other side of the garage. "What do you think? I could drive you in this one."

Christian grabs a set of keys off the rack before tossing it to me. "That one it is. Security team is going to follow behind you to make sure that you get home safely once you've dropped me off."

I nod as I catch the keys before sliding into the sleek lime green car. As I press the button for the garage door, Christian drops his bag into the trunk before sliding in beside me.

The engine roars to life as I twist the key in the ignition.

The drive to the private airport Christian flies from is short and filled with music.

I don't know how much he paid for the sound system in this car, and I don't want to know.

The bass pounds, shaking the mirror as I pull into the airport and come to a stop in front of the hangar.

Christian's plane is sitting there, gleaming in the bright sun.

The pilot stands beside it, scrolling through something on his phone.

Christian leans over the console to kiss me.

"I'm going to miss you," I say, my vision starting to blur as tears gather. I bite them back and smile as he kisses my forehead. "Have a safe flight and let me know when you get to Georgia."

He gets out and leans down to look at me. "I promise that I'll send you a message the moment the plane lands."

"Good." I smile and tighten my grip on the wheel, still trying to hold back the tears. "I love you, Christian. Stay safe."

"I love you too."

He closes the door and grabs his bag from the trunk before heading for the plane.

The pilot takes the bag from him, and the two men climb the steps into the airplane.

As the door shuts, a lump rises in my throat.

I wait for a moment longer, smiling when his face appears in one of the windows. He winks at me before disappearing.

I take a deep breath and turn the car around, heading back out of the airport and to the main road.

When I glance in the mirror, the security team are following behind me.

The tightness in my chest eases.

Even though Christian says that nobody is going to be coming after us anymore, the entire situation with Demarco has me worried.

I turn up the music, trying to drown out the worries that I still have.

Demarco is dead. The people coming after us are dead. Christian is going to be fine while he's in Georgia. He'll be talking business with his friends.

I'm going to be fine at home. Camila is going to stay with me while Christian is gone, and Ruben won't be far away. Everything is safe.

The only thing I have to worry about is the performance schedule.

If I'm going to impress the agents and have any chance

to get signed to a record label, I have to put on a couple of good shows this week. I have to be able to make them fall in love with my music in only a short time.

Nerves race through me as I start to go through a setlist in my mind. I have several new songs that I want to perform but covers of some of my favorite songs could be a better idea.

Although, I want to get signed for the music I write.

This is going to be a long week.

I take the long way home, needing the time to think about what I'm going to do once I get back in the studio.

The studio is where I'm going to spend most of my time until the performances, working on recording as many of my songs as I can. I need something to occupy the time that I would otherwise spend worrying about Christian.

As I pull up in front of the house, I know that no amount of hiding in the studio is going to erase the worry from my mind.

Stop that! Christian is a grown man, and he can take care of himself. Everything is going to be fine.

When I stop the car, I take a look toward the door.

My father is sitting on the doorstep, his hands clasped in front of him.

My eyebrows knit together as I look at him.

He doesn't look at me, instead staring off into the distance.

I sigh and get out of the car, trying to mentally prepare myself for whatever game he's about to play.

That sitting there and looking into the distance is the same trick he used to use on me when I was younger. He would sit there, looking miserable and then proceed to tell me how much I had disappointed him that day.

Nothing I did was ever good enough.

Though I have no idea what I might have done this time, guilt rolls through me in waves as I climb the steps and take a seat beside him.

I love my dad.

Even though there are times when we aren't on the same page, or even in the same book, he's still my dad. He loves me. He just has a hard time loving the person I became instead of the one I used to be.

"I didn't know that you were going to be coming over," I say, my tone guarded as I stretch my legs out in front of me.

"You know, if anyone asked me how my youngest daughter would be spending her life, this isn't what I would have said. Seeing you get married to a criminal is a travesty, Zoe."

Dad sighs and looks at me from the corner of his eye. "I thought that me and your mother raised you better than that. I thought we taught you to know right from wrong."

I sigh and pinch the bridge of my nose. "Dad, you were arranging for me to get married to Christian in the first place."

"I needed to arrange the marriage. But I found a way to call it off. And then you go off and get married to him anyway." Dad sighs and sits up, crossing his arms. "Can't you see that this isn't the life I want for you?"

The security teams are sitting in the car in the driveway, giving us space but watching us.

I nod to them, letting them know that everything is alright. If they get out of the car and come over here, then Dad is only going to get more agitated.

"This isn't the life that I thought I wanted for myself."

Butterflies beat their wings against the inside of my stomach. "But now that I'm living it, I'm happy."

Dad scoffs and shakes his head. "You don't even know

what happiness is. Not if you think that you've found it here with him."

"I love Christian. I am happy here. I get to live out my dreams, and I don't have to fall into the little box that you and Mom made for me."

I run my sweaty hands down my pants, trying to dry them out. "I love you too, Dad, but you don't get to decide what life is and isn't right for me. I like it here. I love being with Christian. He's a good husband."

"I'm not going to allow this." Dad glares at the bushes that line the path from the driveway to the side door of the house.

His eyes fly to mine. Hard and unwavering. "Go pack your bags, Zoe. I know that he's out of town on a trip right now. We're going to get your things packed and then I'm going to take you back home where you belong."

I shake my head and stand up. My chest aches.

The last thing I want is to fight with my father again, but I know I have to. If there is one thing that I've learned in my time away from home, it's that I deserve the life I want.

Even if I have to fight for it.

"I'm not going to be moving back to your house." I tuck my hands in the pockets of my linen trousers. "I like it here, Dad. I have a good marriage with a man I love."

"You don't know what love is. You're too young, and he's years older than you. Do you really think that this is going to work out? You're in two different parts of your life."

Dad scoffs and stands up, looming over me. "You're going to go pack your bags right now, Zoe. I'm not going to let you ruin your life like this. You're coming back home where I can keep you safe."

"No. I'm not." I smile and climb the stairs to the front

door. "This is my home now. I love the life that I'm building with Christian, and I'm not going to give it up."

"Not even knowing that your family is worried about your safety?"

"I appreciate that you're worried about me, but you don't have to be."

He shakes his head, disgust and disappointment clear on his face. "You're going to regret this."

Dad takes off, heading down the driveway and to the road where a car is idling.

My heart aches as I watch him get into the car and take off into the distance.

Though I know that he thinks I'm making the wrong decision, he's going to come around. One of these days, he's going to see how happy I am with my life now, and he's going to support me. Right?

Right now, he's just being overprotective because he's worried about me. Even though there is no reason to worry.

If he just spends a little more time with me and Christian, he'll see that he needs to let go and be happy for me.

At least that's what I tell myself as I head to the studio to pour everything I'm feeling into a song.

27

CHRISTIAN

The rain is pouring down as I send a message to Zoe and step off the plane in Georgia.

The tension that I've been feeling for the last couple of weeks starts to fade as I take my bag from the pilot and head over to the waiting SUV.

Alessio and Jovan grin at me from the front seat as the back door flies open.

Billie throws herself out of the car and pulls me into a big hug, despite knowing that is the last thing I want. She laughs even as my arms hang down by my sides, and I don't hug her back.

"One of these days, Christian, you're going to be as excited to see me as I am to see you." Billie steps away to take my bag, her wet hair hanging down in her face.

I hold my bag out of her reach and head for the trunk. "I can carry this on my own, thank you."

Billie rolls her eyes and follows me to the trunk, not caring about the way her mascara runs beneath her eyes. "So, how are things going with the wife?"

I toss the bag into the trunk and shake my head. "We're not going to stand here and discuss my love life."

"You know that I love to talk about your love life." Billie smirks as we get into the back of the SUV where Hadley is waiting.

"I want to talk about your love life too," Hadley says with a grin as I squeeze in beside her.

Billie slides in after me, slamming the door shut.

Hadley nudges me with her elbow. "After all, it's been a while since we saw you last. You're going to have to tell me how things are going. I could use a little entertainment."

Jovan twists in his seat to look back at me. "You know the two of them are never going to leave you alone. Not unless you tell them about your wife."

I sigh and lean back in the seat as we pull away from the airport. "Why do we need to talk about Zoe?"

Alessio glances in the mirror. "Because the pair of them have been talking about nothing else since Jovan and Hadley landed here last night. I have to say, I'm a little disappointed you didn't bring her with you. I was looking forward to meeting her."

"You'll get to meet her eventually."

I glare at Billie as she jabs her finger into my shoulder. "What the hell was that for?"

"You should have brought her to meet me now. I help you with girl advice. That means that I should get to meet Zoe before your real wedding."

I bite back the smile that tries to curve the corner of my mouth. "And what makes you think that there's going to be another wedding? I already married her once."

Billie glares at me as Hadley starts immediately protesting. The pair of them start to ramble about how we should be getting married in the wedding of our dreams instead of a secret event in the dead of night.

Jovan and Alessio laugh in the front seat, neither of them helping.

"You have to ask her to marry you properly this time," Billie says, her tone stern as she crosses her arms. "You need to get down on one knee and ask her to marry you. Tell her how much you love her."

Hadley nods. "And then you have to help her plan the wedding. Don't just sit there and ask her to do it. It's your wedding too, and she'll love you even more for it. Make sure she knows that getting married matters to you too."

I toss my hands up in the air. "I never said that we would be having another wedding."

"To be fair," Jovan says, his smirk growing wider. "You should probably give her the wedding of her dreams. Women like that sort of thing. They dream about it. It's not fair to rob her of that."

As I run my hands down my face, I know that they're right.

I should do something for Zoe. I should give us the fresh start at a marriage filled with love. She might want that.

If she does want a dream wedding, then I'm going to do everything in my power to give it to her.

"I'm going to be your best man." Billie says it with a tone that lets me know her decision is final.

With a scoff, I shake my head. "I can't believe that you just decided to be my best man. Just like that. What if I want someone else to be my best man?"

Billie smiles and crosses one leg over the other, invading more of my personal space.

I swear, she only does it because she knows it bothers me.

The tip of her toe taps against my shin as she moves her foot along with the beat of the song.

"Fine!" I push her foot away from me. "You can be my best man. Just stop driving me insane."

The car bursts into laughter as we park in front of Billie and Alessio's house.

Billie and Hadley get out of the SUV, taking off for the front door while I sit with Jovan and Alessio.

As much as I enjoy spending time with the group, this isn't a social call.

"Want to go to my office and talk business, or do you want to get settled in first?" Alessio asks as we get out.

The rain soaks through my clothes as I nod and grab my bag from the car. "We may as well get business out of the way first. That's why I'm here."

The three of us head into the house and down the hall to Alessio's office. I drop my bag in the corner before taking a seat in one of the chairs.

As I lean back in the chair and brush my wet hair back, Alessio pours us all glasses of bourbon. He hands me a glass, the dark liquid sloshing up the sides of the cup.

"We have to talk about Finnigan Byrne," Alessio says as he sits down at his desk.

I take a sip of the bourbon before nodding. "It's only a matter of time before he gets out. My contacts at Ryderson tell me that his time is going to be coming up soon."

Jovan sighs and downs his drink in one go before pulling another. "There is no way that he can come to Florida. I might not have a problem with him, but several of my suppliers do. His best bet is staying in Tennessee."

"I doubt that he's going to stay." I cross one leg over the other. "Who in their right mind would stay in their last known location when their enemies want to kill them?

Besides, I'm not sure I want him there either. Not with his father being who he is."

Alessio tilts his glass in my direction. "You're right."

"I'm sure Byrne is going to get out of Tennessee as fast as he can. He knows his enemies are waiting for him."

I take another sip on my drink as my stomach lurches. "I'm not going to be able to keep him protected once he is out. The favors that I was able to call in this first time have already run out."

Finnigan Byrne is a good man who got mixed up in a dangerous world. Though I don't want him to stick around Tennessee, I don't want to see him die either.

Alessio nods. "Any chance you can talk to him about where he stand on this?"

"I'll pay him a visit and tell him that Georgia, Florida, and Tennessee are not desired destinations for him." I finish my drink and put the glass on the desk.

"Good." Alessio says, his eyebrows knitting together. "We've had enough trouble between to three of us to add a war with the Byrnes to our plates."

I rub my hands over my eyes as I yawn. "Agreed. I think the first few months out aren't going to be easy for him. Do you think he's going to head back to Seattle?"

Jovan gets up and paces over to the window, looking out over the yard as the rain continues to pour. "Don't know. Wherever he goes, I just hope he can stay out of trouble."

There is a knock at the door before it opens and Billie steps inside. "Dinner is ready."

The conversation comes to an end as we filter out of the room behind her and head for the dining table.

As I sit down for the meal, all I can think about is what Zoe's doing right now.

Hours later, I'm in bed and can't sleep. I sigh and roll onto my side, grabbing the phone. I scroll to Zoe's number, hoping that she is still awake.

It's been a long day filled with conversations about Finnigan, and I'm ready to talk about something else.

"Hey," Zoe breathes as the call connects, a faint hum fills the silence in the background. "I didn't know if you were going to call tonight or not. How's everything going there?"

"It's going alright. The day's been long, and I wish that I was back home with you. Or that you were out here with me."

"I wish I was there too," she says as the vibrating hum comes to a stop. "I miss you."

With a smirk, I pull down my boxers and grip my stiffening cock. "Zoe, was that a vibrator?"

She makes a soft strangled sound.

I can picture the bright red blush spreading across those freckled cheeks. "It might have been. I couldn't sleep."

I chuckle lowly, sliding my hand from the base to the tip of my cock. "You know, if I was there, we would be having some fun right now. Hell, I might even play nice and let you use that vibrator for me."

"You want to watch?" Her breathing quickens.

"Fuck yes. I want to watch you play with yourself. I want you to hold that vibrator against your clit. Your pussy would be dripping wet. Is it wet right now? Does thinking about me watching you play with your vibrator soak you?"

Zoe gasps, the slick sound of her fingers sliding through her wet folds coming through the phone. "Yes. I want you to watch me."

"Good. You know what else you're going to do for me?" My cock throbs as I stroke it faster, squeezing harder with each pass. "You're going to plunge your fingers into that tight pussy. You're going to fuck your fingers, dripping wet as I watch you."

"I am."

"Good girl. Fuck your fingers for me. Make yourself come."

"I need you," she whimpers as she dips her fingers into her pussy.

I moan at the sound, wishing that I could see her right now.

"I need your cock. I want to feel it stretch me."

"Later, Zoe. Tonight, you're going to get yourself off for me. You're going to think about the way I would fuck you if I was there. The way I would hike one of your legs over my shoulder as I slam into you. You'd be moaning as your pussy milks my cock, trying to draw out every last drop."

"Fuck, yes. I want that. I want you to come inside me. Fill me up. I need it."

Right now, I'm sure her back is arching off the bed as she plays with her pussy.

I wish that I was there with her.

I would dive between her legs, burying my face between her thighs.

I'd be rock hard as I licked her pussy, the taste of her arousal on my tongue when I kissed her later.

"How close are you, Zoe? Are you fucking your fingers like a good girl? Are you thinking about how I would flip you onto your hands and knees? Drive into you from behind while I pull your hair? Pinch your nipples until you're writhing around? Are you going to come?"

"I'm close," she gasps as I smirk and keep pumping my cock.

It stiffens as I think about the way her pussy pulses around me.

"I'm so close, Christian."

"Good little slut. Keep fucking those fingers for me. Keep thinking about my cock and everything that you would do to have it. What would you do for my cock right now, Zoe?"

"Anything. Everything."

"Such a horny little slut, aren't you? I can hear how wet you are for me. Move your fingers faster, Zoe. I want you to come for me."

The sound of her sliding her fingers in and out of her pussy faster is enough to send me over the edge.

I groan as I pump my cock faster until thick ropes of hot come land on my stomach.

"Get on all fours and ride your fingers, Zoe. Make yourself come for me. Right now." I lean back into the pillows, my cock still aching for her.

It's going to be a long couple of days.

The sheets rustle as she gets onto her knees.

Her moans are music to my ears as she fucks her fingers.

I groan as her whimpers grow louder until she comes.

Her breathing is heavy before the sheets start rustling again.

"I don't know how I'm going to last a couple more days until you get home," Zoe says, her breathing still ragged.

"Don't you worry about the wait. I'm going to make it worth your while."

The things I plan on doing to her when I get back home should be illegal.

"Oh, are you?" she teases.

"You're not going to be able to walk for a week."

Zoe laughs, making me miss home more than I ever have before.

All I want is to get on a plane and go back home to her. Maybe reenact our phone call until she's on her knees and begging for more.

"I miss you," she says, her tone softening.

I sigh, warmth spreading through me. "I miss you too, Zoe. Only a couple more days. Then I'm going to be home. Are you ready for your show tomorrow night?"

"Not even a little bit."

"Well, tell me all about what's bothering you," I say, yawning as I cross one leg over the other. "Maybe we can figure it out together."

As Zoe starts to ramble about her fears, I close my eyes and listen to the sound of her voice.

I didn't think that leaving her was going to be this hard.

She's struggling, and she needs me right now, but there's not much I can do to help her from here.

We talk until she falls asleep, the soft sounds of her snores coming through the phone.

I end the call with a smile, tossing it to the side of the bed before getting up and heading for the shower.

If I had known that loving her was going to be this good, I would have done everything in my power to give her the relationship she deserves earlier.

Since I can't go back in time and change the past, I'm going to give her the future she deserves.

28

ZOE

Ava hugs me before heading for the front door.

"I would stay tonight if I could, but I got called back to the prison. There was a fight and it's all hands on deck. Are you sure you're okay on your own?"

I nod and walk with her to the door. "Camila is going to be home sometime after midnight. Not sure when, but I'll be okay until she gets here. Don't worry about it. Go take care of the people who need you."

Ava nods and hugs me again. "Call me if you need anything, and I'll come back here as soon as possible, okay?"

"Go!" I laugh and untangle myself from her embrace as I give her a gentle push out the door and to her car.

She looks back at me before getting into her car.

Though I know that she's worried about me, there's nothing to worry about.

Ruben is staying in the little guest house not too far from the main house. The security team is roaming the property. Everything is safe.

I shouldn't have told her about the situation with Demarco and the nightmares.

But as much as I want to protect my sister from the darker parts of the life I now live, she's also one of the few people who understands.

She spends her days working in a prison, close to criminals.

Ava sees the prisoners as humans, not just people who have to suffer due to what they did on the worst day of their life.

She honks before driving off into the darkness, leaving me standing in the doorway.

I watch her taillights disappear before going back inside and locking the door.

A movie might be a good way to distract myself until Camila gets here.

I head to the living room and drop onto the couch, sighing as I sink into the cushions.

Tomorrow night, Christian is going to be here, and I can tell him all about how my shows went.

Excitement bubbles through me just thinking about the opportunities at my fingertips.

I want to talk to him and go over the contracts together before figuring out which record label is my best bet.

Although, I've been toying with the idea of creating my own label lately too. Something that is entirely mine that no other person can control.

I would be able to make the music I want to make and run my career the way I want to.

I have the equipment I need in the studio. Producing and releasing my own music wouldn't be that far of a jump.

Yet another thing I want to talk about with Christian.

My phone starts ringing before I can pick a movie.

I groan and reach over, seeing Dad's face on the screen.

For a moment, I consider not answering it. I'm not

sure that I can handle another conversation with him about my life right now. Not when he isn't willing to see my side.

But he's still my dad, and he doesn't call me unless it's important.

"Hi Dad," I say, leaning back into the cushions and kicking my feet up on the coffee table. "Is everyone alright? Did something happen at home? How's Mom?"

My stomach growls as I try to relax.

Within a couple seconds of getting comfortable, I'm up and walking for the door.

There's a pizza place not far from here that makes the best calzones.

"I was just calling to see how you were doing. I know that the last conversation we had didn't end so well, and I wanted to try to talk to you again about your choices."

I sigh and slip on my shoes. "Do we need to talk about this right now? I'm walking down to that small pizza place not too far from my house. I don't want to be arguing with you in public."

Dad sighs. "There is no argument that we need to have, Zoe. Just tell me that you're ready to come home, and I will come get you. I can leave right now. You don't have to stay there just because he wants you to."

"I'm going to say this for the last time," I say, my tone firm as I leave the house and lock up behind me.

The night air is cool against my skin as I head down the driveway and to the road.

One of the security guys follows behind me, his hands tucked in his pockets.

"Zoe," Dad cuts me off. "There is no need to say it again. You don't know what you're doing. Your marriage is going to get you killed one of these days. Do you think I want to put my daughter in the ground? Please, just come home where I can keep you safe."

"I love you, but I'm not going to do that, Dad. I can't be your perfect little girl anymore. I can't keep putting aside my wants and needs for the good of the family. Especially not now that I realize how much I've had to give up over the years."

"The family needs you, Zoe."

I bite back the tears that gather in my eyes.

It's the same line that Dad has used over the years. It's the line that comes up any time he wants me to put my life on hold for his own needs.

As much as I love him and my family, as imperfect as they are, I can't keep doing this. Not anymore. I have to be my own person, and heading home is only going to result in the gilded cage closing in around me again.

"I can't, Dad. You need to understand that. I will be there for the family when it matters, but my coming back to your house is only you trying to regain control over my life. I know that letting go of me and letting me live my own life is scary, but you have to let me be free. I need to spread my wings."

Dad sighs. "Please, Zoe. I don't want to do this. I thought that you were my little girl."

"I can't be your little girl forever. I have my own life to live." I swallow hard, trying to get rid of the lump in my throat. "Dad, I need you to be there for me and support me in this. I know that you don't like Christian, but he's my husband. You have to find a way to be okay with that."

"I'm sorry, Zoe."

The call ends before I can say anything else.

I resist the urge to throw my phone at the ground and watch it shatter into a million pieces.

I never thought that going out and having my own life would be this difficult. I thought that my family would be happy for me. I thought that they would support me while I grew up.

Ava supports me. Christian supports me. Why can't Mom and Dad?

Maybe they can, in time.

Still, it feels like Dad has driven a knife through my heart.

I know that this is hard for him, but I thought he would see that this is what's best for me.

He's stuck in his ways. I can only hope that one day he'll come around. Because I don't want to lose my father, no matter how difficult he can be at times.

I tuck my phone back in my pocket as the breeze blows harder and clouds drift across the moon.

The streetlights shine a dim glow in the night as I turn the corner.

I hope the walk to the pizza place and back is enough to clear my mind.

As I look over my shoulder, the security guard gives me a small smile. He's still a few feet behind me, giving me the space I need.

A car comes out of nowhere, whipping around the corner so fast the tires squeal on the pavement.

My security guard turns around, his gun drawn, but he's too slow.

A man leans out of the back window, and as if the world is in slow motion, I witness the man in the car shooting my security guard.

The car screeches to a stop beside me before I know what's happening.

Two men jump out, hands grabbing at me.

I scream as loud as I can, hoping that someone will hear me even though there are no houses in this section of the neighborhood.

"Shut up, bitch," one of the men growls as he reaches for my bicep.

I turn and slam my fist into his nose, hearing the crunch as it breaks.

He wipes away some of the blood with the back of his hand, grinning.

The other man grabs me from behind, holding my arms back.

I flail and kick, trying to hit something solid.

The man with the broken nose gives me a sinister smile before slamming his fist into my gut. All the air whooshes out of me as I try to double over, but the other man holds me up.

"I told you to shut up." The man chuckles and nods to the car. "Now, get the fuck in there."

"Fuck you." I wheeze and spit at him, throwing my head back into the other man's face.

His nose crunches and hot blood splatters against my neck.

I pull my arms free and lunge at the first man, scratching at his face.

If they're going to kill me, I need their DNA all over me. Christian needs to be able to find them and get revenge. He'll never be okay if he doesn't.

Even as terror grips my heart, making it race, I keep trying to fight.

I drag my nails down the man's face as he pulls out his gun. The scratches on his face trickle with blood as he slams the pistol onto the side of my head.

The world goes fuzzy before fading to black.

When I come to, I'm cold, and my head pounds.

My vision spins as I look at the metal bars in front of me and the cot to my right. There is no window or another door.

Wherever I am, I'm trapped. There won't be any getting out until whoever took me comes to finish the job.

My heart pounds, and bile rises in my throat.

I turn to the corner where there's a little bucket. As soon as I spot it, I crouch down, the contents of my stomach coming up.

With a groan, I lean back against the cold wall and wipe my mouth with the back of my hand.

There is only a wall on the other side of my cell door.

Though I don't know where I am, I'm surprised that I'm alive. I thought the men were going to kill me.

All I can do now is hope that Christian gets here in time to keep me that way.

He's going to notice that there's something wrong when he calls tonight, and I don't answer. Or when the security team starts to think that I've been gone too long.

Maybe Camila will get to the house first and find me missing.

Either way, Christian is going to find out I'm gone and he's going to find a way to save me. He's coming for me.

I know he is.

Footsteps echo in the hallway.

The dim light shining overhead casts the shadow of a person on the wall opposite me. The person comes into view and tears spring into my eyes.

My pulse races as I look at my dad.

"Daddy. Thank god, you're here?" I swallow a sob that

threatens to surface. I stagger to my feet even though my entire body hurts. I'm sure that even my bruises have bruises. "Can you open this door now, please?"

Dad looks down at the ground, exhaling slowly.

When he looks up at me, there is only a distant expression on his face. It's as if he's seeing through me rather than looking at me.

He sighs and leans against the wall, crossing his arms.

"Dad?" Why is he acting like this?

"Go ahead, Jeremiah," a man says as he appears beside my dad. He's the man I slammed my head into. There are purple bruises beneath his eyes and a bandage on his nose. "Tell your daughter why I had to go and get her tonight. Tell her what you did."

I look between the two of them, my eyebrows knitting together.

The man laughs and shakes his head.

Dad seems to shrink in on himself, but he keeps quiet.

I'm going to throw up again.

My pulse pounds in my ears as I look between the two of them.

None of this makes sense. Why would Dad have me kidnapped and put in a cell? Is he still trying to get me away from Christian?

I can't wrap my mind around it. "What's going on, Dad? What's he talking about? Why am I here? You're not trying to get me to come back home, are you? I already told you that I'm happy with my life."

Dad shakes his head. "That's not what's happening here, Zoe. I should've told you about this sooner, but there's no way that you would have done what I wanted."

"What are you talking about?" My heart plummets to

my feet as the man beside Dad grins and approaches the bars.

"He really didn't tell you anything about what he's been up to, has he?" The man clicks his tongue and looks at Dad. "Naughty boy, Jeremiah. I would have thought that you would talk to your daughter about what your actions have cost her."

The room is shrinking in around me as I look between the two of them.

Though I don't know what's going on, Dad is the reason that I'm here. He's the reason that I got hurt tonight. He's why I'm locked in a cage.

"Dad," I say, my voice hollow as I try to keep my hands from shaking as I grip the bars. "What's he talking about? What did you do?"

"It was supposed to be Ava. It was never supposed to be you." Dad swallows hard, his face growing red. "I could have never done this to you, Zoe."

"But whatever this is you could have done to Ava?" Hot tears track down my cheeks. "What the fuck is going on here?"

"There's a debt to be paid," the man says, coming over to the bars. He runs his fingers over mine, smirking when I recoil at his touch. "You're going to have to learn to like the touch of strange men soon, sweetheart. My bidders have no interest in a frigid bitch."

My heart plummets to the ground as I keep my gaze trained on my father. "You need to tell me what's going on. Right now. I need to know."

Dad shakes his head and crosses his arms. "It's better if you don't know what's going to happen, Zoe. Trust me."

I glare at him through the tears that stream down my

cheeks. "How can I trust you when you're the reason that I'm in here?"

The man laughs and elbows my father. "She has a point, Jeremiah. Now, I think that it's time to collect on that debt you owe me, don't you? After all, I've been waiting a very long time for this. And there is still the small matter of the interest you owe on the debt after that little stunt you pulled with the cartel."

"It's not my fault she married him!" Dad scowls at me like all I've done is complicate his life. "I've been trying to get her to come home so I could pay you."

"I'm going to have to charge you a finder's fee for this as well. I shouldn't have had to go and get her myself, Jeremiah."

The man's tone is patronizing. "Your debt just keeps growing. I'm so glad that the time to collect has finally come. Now, get out of here before I force you to join her in the cell."

"You can have my other daughter."

The way he says the words is cold. Detached. Like me and my sister are just possessions to be passed on.

"You fucking bastard!" I scream, throwing myself at the bars. "How could you do this to us?"

I'm going to kill him if I get my hands on him. There's no way that he's going to hurt Ava.

"Don't worry, sweetheart," the man says, his tone sickly sweet as he looks at me. "Your sister isn't useful to us. Your father will have to find another way to pay his debt."

Dad scowls at him and brushes by him.

The man winks at me before pulling out a gun.

The loud crack of the shot echoes inside the walls as my father's steps faulter before he slumps to the floor.

I scream, dropping to my knees as my father's body lies

unmoving where it fell. Blood pools on the floor, trickling toward me.

I grab the bucket and throw up again.

The man laughs and tucks the gun back into the holster at his hip.

He crouches down in front of me, that sinister smile sending a chill down my spine.

"Who would have thought that a father was capable of selling their daughters to a sex trafficking ring?" The man snorts and shakes his head.

He reaches through the bars and runs his fingers along the side of my face. "Everything is going to be okay, sweetheart."

"You're a bastard." I nearly choke on the words as I glare at him.

The man shrugs. "You know, some would call me a bastard and others would say that I'm just doing what it takes to survive. The real bastard here is your father. He tried to sell your sister, and when that didn't work, he sold you. How do you manage to cry for someone like that?"

He's right, but he's still my father.

And right now, it's hard to see the truth about Dad when he's lying dead only a few feet away from me.

The man pulls out a set of keys and unlocks the door.

I scramble backward as he advances on me.

"Now, I hear that you're married to Christian Herrera." The man moves faster than I anticipate, grabbing me by the hair and hauling me to my feet.

I bite down hard, blood pooling on my lip.

Tears run down my cheeks as pain flares across my scalp.

He gives me that sinister smile and yanks my head back.

"Don't be stupid, Zoe. If you want to save your life, you're going to tell me what I want to know."

"Go to hell."

He chuckles and throws me to the ground.

I yelp as my arm smashes into the hard floor.

The man kicks me hard in the thigh.

I scream, unable to hold it back this time.

Pain shoots through my body as I look up at him.

"You want to live? You're going to start talking."

He slams his foot into my other thigh, the heel of his boot digging into my flesh.

I scramble back, trying to get as far away from him as possible.

I'm not going to betray Christian.

"He's sending a big shipment of guns overseas. Where is it going, and how is he getting it there?"

I glare at him through the tears.

My lips press into a thin line as my head throbs from the pain.

The man slams his fist into my ribs.

When all I let out is a small whimper, he punches me again.

"Useless bitch. You're lucky you're going to the brothel. If you weren't, I would be breaking that nose of yours right now."

Two other men appear in the hallway as the man stands tall. They drag away my father before coming back and stepping into the cell.

My heart pounds as I look at the three of them.

Though my stomach tosses and turns, I have nothing left to throw up.

I try to move backward, but a cold wall presses against me.

I could try to get to the door and slam it shut on them. Except, I don't know where I am or who else is here.

I'm trapped and there's nothing I can do about it.

"Take her to the brothel to heal and prepare for the sale of her virginity," the man says, looking at the other two. "If this bitch doesn't want to cooperate, then her sale date is being moved up. I want her out of my sight immediately."

The men lunge at me, each taking an arm and hauling me to my feet.

Dark shadows line the corner of my vision as the pain flowing through my body overrides every other thought I have.

As they carry me out of the room, the man in charge leans closer to me.

"You only have your father to thank for being captured tonight. He was nice enough to let me know you were going out for pizza. I never would have been able to get to you without him."

29

CHRISTIAN

I sigh as I stare up at the ceiling with my phone on the bed beside me. The rest of the room is dark.

I've been trying to fall asleep for the last hour, but I can't. It feels strange to be in a bed without her. I'm too used to the way she cuddles against me and sighs when she falls asleep.

More than anything, I want to be in my own bed with her and drifting off to sleep.

Maybe I should head home early. I could cut my trip a day short and fly back to her sooner.

I miss her, and I never thought I could miss her this much. It feels like there's a piece of me missing. And I'm not going to feel whole until I'm back home with her.

A call should be enough for now. Something to hold me over until I can have her in my arms again.

I grab the phone and call her, listening as the phone rings and rings before going to voicemail.

I try her number again. When I get her voicemail a second time, my chest constricts.

It's not like Zoe to not answer her phone.

Where the hell is she?

When I call her for a third time and there is no answer, I get out of bed and turn on the light.

Maybe she went out with her sister before spending the night with Camila.

Ava had been talking about stealing Zoe away to go dancing.

I had given her the okay with the stipulation that they took security with them.

There's nothing to worry about.

I'll just call her again and leave a message, and she'll call me back when she gets home.

I pace back and forth the room as the phone rings again before going to voicemail. "Hey Zoe, call me when you get this. I just wanted to talk to you before bed. I miss you, and I love you. If you're out dancing tonight, have a good time. I'm having a hell of a time trying to fall asleep without you. Just call me when you get this."

After hanging up, I toss the phone on the bed and head over to the desk near the window.

I pull out my laptop, needing something to do until Zoe calls me back. I already know that I'm not going to get any sleep until I hear from her.

She's just out dancing, nothing to worry about.

Except anything could happen while she is at a bar.

Zoe is smart, though. She knows how to take care of herself, and she has always been great about taking security with her.

Or maybe she picked up another show while I was gone.

Yet another valid reason for her not to answer me. She could be on stage, singing her heart out.

Zoe wouldn't have her phone on her while she's performing.

No matter what she's doing, she's safe.

Her father won't risk coming after her when I have security watching her. Not when I already made it clear to him to stay away.

Everything is fine, and I'm worrying for nothing.

I need something to stop obsessing over this. So, I pull up the profit and loss statements for the last quarter. There is more than enough information there to keep me busy for a while.

An hour after I left Zoe the message, my phone starts ringing.

My heart leaps in my chest as I dash across the room and grab the phone.

Ava's name flashes across the screen, and a pit opens in the bottom of my stomach.

"Hello?" I say, my voice tight.

"Is Zoe answering messages from you? I was with her earlier tonight, but I got called into work, and I had to leave. I've been trying to message her, but she hasn't answered me."

I drop to the ground and drag my bag out from under the bed. "No. I called her a few times an hour ago and left a message, but I haven't heard from her since. Was Camila there yet when you left?"

"No. I had to leave before she was supposed to get there." Ava sniffles. "Ruben checked the cameras. He saw her leaving the house."

"You're with Ruben right now?"

"Yes. When she didn't answer my messages, I told my boss that I had a family emergency." Ava whimpers, and

Ruben says something in the background that I can't quite catch. "I'm at the house right now and there's no sign of her."

I haul my clothing out of the dresser and stuff it into the bag. "I'm going to get on a plane right now. I'll be there soon. You need to stay at the house with Ruben until I get there. Do not open the door for anyone other than me or Camila, got it? Nobody, Ava."

"What if my parents come over? They know that she's missing. Dad said that he was going to go out and look for her, but that was an hour ago."

My chest constricts as I head through the silent house and out into the night, grabbing a set of keys from the rack by the door as I go.

Alessio won't blame me for taking his car right now. I'll send him a message so he knows where it is.

There is no time to wake him up, though. I have to get to Zoe before something happens to her.

Before her father hurts her.

"Do not let them in. Me or Camila. That's it. Do you hear me? Make sure Ruben knows. I've got to go. I'll be there soon."

Ava sniffles again and ends the call as I unlock the car and toss my bag inside.

My heart pounds in my chest, and my hands shake.

I don't know where Zoe would have gone, but I'm sure that her father took her.

He's been trying to get her away from me, and he would be stupid enough to go after her while I'm out of town.

I slide into the car and start it up, heading for the airport as fast as I can.

I'm coming, Zoe. Just hold on until I get there.

Camila is standing outside the house when I get there. Her mouth is set in a thin line even as the tears track down her cheeks.

Ava is sitting on the ground with her arms wrapped around her knees. She looks like she's seen a ghost.

"What do we know?" I ask, looking at Ruben as I pull the gun out of my waistband and check it over.

"My friend called me. She was in the pizza place around the corner when she heard a gunshot." Camila's voice wavers slightly as she speaks.

She takes a deep breath, "She noticed a man was on the floor bleeding and someone was grabbing Zoe, but she couldn't get to her before she was put into a gray van. Copperhead Shipping was written on the side of it."

"Copperhead Shipping? Is she absolutely sure that's what it said?" My stomach knots itself as I abandon the taxi I took here.

Camila nods as Ruben gets my bag.

Fuck.

I head for Camila's car. "That's a cover for fucking sex traffickers. Take Ava inside and keep her safe."

"And where the hell do you think you're going?" Camila asks as she tosses me the keys. "You don't think that you're going to get out there and take care of this on your own, do you?"

I scoff and get in the car. "I'm going to get my wife back, and then I'm going to kill the bastards who took her. One by one."

Camila jogs over to the passenger side of the car and gets in. "I'm going with you. She's my sister now too, Christian, and we both know that you're going to need backup."

I sigh and nod. There isn't enough time to waste arguing with her. If we don't get on the road now, we may lose her forever.

If we aren't already too late.

The streets are dark and empty as I head toward the warehouse district.

Copperhead Shipping operates out of a small warehouse at the end of the district. They've been known to move kidnapped women in and out of there in the blink of an eye.

Their leader, Shayne, has tried to do business with me more than once. Every time I tell him that I'm not interested in trafficking people, he sulks like a child and comes back a few months later.

I should have killed him the last time I saw him.

As we get closer to the warehouse, I turn off the headlights and park behind a shipping container.

Camila and I get out of the car, guns drawn.

I take a deep breath, my pulse pounding in my ears.

We head toward the warehouse, keeping to the shadows.

The rest of the world around us is silent as I make my way to the side door and pull on the handle.

The door opens easily.

Camila touches my back as we enter the building.

I feel like I'm going to be sick as I lead her through the winding stacks of crates to a hidden door in the back.

During one of Shayne's many pitches to work together, he offered a tour of his facility.

At the time, I thought that it would be a bad idea to waste more time with him, but I could see the benefit of understanding his operation too. If there ever came a time when he crossed me, I would have been able to take him down.

Now, that information is coming in useful.

His hidden brothel is the only place he would take her. It's a safe enough place, hidden in his legitimate business and only accessible if you get an invitation.

I open up the hidden door, revealing a staircase lit by dim lights on the wall.

Camila and I descend into the basement, careful not to make a sound as we walk.

The door at the bottom of the stairs is open, and the lights are on.

It looks like the brothel is closed tonight.

Good. There won't be any innocent people in my way.

I look over my shoulder at Camila before pointing to a door nearly hidden by the thick black curtains that drape around the main room. It's just to the right of the stage.

If there were women in here tonight, it would be completely obscured by the bodies moving around the room.

"I thought that I might find you here soon," Shayne says as he steps out from behind one of the curtains.

His smile is downright disturbing. "I have to tell you, when I found out that Jeremiah allowed his precious little virgin daughter to marry you, especially after he sold her to me, I was shocked."

"Where the fuck is Zoe?" I raise the gun and aim, my finger wrapped around the trigger.

Two more men step out of the shadows. Their guns are pointed at Camila, and they grin.

Shayne stands between them, arching his eyebrow like he's in control here.

He's dead. He just doesn't know it yet.

"You don't want to do this, Christian. I'll kill your wife and your sister in the blink of an eye." Shayne smirks as he looks at Camila. "I should have waited until you were with her. I would have been able to take both of you."

Camila points her gun at him. "If I were you, I would stop goading him."

Shayne tucks his hands in his pockets and shrugs. "Her father sold her to me, Christian. Just because you married her doesn't mean that she's yours. I've collected my debt, and in a matter of hours, she is going to be sold off to her new home. Men pay a pretty penny for a virgin these days."

I tuck the gun in my waistband. All I can see is red as I lunge at Shayne.

Guns point at me, and shots are fired. Two bodies drop to the ground.

He shouts as I tackle him to the ground and slam my knee into his chest.

He wheezes, the air forced from his lung.

As I move to straddle him, he writhes.

There is no getting free. Shayne is going to die for what he did to my wife.

I slam one fist into the side of his face.

His nose gives way under my other fist.

"Get the fuck off me," Shayne says, spitting out blood as he thrashes beneath me. "I don't want to die."

I chuckle as I pull out the butterfly knife I keep in my back pocket.

I slip it open and drive the knife into his shoulder.

"You should have thought of that before you decided to fuck with me and take the woman I love."

Tears stream down his cheeks as I drag the knife across his neck, slitting his throat.

Blood drains onto the white carpet, mingling with the blood spreading from the other bodies.

"Are you alright?" Camila asks as we leave the bodies behind us and head to the hidden door.

I open the door and see the body of Jeremiah Redford on the ground in front of me. "I would have been better if I got to kill this bastard myself."

There are no other people in the hall as we make our way to the only room with a closed door.

I take a deep breath, my heart racing as I try to prepare myself for what I'll see in there.

Though Shayne insinuated that she is still alive and has not yet been sold, it doesn't mean that she isn't hurt.

"Everything is going to be okay," Camila says, her voice chocked as we stop in front of the door.

I nod and open it up, the air knocked from my lungs as I see Zoe's crumpled body in the middle of a bed.

The sheets and pillows are a mess around her.

She sits up and scrambles back on the bed, terror in her eyes.

"It's just me, Zoe. It's just me. I'm here and nobody is ever going to hurt you again." My voice is strained, and my vision blurs as I make my way across the small room to get to her. "Did they hurt you?"

"Thighs and ribs," she gasps and lifts up her shirt to show me the dark bruises spreading across her body.

Tears stream down her face as she looks up at me. "Are they dead?"

"They're dead." I pull her into a hug, careful not to hurt her more.

Hot tears track down my cheeks as I pick her up and hold her close. "We're going to take you to see the doctor and then I'm going to take you home."

She nods, sobbing into my shoulder as I carry her past the dead men and out to the car.

Camila calls the cleaning team as we race to the doctor's.

Zoe groans from the backseat with every bump in the road.

I feel horrible, but this is the fastest way to get her help.

As I glance in the mirror at her, some of the tension in my body starts to ease.

Zoe is safe. Zoe is going to be fine.

As ZOE CLIMBS into our bed later that night, I try to scrub the blood out from beneath my fingernails.

I don't want there to be a memory of tonight.

"Christian, please just come to bed," she says, her voice wavering. "I'm not going to be able to sleep without you."

I glare down at my nails, inspecting them until I'm sure that there is nothing there.

When I can't stall any longer, I walk over to the bed and get in beside Zoe.

My chest tightens as I wrap her in a tight embrace and hold her to me.

I almost lost her today. I came so close to getting there too late.

If Shayne had managed to sell her, she would have disappeared from the city before morning.

I can't go through life without her.

Zoe presses her face into my chest, and her tears start all over again.

I drift my hands up and down her back, offering her the only comfort that I can right now.

There are no words to make everything better. I can't erase her father's betrayal or take away the pain she feels.

All I can do is hold her and help her get through this.

I'll hold her for as long as it takes.

30

ZOE

I tuck my hands in the pockets of my black dress and glare at myself in the mirror.

There is no way that I can do this. I can't go to the funeral of a man who signed my life away, even if he was my father.

There is no forgiving what he did to me.

Ava enters the room as I reach for the zipper. "Aren't you coming to the funeral?"

I turn around and look at her.

A lump threatens to choke me as I try to find the words to tell her that I can't honor that bastard. He might have been horrible to me, he might have tried to sell us both. But he is still her father.

Ava knows what happened. To a degree.

She knows that I was taken by sex traffickers and that Dad arranged it all. She knows that the traffickers killed him. Everything else, I've kept a secret.

She doesn't know that Dad was the one who called the traffickers and told them where to get me. He was the one who saw me in that cell and chose to walk away because his debt was paid.

It would kill her to know the entire truth. I can't hurt my sister like that.

I'm not my father.

"I can't, Aves," I murmur as I unzip the dress and tug it over my head.

I toss it to the side before grabbing my robe and pulling it back on. "Not after everything he did to me."

Ava's eyes well with tears but she nods. "I have to go. I need the closure."

I hug her, hissing softly as my ribs ache. "It's fine, Aves. He was a different man to you than he was to me. He protected you."

This is the only truth that matters. Her truth.

God knows the real truth helps no one.

Dad is dead and Shayne is dead. Nobody will be coming after her.

Telling her that Dad was going to sell her too isn't worth the pain it will put her through. It's a weight that I'll bear alone.

I love her too much to ruin her life like that.

Ava deserves the best out of life, and now that Dad is gone, I'm sure that she's going to get it.

HOURS AFTER THE FUNERAL, Ava walks back into the house.

Christian looks up from where he sits on the couch as she enters the room.

Smeared mascara marks her cheeks, but no tears fall.

Ava stands in the middle of the room, looking at me with a distant gaze.

"I'll leave the two of you alone for a bit." Christian stands and kisses the top of my head before leaving the room.

Ava sighs and sits down on the couch beside me. She buries her face in her hands as I set my book to the side and cross my legs. Her shoulders rise and fall with her deep breaths.

When she finally looks up at me, the only sign that she's been crying are her red-rimmed eyes. The smeared makeup is wiped away and her mouth is set in a hard line.

"I need to know what else he did," Ava says, her tone hollow as she looks at me. "I know that you're hiding things from me. I need to know the truth, but I can respect that you don't want to talk about it."

"I don't." I reach out and squeeze her hand. "Ava, one of us deserves to remember the good parts of him. That's ruined for me, but you don't have to ruin it for yourself. Sometimes, things are better left unknown."

"I need to know, Zoe. I need to know everything that he was involved in, and I know that I'm not going to be able to let this go until I do." She leans back against the cushions and stares up at the ceiling.

"Are you sure?"

Ava nods, her bottom lip quivering slightly. "I have to. I need to know."

"You'd probably be happier if you didn't."

My heart aches for her.

I know that neither of us has made peace with what our father did, but I can't imagine wanting to know everything about him.

I already know enough about what our dad was capable of for a lifetime.

"I don't care if I would be happier." Ava stands and looks down at me. "I'm going to do this, Zoe. And maybe someone in Ryderson can help me."

"I can't be part of that. I know all I need to know. More, even. Now I just want to move on with my life."

Ava stoops to hug me, her embrace tight. "I know. I have to do this, though."

She lets me go and I nod.

"Be careful, okay?"

She nods before leaving, the door slamming shut behind her.

I bite back tears that threaten to fall.

If this is what she needs to move on, then I'm going to do my best to support her.

Even if I think it is a terrible idea.

Christian walks back into the room and sits on the coffee table across from me. "How did that go?"

"I don't want to talk about it." I sigh and shut my eyes for a moment.

When I look at Christian again, there is concern shining in his eyes. "I don't want to talk about anything."

"Well, what do you want to do?" He takes my hands in his and holds them tight. "Anything."

I want to go to bed and pull the sheets over my head. I want to spend an entire night pretending that this never happened and then tomorrow I want to pick up the pieces.

But I know that won't bring me the closure I need.

"Can we take my dad's pictures to the beach and burn them?"

Christian leans forward and pecks me in the lips. "Absolutely."

It doesn't take long for us to print off every picture I have of my father.

We load the truck bed with the pictures and some blankets before heading out.

The ride to the lake is silent, but that's what I need right now.

I don't need Christian sitting there and asking me if I'm okay when we both know that I'm not.

Thankfully, he doesn't. He holds my hand as we drive, his thumb drifting in slow circles over the back of it.

By the time we park, the moon is high in the sky, and the stars are shining overhead.

Christian hops out of the truck and gets a fire going while I grab the box of pictures.

My heart pounds against my ribs as I sit by the fire and slip picture after picture into it.

When the last picture is in the fire, we climb into the bed of the truck.

Plumes of smoke twist and turn high in the sky as we lay down and look at the stars.

"When we have children, I never want them to have to go through what my parents put me through," I say, my voice soft.

Christian props himself up on an elbow to look down at me. "We're going to make sure that they have a better life than either of us ever had. We're going to give them the world, and they're going to know exactly how much they are loved."

I swallow hard as tears blur my vision. "And I don't want them around my mother either. Not ever. She was a horrible mother, and I don't want that poison in our lives anymore."

"I have no problem with that." He smiles.

I try smiling back. "I want us to have a good life together. One where our children feel safe."

"So," Christian says, wiggling his eyebrows at me. "When do you want to start practicing for these children?"

I laugh, feeling better than I have in days.

Somehow, he always knows what to say to make me feel better, even if it is just for a moment.

"I love you." I reach up to run my fingers through his hair, pushing it back from his face. "I'm bruised up, though. I'm not going to be much fun tonight."

He grins. "I love you too. You don't have to worry about doing a damn thing, Zoe. Just lay there and let me worship that body."

Heat floods through my body at his words, wetness pooling between my thighs.

He smirks as he moves to hover over me.

When his mouth collides with mine, stars dance behind my eyes.

With a moan, I sink my fingers into his hair and pull him closer.

He presses his hips against me, the curve of his cock digging into my hips.

I hook one leg around his waist as he slides a hand beneath my shirt and cups my breast.

"I'm never going on another trip without you," he says as he kisses his way down my neck.

I sit up enough to pull my shirt over my head.

Christian groans as he opens the front clasp of my bra and takes it out, tossing it to the side.

I lift my hips, and he shimmies the rest of the clothing down my legs.

"I've missed tasting you," he says as he kisses his way back up my leg.

He sucks on my inner thigh as my back arches off the pile of blankets.

Christian smirks and flicks his tongue against my clit before pulling back.

He sheds his clothing, taking his sweet time before diving back between my legs.

"Fuck, that feels good," I say, my voice breathy as I run my fingers through his hair. "Don't stop."

"Wouldn't dream of stopping." He slides his fingers into me, stretching my pussy as his tongue circles my clit.

My pussy clenches around him as he rocks his fingers harder and faster.

I pull on his hair as he sucks on my clit.

When he crooks his fingers and presses against the spot that drives me wild, I come hard and fast.

As he kisses his way back up my body, my legs are shaking.

His fingers keep thrusting as his mouth captures mine again.

Our tongues tangle as I slide my hands down his back, my nails digging into his skin.

"Fuck, I need to feel you wrapped around my cock," he says as he replaces his fingers with his hardened length.

I moan and hook a leg around his hip as he enters me slowly.

With a quick thrust, he enters me fully and buries himself to the hilt as my pussy aches.

My nails rake down his back as he rocks his hips.

Christian's hand slides under my thigh to lift it higher, changing the angle until he is thrusting deeper inside of me.

I hold onto him, lifting my hips and meeting him thrust for thrust.

His cock throbs as he sends me over the edge of another orgasm.

My pussy milks his cock as he comes, pulsating around him until he slumps to the blankets beside me.

"That was a pretty good practice round," he says with a smirk. "I think I could spend the rest of my life practicing with you, Mrs. Herrera."

I smile and roll into his side, nestling against him as the stars shine overhead.

"Well, that's probably a good thing, Mr. Herrera, because I plan on spending the rest of my life with you."

31

CHRISTIAN

Zoe sits in the studio, strumming her guitar.

Every now and then she stops strumming to lean forward and scribble something in her notebook.

I sit on the couch, watching her with a mug of coffee in my hand. The corner of my mouth tugs upward as I watch her.

How the hell did I get this lucky?

"You're staring at me again," Zoe says, glancing up at me with a small smile. "Am I going to have to ban you from the studio so I can get some work done?"

I shake my head and stretch one arm over the back of the couch. "I'm just glad that you're starting to feel better."

Zoe laughs and sets her guitar to the side. "Well, you kept me in bed for the better part of two weeks. After that long, anyone would start to feel better."

"You went through a lot." I put my coffee on the table as she gets up and comes over to me.

She sits beside me on the couch, tucking one leg beneath her as she leans into my side.

"I know. Ava is still worrying me, though. She wants to

go out and find the truth about our father. She is even talking about asking someone at Ryderson for help. I'm terrified about what she'll find."

"Are you still sold on not telling her about him trying to sell the two of you?" I rake my fingers through her soft hair, my heart racing.

Even though it's been two weeks, the thought of what Zoe's father tried to do still has me on edge.

At night, I wake up in a cold sweat from dreaming about what could have happened to her if I hadn't gotten there in time.

I don't want to think about it anymore, but the thoughts still linger in the back of my mind.

She's safe now. She's home with me and everything is going to be okay. We're going to move forward with our lives.

Zoe closes her eyes and nestles deeper into my side.

"I know I have to tell her one day, but now isn't the right time. Everything is still too fresh. I need a little time to wrap my mind around what happened before sharing it with her."

"She's going to want to hear it. You know that, right?"

"I know. I just feel bad. Once she finds out that he was going to sell her to a trafficking ring, she's never going to recover. Ava is strong, but she isn't *that* strong."

"You don't have to be that strong either." I pull her into my lap and wrap my arms tighter around her. "I keep waiting for you to fall apart, and it hasn't happened."

She sighs and tilts her head up to kiss the base of my throat. "I've been falling apart since the day we met. I'm still upset about what happened. And angry. I don't think that the anger is ever going to go away."

I kiss the top of her head. "You can be angry for as long as you want."

"I will be." She grins up at me, but there are tears shining in her eyes. "Thank you for saving me that night."

"Don't thank me for protecting you, Zoe. It's my job."

"It's *not* your job, though." She traces my jaw with the tips of her finger. "Camila's been teaching me how to shoot and fight, but I want to get better. This is my life now, and I want to be able to handle myself the way a cartel wife should."

I smile and turn my head to kiss her fingertips. "I'll teach you everything you need to know."

I'll teach her to be the best damn fighter in my cartel if that's what she wants, But all that happened makes me think that I should *consider stepping down.*

I don't want to have to risk losing her again.

Zoe hums and glances over at the clock on the wall. "Come on, we have to go get ready for my show. Ava and Camila are going to be waiting. Ruben said he might be coming to the show tonight too."

I stand up with her in my arms and leave the studio, heading for the house. "We still have a little time to kill if you want to have a shower together."

"Mr. Herrera, are you propositioning me?" she teases.

"Mrs. Herrera, I'm going to spend every day of our lives propositioning you."

The crowd goes wild as Zoe finishes her set.

She jumps around the stage, waving to everyone around her.

I stand and whistle, clapping as loud as I can.

Ava stands on the booth with Camila, beaming smiles on their faces.

"She's going to be a star," Ava says as she turns to look at me with wide eyes. "She's really going to make it as an artist. I always knew that she would, but seeing her up there like this, it's like she's finally figured herself out."

Zoe steps off the stage and makes her way over to our booth.

Her gaze is fixed on me as she weaves through the crowd.

When she's close, I open my arms and pull her to me. As I kiss her, Ruben and Camila whistle.

"Damn, get a room," Camila says as Zoe pulls away from me with bright red cheeks. "You know, when you eventually get your own tour, I'm going to need tickets to every show."

Ava launches herself at Zoe, nearly tackling her. "You were amazing. I mean, you've always been amazing up there, but this was different. It was so special! I'm going to need front row seats to every concert when you're famous."

Zoe laughs and hugs her sister, rocking back and forth. "What if I get you backstage passes? Maybe a special meet the artist pass."

The pair of them dissolve into a fit of giggles as they slide into the booth together.

Camila drops down from where she stands, sitting beside Ruben with a grin.

I sit down beside Zoe, nearly bursting with pride.

"You're so damn talented," I say as I grab the drink menu and look through it. "One day, when you're famous, promise that you won't forget the little people."

Zoe leans her head on my shoulder as she looks around the table. "I could never forget the people who made me. Without all of you, none of this would be possible."

I shake my head. "No, Zoe. One way or another, you

would've made this happen all on your own. There is no way that you wouldn't have. Being on that stage is what you were meant to do."

"It was," Camila says, looking over at me.

She arches an eyebrow and I nod.

The pair of us are going to have a lot to talk about.

There is no doubt in my mind that Zoe is going to get signed to a label soon. After that, it's only going to be a matter of time before she goes on tour.

I'll be damned if I'm stuck in Tennessee and missing months of our lives together.

She is more important to me than the cartel ever has been.

If Camila isn't ready to step up by the time Zoe goes on tour, I'm sure that Ruben will be happy to take the lead.

There's time to think about that later,

Tonight, I just want to enjoy a night with my wife and our friends. I want to celebrate the fact that we're all still alive and happy.

It's been a hard few months, but we're here, and we're safe.

Though this might not be the path I thought my life would take, I wouldn't go back and change a single moment of it.

"Zoe?" I look into her eyes. "I love you so much."

"I love you too." She beams as she reaches up to kiss me.

When the kiss ends, I slip to the floor on one knee. I take a little box from my pocket.

"What are you doing?" She is frowning, but her eyes are shining.

"What I should have done that night we met on that bar." I smile.

Opening the box, I hold it out to her, the diamond on the ring glinting even in the dim lighting of the club.

"Zoe, love of my life, I took away the chance for you to have the wedding of your dreams. Now, if you'll let me, I'd like to right that huge wrong. So, Zoe Herrera, will you do me the absolute honor of marrying me? Again?"

Her eyes are wide and her mouth his ajar, her hands covering it.

My heart is trying to gallop its way out of my chest as I wait for her answer.

Yes, we are already married, but that was never her choice. Her answer today means everything to me.

She nods, a slight up and down of her head at first until she is almost frantically nodding.

"Yes. Oh my god, yes. Are you serious?"

I nod and laugh as I slide the ring onto her finger.

I hold her to me and kiss her with all my love.

This woman is my wife. My world. My life. My soul.

Ava, Camila, and Ruben hug and congratulate us, cheering and ordering champagne for the table.

As I look at our little group, our family of sorts, I'm overwhelmed with happiness and love.

This moment right here is the best moment of my life.

The love of my life chose to spend the rest of her life with me.

And I'll do everything in my power to make her the happiest woman in the world.

Just as happy as she makes me.

EPILOGUE

Christian

ONE MONTH LATER

"Have I told you how beautiful you look tonight?" I ask as Zoe's white dress flares out around her as we spin across the sand together.

Her face turns a pale shade of pink.

I smile and kiss her cheek, still in awe of how we finally got to this point.

A second wedding may not be traditional, but we needed it.

I needed to give Zoe the wedding she deserved, even though she tried to say it was fine.

She rolls her eyes, that stunning smile still in place as I dip her low.

"You've only told me about a thousand times tonight. I keep thinking that sooner or later, you're going to get tired of saying it."

Chuckling, I pull her closer as our final song starts to play.

Our friends and family pile onto the dance floor with us.

Ava smiles as she sways by herself, a glass of champagne in her hand.

Camila grins as she coerces Ruben into a dance.

It's not going to be long until the two of them are arguing with each other in the middle of our wedding.

Zoe seems to be thinking the same thing as she gives me a knowing look. "You know, we might have to bury a body tonight."

"Camila isn't going to do anything. Not when she's training to lead the cartel now. She needs to show everyone she is capable of being a good leader even though we all know she's going to be a great one."

Zoe nods and looks over at Ava. "I still wish that Aves wasn't leaving in a few days."

"She's happy."

"I'm going to miss her when she's gone. It was a good thing we pushed this wedding forward, or I'm not sure she'd be here."

"Zoe, your sister wouldn't miss our wedding for the world." I kiss the tip of her nose as we spin beneath the twinkling lights draped beneath the trees.

The soft sound of waves crashing against the shore blends with the music as the final song comes to an end.

Zoe sighs and looks up at me with tears shining in her eyes.

Tendrils of her hair hang down around her face.

I wrap one of those tendrils around my finger and give it a slight tug. "Don't look so sad, Zoe. It's not over yet. We still have one more private dance. Just the two of us before we take off for the airport."

Her entire face lights up as I lead her away from the party and into the line of trees.

We keep walking until I find the little clearing lined with wildflowers.

Dimly glowing lanterns hang in the trees and a speaker sits to the side.

I pull out my phone and select the song she wrote about us.

"May I have this dance?" I ask, a teasing smile on my face as I bow low and hold out my hand.

Zoe laughs, tears welling in her eyes again as she slips her hand in mine. "Only if you promise to love me forever."

"Zoe, time itself could come to an end, and I would still keep on loving you."

I pull her to me, and she leans her head on my shoulder.

The familiar scent of her perfume envelopes me as we sway together to the soft melody.

She hums along with the song as I hold her tight.

This is the wedding that I should have given her. Right here on the beach that brings us closer together every time we visit, with the people we care most about in the world.

It's the place where I first told her I loved her. Where I realized that life was more than being a monster.

The beach at the lake is the place where I figured out what it meant to love someone with my entire being.

Zoe brought me back to being human. She changed my life for the better, even after I gave her every reason not to.

Though she could have given up on me at any point, she didn't.

The decision to step back from the cartel was clear after she was kidnapped. I didn't want to waste another minute of our lives away from each other.

If she was going to travel the world and perform, then I was going to go with her.

Camila didn't need any convincing.

As the song ends, I glance at my watch. "We better get going. We don't want to miss the plane."

"We could dance for a little while longer." She reaches up to run her fingers through my hair.

"I will dance with you all you want on the plane and at your shows, but we really do have to be going. We have a honeymoon to enjoy."

She laughs and nods, stepping away from me.

I lace my fingers with hers and pull her through the trees and to the road where our car is waiting.

As we get in the car on the way to start the next chapter of our lives, a weight is lifted from me.

I feel like I can finally breathe. That puzzle piece in my life that's been missing for so long is finally back.

It came in the shape of a woman who is far too good for me.

Zoe smiles at me, leaning her head on my shoulder.

I kiss her temple and hold her close as we head to the airport.

A lifetime spent with Zoe is all I need to feel complete.

Printed in Great Britain
by Amazon